SAM IN FULL

THE STORY OF A HARRIS COUNTY LEGEND

ED OLIVER

authorHOUSE®

AuthorHouse™
1663 Liberty Drive
Bloomington, IN 47403
www.authorhouse.com
Phone: 1-800-839-8640

This book is a work of fiction. People, places, events, and situations are the product of the author's imagination. Any resemblance to actual persons, living or dead, or historical events, is purely coincidental.

First published by AuthorHouse 9/8/2010

ISBN: 978-1-4520-6202-0 (e)
ISBN: 978-1-4520-6200-6 (sc)
ISBN: 978-1-4520-6201-3 (hc)

Library of Congress Control Number: 2010911047

Printed in the United States of America

A special thanks and appreciation to CLIFF CASEY, artist, for his rendering of the front cover illustration (SAM AT SUNRISE). CLIFF CASEY, 2219 Nashville Drive, Norman, OK 73071

ABOUT THE AUTHOR

Ed Oliver is a teacher/coach in the Harris County School System in Harris County, Georgia. Previously he spent eight years at Columbus High School in Columbus, Georgia, where he was assistant baseball and football coach to Bobby Howard. He was also head coach for fast-pitch softball. Coach Oliver's teams have been state contenders many times and five of Columbus High's baseball teams were state champions while Coach Oliver was on the Howard staff. His 2000 fast-pitch softball team won the first state championship ever for the Harris County school system.

Ed's passion for wildlife has been a lifelong affair. He is a conservationist first and foremost, and a longtime student of the white-tailed deer. Ed shot a huge buck in 1989 that appeared on the cover of *Georgia Sportsman* magazine. He has also been featured in several other wildlife publications. Having long been a pioneer for what he calls, "Give the young ones a chance," Ed was an early proponent of Quality Deer Management (QDM).

"I'm not a great hunter by any stretch of the imagination," Ed says. "Instead I'm a man who has a great appreciation and love for whitetails and for the great outdoors. The chase, the challenge, and the associations I've had with other hunters are the things that are most important to me."

Ed has been married for 43 years to Martha Jo Reese, of Cordele, Georgia. They have four children: Susan (deceased), Spence, Sim and Bess. The two boys have been very much a part of Ed's deer-hunting experiences and he declares, "There is absolutely nothing more rewarding than hunting with your sons on a cold crisp morning. Sharing the peaceful solitude of daybreak and the world of nature coming alive around you, builds bonds that are difficult to equal."

PREFACE

Each year, virtually thousands of hunters race to the woods in search of a giant set of antlers. Every year is filled with anticipation of bringing home a new state record! I've been in that sea of hunters. I'm one of the thousands who have watched the seasons come and close without taking a special deer. However, the lessons I've learned are more important than any set of horns!

On a few occasions, I've been fortunate enough to be in the right place at the right time and I've taken several outstanding trophy bucks. One of those deer inspired this work. That buck had a mid-160s gross Boone and Crockett score and was taken in the location referred to as the Park in this story. The harvesting of that buck was the result of eternal hope. Those of you who brave the cold weather, the rain, the wind and countless hours alone in a deer stand will understand what eternal hope is!

Eternal hope is that fire that burns in your gut. It's that urge that drags you out of a warm bed on a terrible day. It's that determination to sit one more minute while freezing to death. It's that one last look while descending from your deer stand.

It's that internal feeling that tells you, *this is the year all my hard work is going to pay off!* It's the feeling that says, *this is the year I will take the big one and maybe my picture will appear on the cover of a trophy hunting magazine.*

Many of the characters, descriptions, locations and adventures involving the individuals in this story were born in my mind while deer hunting. Some were born while positioned high in a tree stand along a quiet creek. Others were born while sitting on an old bucket; and, always while looking for a glimpse of a really good deer. Harboring eternal hope allows us to believe that today will be the day the deer I've been looking for will pass my way!

It is my prayer that all who read this book will enjoy it as much as I have in creating it. And that somewhere in these pages a smile will come to your face!

Ed Oliver
Harris County, Georgia
August 2010

DEDICATION

This work, as humble as it is, is dedicated to all those who love the great outdoors. It is especially dedicated to those who appreciate and love the ways of the white-tailed deer. It is dedicated to my family and specifically to my wife, Martha Jo. She has been patient all these years while I was out in pursuit of a personal passion – "hunting."

This book is also dedicated to my daughters Susan and Bess and to my sons, Sim and Spence. The two boys have hunted with me for most of their lives. They have been the source of so much hunting pleasure and pride. The book is dedicated to all my friends in the Whitetail Hunting Club of Harris County, Georgia. It is dedicated to Roger Holcombe, Thomas Martin, Robert Shirley and all the club members.

Lastly, this work is dedicated to all others who hold a warm place in their hearts for the joys of hunting and have a deep appreciation and respect for the great American white-tailed deer! It is dedicated with great pride to those hunters who have the patience and humility to let a young buck walk in the hopes of a better hunt on a better day!

Ed Oliver

ACKNOWLEDGEMENTS

Every story has a character and every character has a story! Everyone tells his or her story in some manner. Some tell it through books. Others tell their stories simply by the way they live. We are characters in life and our story is read through the eyes of those who know us. I want to acknowledge the characters that influenced this book. Without the help, encouragement and friendship of Shane Holcombe, this story never would have gone to press. Thanks, Shane for believing in the manuscript and your support. To Roger Holcombe, Robert Shirley, Stan and Patrick Olive, Thomas and Robbie Martin, Wayne Parker, Joey Shirley, Melvin and John Cochran, Allen Rucker, Danny and Josh Payne and certainly, Foster Cagle – "Thanks for your friendship." These men are some of the most knowledgeable outdoorsmen I know and are my close friends.

To Mr. Charles Hogg, who can spin a yarn with the best of them, and to Mr. Perry Williams, who can make me laugh 'til my sides hurt I say, "Thank you very much for sharing your humor with me!" These men are great neighbors and funny characters. To my wife, Martha Jo, my sons Spence and Sim and my daughter, Bess Oliver Carter, "I love you and thank God for you!" To Sam, Big Sam and the other fictional deer characters in this story, I say, "Thanks for allowing me to express my thoughts and philosophies of life through your adventures."

CHAPTER 1

Harris County, Georgia…

It was a cold, rainy night in late October when a young buck deer, known as Sam, and his mother reached their bedding area. They had fed late into the night and the fog was beginning to settle around them. They were glad to be home! They had browsed all the way from Curtis Avery's fields to their sanctuary of short pines on the Hogg place.

Not long after they settled in, Sam heard his dad, "Big Sam," raking trees and coming up the trail he and his mother had browsed in on. With his nose to the ground and his tail at half mast, "Big Sam" rushed into the bedding area. He was full of nervous excitement. The doe scolded him and told him to settle down. It was late and she was very tired. Big Sam told his mate and his son that he had stopped by only to let them know that he was heading over to Troup County.

Obviously put out by his antics, the doe jumped to her feet and said, "Big Sam, it's a bad night to be out running around and chasing something you don't need! You'd be smart to settle down and stay here with us. Just because you think you are bullet proof, doesn't mean that you are! Confidence and ego will be your demise and your hardheadedness overlaps your intelligence!"

Big Sam began to fidget as he prepared to leave. "I've got some business to take care of in Troup County. I'll be home before daybreak!" he exclaimed.

The doe pleaded her case. She told him there was nothing in Troup County that he couldn't live without. "Don't you have all the business you can take care of between Mote Road and Flat Shoals Creek?" she asked. "In fact, you may have *more* business here at home than you can take care of." She said that to Big Sam with a twinkle in her eye and her son, Sam, understood exactly what she was talking about.

Big Sam chuckled and twitched his tail twice. He then went over and gently bumped horns with Sam before wheeling around and trotting off down the trail. In a few minutes, they heard him hit Flat Shoals Creek. What a sound! It could be heard for half a mile.

The doe laughed and said, "That's your dad, Sam! No deer crosses Flat Shoals Creek like Big Sam! That's his calling card! He hits the big creek like a logging truck. Every deer in both counties, Troup and Harris, knows when he's traveling. He's been doing it for years and everyone has grown accustomed to it.

"Your dad is special, you know," the doe continued. "Without question, he's the most influential deer in these parts and he's so proud. His ancestors came from a cold northern section of Wisconsin and the love for cold weather is in his blood. My stock all descended from the brush country of South Texas and I hate cold weather. They say that Big Sam's relatives and my parents were shipped into these parts the same year, and it's odd how we met and that we've been together all these years. He's from Wisconsin and I'm from Texas. It's strange that we met in Georgia!

"He's been a great father to you and he's protected us all these years. I just wish he would settle down a little in his old age. He embarrassed me tonight while we were on the Avery place. You know how deer gossip? Two of the does over there were whispering tonight – whispering but talking loud enough to make sure I heard. They said that Big Sam had been seen running with a bunch of whores over on O'Neal Road."

"He was seen in an uncompromising situation and I know that he's had some improper relationships over there. Son, they have no idea that I've seen him with both of them! They're just jealous! No matter what you hear about your dad, he's still your dad and he's the most imposing animal in our territory. Be proud of what you are and who you are. Be proud that the blood in your veins is pure. We're all imported and there's not one basket-racked crossbreed in your pedigree. You are from royal stock!

"Never has an outside buck passed through our area, much less taken a doe with him. Big Sam has kept us pure and that's why we look the way we do. We are strong and have great size and character! Someday you'll understand and someday it'll be your responsibility to preserve it. Big Sam will pass that torch to you!"

***

The night passed slowly. Sam's mother was up several times and once woke Sam and asked if he'd heard from his dad. She was very worried. It was almost daybreak by then and they hadn't heard Big Sam hit Flat Shoals. He was *always* in before first light. The doe had a bad feeling, and she had not slept a wink. Something, maybe that sixth sense that all deer possess, had worried her that Big Sam was in danger and that's why she had pleaded with him to stay home in Harris County on such a cold, foggy night.

Big Sam was the biggest and strongest deer that young Sam had ever seen. He was huge, yet gentle with him and his mother. The doe often referred to him as a giant of a deer with the heart of an angel. His huge size and presence kept him out of trouble most of the time. Few bucks in the area dared challenge him, and he'd not fought since he was four years old. It was understood in the area that Big Sam was *the* man and that was that!

As they waited that foggy morning, the doe talked a lot about her mate. She told young Sam that she had loved Big Sam through thick and thin. She told him that she often appeared ignorant about his carrying on, but she knew better! She ignored his antics just to maintain peace in the family. She told young Sam the real reason his dad had gone to Troup County was to check a scrape line he had laid there three days earlier. Big Sam hadn't told her that, but she always had a way of knowing those things, and this time was no exception. His business there was of a personal nature, and the intuitive mother doe knew he had put himself and the family in danger by hanging out in an unfamiliar area on such a terrible night.

Daylight began to break! In the far distance, across the Troup County clear cut, they heard the lone howl of a wild dog. It was followed by another and another and another. The howls were complimented by yelps and barks

3

that soon developed into a full chase! The doe jumped to her feet. "They're after Big Sam," she screamed, "and he'll bring those mongrels right in here and we'll have to run for our lives all day! I begged the bastard to stay home!" She was really upset.

The chase was definitely headed their way, and it was obvious that the sounds were made by wild dogs, not coyotes. The doe began to prance around and wind the foggy air. Her nose was straight up when she and Sam heard the shrill sound of a truck horn out on Highway 18. The sound of the horn was followed by screaming, skidding tires and a loud crash!

"Oh, my God, that's Big Sam!" she screamed, and leaped from the bedding area in a mad dash toward Flat Shoals Creek.

When they hit Flat Shoals, young Sam couldn't help but think that both of them made a simple little splash compared to the thunderous crash that Big Sam always made whenever he crossed. They continued through the pines. As they reached the ridge above the road, they saw lights shining and two men in orange vests standing by an old yellow pick-up truck. One headlight was shining ahead and the left fender was smashed almost to the tire. The men, one short, dark, Italian-looking guy and the other, a great big fellow with a beard, were holding flashlights on something in the ditch. They appeared to be in total admiration of a huge buck in their lights.

The big guy took the lead and dragged the massive deer up the shoulder of the road. The Italian let down the tailgate and after they counted, "One, two, three," the heavy deer hit the truck bed with a thud! The old truck sank to its springs under the weight. The big deer's horns could be seen well above the bed liner and there was no doubt in young Sam's mind that the deer they had loaded was his dad, Big Sam.

The doe raised her right hoof and dropped it with a thud. She winded the trail they were standing on and they both knew it was the same route Big Sam had taken earlier that morning. The doe dropped here hoof again and listened. She continued this as the old truck turned in the road and passed in front of them. As it passed, she gave a loud, shrill nasal blast and stomped several times more. She had done this for Big Sam many, many, times to warn him of danger. However, they both knew that this was too little, too late.

As the truck passed, the doe dropped her nose to the trail again. Then she raised her head high in the air and winded a scent from afar. The last familiar odors of Big Sam were passing before her and there was nothing she could do! Sadly, she would never smell that familiar scent again and her heart was broken. They stood for a brief moment as the doe seemed to be trying to escape from the tragedy. Then she gave a twitch of her tail that said, "Let's move on," and she started back toward the bedding area. It was almost as if she were trying to deny that it had actually happened. She wondered if it was only a bad dream. She seemed to be thinking, *Maybe it wasn't Big Sam after all; maybe he'll be home when we get there. Maybe he'll come back tomorrow... That couldn't have been Big Sam....*

Young Sam's thoughts were of a different nature. He watched as the old truck topped the next ridge and turned left on Drummond Road. He could still see those big horns sticking up above the truck bed and he knew he'd never see his dad again!

Without question, Sam's first year of life had been 12 months to remember. His mother was growing older and she was never the same after Big Sam's death. She spent more and more time to herself and had little or no patience with young Sam. The fast-growing yearling soon found himself moving in different circles, and only on rare occasions did he spend time with her.

Later on, during the following spring, the doe failed to give birth for the first time in seven years, and everyone knew why. She simply withdrew and showed little zest for living. The love of her life was gone and nothing seemed the same. Life simply was not as sweet. She really had nothing to look forward to. Her son was almost mature and needed a life of his own. Friends suggested that she get out and mingle with other deer in the area. Some even suggested that she find another mate. To them she boldly said, "Until you walk in someone's shoes and until you've felt their pain, don't go advising them about what they should do!"

***

The following fall found the doe thin, gray and frail. Her teeth were worn down to the gums and she spent most of her feeding time in open pastures and fields. Her spirit was clearly broken, and the only time she showed any sign of being the grand lady that she had always been occurred when she visited places she and Big Sam had frequented. She would always perk up and show excitement when she entered old feeding or bedding areas they had shared and called home.

A full year passed after Big Sam's death, and Sam gained weight. His status in the social order changed. Fully 2 1/2 years old now, he carried some clout in his clan and there was a challenge around every corner. His mother had often told him about Big Sam's battles to become the dominate buck that he was, and Sam certainly appreciated those stories now. However, being the heir apparent to his dad's territory was not a foregone conclusion. Instead of things being easier for him, they were harder. Old enemies of the family came out of the woodwork and he had to fight daily for respect and rank.

On one occasion, after battling two, 3-year-old bucks all afternoon, Sam wandered into his old bedding area. It was the same area where he and his mother had bedded on the night of his dad's death. To his great surprise, his mother was there. Sam was sore to the bone and scraped up to the point of bleeding around his shoulders and ribs. One ear was split and he had a broken brow tine. His mother looked old and tired but happy to see him. As usual, she showed patience and love. It would be the last night they would ever spend together and one that would have a lasting effect on Sam's life. She told him that she was glad that he had come, but that she understood why.

"If you were healthy and strong tonight, you wouldn't have come," she said. "Your daddy was that way. Son, your daddy was the most hardheaded buck I ever knew. I know he loved me, but sometimes it took getting his ass kicked to make him show it! Sometimes a good comeuppance is what you need too! Your dad became a great leader from both strength and getting his ass kicked. He couldn't have reached his potential without both.

"Remember, son – strength alone will lead you down a lonely path! Learn some humility and patience early in life and they'll pay you rich dividends. Many deer in our clan have met untimely deaths from lack of patience, caution and discipline. I knew your dad had no business going into Troup County last October. However, during the rut, I couldn't do anything with him. We all think that an old yellow truck killed him, but Son, it wasn't that truck that killed your dad! It was that scrape line he laid in Troup County. It was in an area he had no business being in!

"Son, a cool and intelligent head is always more beneficial to you than an abundance of testosterone! Don't you ever forget that! Wayward females have been the demise of many a good buck. Find yourself a good doe. Find her while you're young, and run with her and lay down with her. I know you'll have business to take care of, but don't let your cravings run your life. I always tried to tell your dad that, and he abided by it until the rut came each year, and then he went into a testosterone-driven rage! One of the last things I remember saying to him was, 'Big Sam, there ain't no fool like an old fool!'

"You know what? He thought I was talking about somebody else! It went right over his head! Love of family and duty is what's important, Son! Take care of business in your own area and learn to love. Fight for what's rightfully yours. Defend what's yours with your last breath, but you'll get yourself killed trying to serve every hot doe in two counties. Just look at your dad!"

Sam and his mother spent the whole night talking. The things she told him that night stayed with him all his life; things like the importance of love of family, pride in who he was, fighting for what was rightfully his and taking care of business in his own home territory. She told him that finding someone to love and lay down with, cultivating humility, patience, caution, and most of all, having a cool, intelligent head, was always more beneficial than an over abundance of testosterone!

The following morning broke blue-bird clear. Sam's mother seemed much happier and Sam's soreness was greatly improved. The doe got to her feet early and walked over to where Sam was bedded. She licked his face and ears. She twitched her tail several times and headed off alone toward the sweetest honeysuckle patch in Harris County. Sam got to his feet thinking about finding that good, young doe his mother had talked about! That was the last time he ever saw his mother. As he remembered her, she was wading in honeysuckle up to her stomach and happy. Yes, he believed that she was happy!

After having grown his third full rack of horns, Sam spent his fourth winter in seclusion. He was tired from the rut, weak from all the battles he'd fought, and depressed from the loss of his mother. He found himself gradually moving east in his territory and always looking and searching for that special doe that his mother had encouraged him to find. By early spring, he felt more secure and his energy level was up. On a beautiful spring day in April of that year, he was browsing in a sanctuary area known as "the Park."

Lush pastures, huge oak trees and lots of cover dominated this part of Sam's territory and the beauty of the place seemed to soothe the pain of losing his mother. Sam thought many times that this place was too beautiful not to share with someone he loved. During the month of May of that year, his dreams came true!

Turkeys were gobbling, birds were singing, owls were hooting, squirrels were scampering, chipmunks were scooting and every bush, tree, and shrub was blooming. It was spring in the Park and the entire world seemed so at peace. It was in this peaceful environment that *she* appeared. Sam was standing in the big oaks that overlook the Avery pastures, and like a perfect story-book ending, there she was on the horizon! Her name was Grace and she was long, sleek, tall and beautiful. She was the only doe in the world that even approached his mother in stature or class. It was love at first sight and Sam didn't even have any horns! He had shed them in February and was just beginning to start new growth. He felt a little embarrassed; yet, he knew this was going to be more than a one-night affair and he remembered his mother's words, "Find yourself a good doe early in life – one that you can run with and one that you can live with."

There was no doubt in his mind that Grace was the most beautiful doe he had ever seen and that his life was about to change. She had Wisconsin imports on both sides of her pedigree. She was as royally bred as any of his tribe and it showed. Patience, humility, caution, and love – the traits his mother always talked about suddenly had meaning. He knew that in the fall, he would have business to tend to. However, there could be no doubt that this was the doe he would run and lay with for the remainder of his life!

The summer passed quickly and his fourth rack grew huge. Grace found it hard to believe that Sam was the same slick-headed buck she'd met in the spring. Mature in every way now, the responsibility of dominating the territory was Sam's and he had no equal in either size or strength. He and Grace ran together daily. At night, they always bedded in the same area.

The fall breeding season came in an orderly fashion with few battles to fight. Sam took care of business in a cautious manner and he was always home with his doe before daybreak. Often he thought about his mother and Big Sam. The lessons learned from them made him strong, and much meaning came into his life through the examples they had set.

The next spring, Grace gave birth to twins; one, a strapping male, and the other, a female of rare quality. Their mom quickly named them Little Sam and Star. The four deer spent the next year in and around the Park. It was a safe and beautiful place with the only danger being an unusual and strange family of hunters. A little ol' man and his two boys hunted in the Park in those days. But it seemed as though their main purpose was to observe the deer instead of shoot them. They seemed to be no threat at all. They became as much a part of the Park as the four deer were, and Sam and his family learned to accept them and have little fear of them.

Little Sam and Star grew rapidly. By the fall of Sam's sixth year, they were big and strong. Little Sam grew a nice 6-point rack for his second season and Star developed into a doe that truly stood out among her peers. They had lived in peace for two years and life couldn't have been sweeter. With caution and love, Grace took great care of them and they were a happy family unit.

CHAPTER 2

Life has a way of humbling us all. In the midst of happiness, danger or turmoil often rears its ugly head. This was true in Sam's sixth year. The rut was just beginning when word passed that trouble was brewing in the far western part of his territory. Sam left his family in an effort to determine what the problem was and how it could be remedied. Grace, Little Sam and Star remained in the Park and waited for Sam's return.

Two days passed and Sam showed up in the bedding area late one frosty night. It was the middle of October and he was furious. Grace tried to calm him down, but she was seeing a side of him that she had never seen before. He was angry to the point of being dangerous and nothing seemed to calm him.

Finally he exclaimed, "You won't believe what's happened over yonder… They're cutting all the big timber on O'Neal Road and things are a mess! Logging trucks are running the roads and chain saws are everywhere, clear cutting everything! I'm telling you, there ain't a tree big enough to rub left in the whole territory. It's a mess!"

Grace spoke in an effort to calm Sam. "That's not our area; we don't belong there Sam. What's your worry and why all the anger? It won't affect us here in the Park. We have plenty here in the Park and always will!"

Having worked himself into a fury, Sam was snorting, pawing and in a dangerous state. "I'll tell you how it affects us," he said. "Those deer over there are out of food! That's Nasty Pete's territory and I know him. Dad

11

fought him for years and he's a no good half-breed! He has no character. He's is a common-bred pervert and he's raised nothing but a bunch of basket-racked bastards."

"Tell us how you really feel about him!" Grace said sarcastically.

"This isn't funny!" Sam continued. "The word is already out that he plans to move his bunch across Highway 219 and claim our western territory, but it ain't gonna happen, honey!

"I'm telling you, we ain't gonna have no basket-racked morons in these parts and I'll fight with my dying breath to keep it that way!" Sam screamed. "Dad would roll over in his grave if he knew what was going on. Big Sam fought his entire life to keep our genetics clean and pure and I can't let him down. Do you understand that, sweetie? Do you understand that? I know what my mom said about peace, caution, and love of family. However, I also remember what she said about fighting for what was rightfully ours. Nasty Pete has no rightful claim to anything east of Highway 219 and I'll fight him every inch of the way.

"You don't know him! He's a sneaky bastard and you can't trust him. He's a big, ugly 9-pointer with no class at all. They say his bunch is so inbred that you can't tell the bucks from the does and that Nasty Pete has bred his own daughters for years. He's no good and his whole clan is an inferior bunch of retards. They'll ruin all we've worked and fought for all these years!"

"Well, what're you gonna do?" Grace asked.

"I'm going over there tonight and lay a scrape line from Sand Creek to the Stage Coach Road. If one of those basket-racked fools even as much as takes a leak in it, it's gonna to be war. I tell you, it's gonna be war!"

Sam turned with a jerk and disappeared into the thick cover. He was headed west toward Sand Creek!

Little Sam said, "Mom, maybe we should go with him."

Grace said, "No, he's in a state of mind that I've never seen. He'll have to settle down before anyone can talk to him. It's his daddy, Big Sam, coming out in him! He loves us dearly but there's a side to him that no one really knows. There are several sides to everyone, Son! Tough times bring out the best and worst in all of us. I understand the urgency of him going tonight but I hope he'll get back into our area before daybreak. It's getting late in October, you know, and there are hunters in our woods!

"By the way, I ran into an old doe today that has lived in the Park much longer than any of us. She told me to tell Sam that those two young boys and that little ol' man were not to be trusted. She said to tell Sam that they would never harm either of you, or me, but that they would bust a cap on your daddy in a heartbeat if given half a chance. Gosh, with all that's going on, I forgot to tell him!

"That same old doe thinks that the little ol' man is responsible for the disappearance of Big Elrod several years ago. Big Elrod simply disappeared one morning in the fall. Some say that he was my daddy, but you know how deer talk! I thought about that today. I wonder why the old doe made a point of bringing that up to me! I wonder if she knows that Big Elrod *was* my father!"

Sam was gone all night. He spent some time looking for ol' Nasty Pete but most of his time was spent laying down his scrape line. From Sand Creek to the Stage Coach Road he clearly marked his territory. Just as daylight was breaking, he started back to the Park. Sam's temper had settled down some by then and he was thinking about his family and the sanctuary of their bedding area.

He had just crossed the R&R Creek and started up Stage Coach Road when his legs suddenly folded under him! *What's happening?* he thought. Pain ripped through his body and blood ran from his shoulder! His entire body went numb and he almost lost consciousness. Shock set in and he was trembling all over. *What's going on?*

With all the energy he could muster and with the help of adrenaline, he scrambled to his feet! Just as he made it up, the ground exploded under him. He leaped forward a few feet and a two-inch poplar sapling exploded in his face! Fear overtook his body and another rush of adrenaline surged through his system. As he struggled to stay afoot, one giant leap landed him in the cover of a thicket filled with brush, bramble and weeds. Another leap and he was literally bounding over downfall timber. While still struggling to stay on his feet, the ground exploded under him once again and the next leap landed him in the middle of R&R Creek. His shoulder was a mess! Blood was rushing down his leg and he was getting weak. For the first time in his adult life, he was afraid. *What's happening to me?* he wondered again. *What's causing all this pain? Could it be hunters?*

The next thing Sam remembered was the sound of human voices. He had collapsed in R&R Creek. His nose was resting on a sandbar. His wounded shoulder was face down to the sandy creek bottom. He was positioned against a steep bank of the creek. He was invisible except for one side of his giant antlers and the bulge of his rib cage. Two hunters were walking the creek bank above him. Their voices were quiet and low, yet they showed signs of excitement. They passed right by Sam and continued downstream.

After they had passed him, one of the hunters hollered, "There he goes!" The man then fired a shot in the direction of the Wyche Farm. Apparently a bedded buck belonging to ol' Nasty Pete's bunch had gotten caught up in this ambush and probably saved Sam's life.

As the two hunters walked by Sam for the second time, one commented, "I thought I hit him harder than that, but guess I didn't. That second deer didn't show any signs of being hurt! I guess it was the same buck!"

Blood from Sam's shoulder quickly mixed with the white sand on the creek bottom and formed a Jell-o-like pad over his wound. After some hours, the bleeding finally slowed but he was too weak to even move. His life hung in the balance!

What a way to die, he thought.

Then he lost consciousness! All day long Sam lay in the cold waters of R&R Creek. His body temperature dropped. As nightfall came, he had little hope. Drifting in and out of consciousness, he became delirious. He began to have strange dreams. At one time his mind and spirit ascended above him. He could see his body in the water and wondered: *What are you doing here, Sam? Get up. Your family is waiting for you in the Park!*

Another time his dad, Big Sam, appeared on the sandbar. He felt Big Sam nudge him with his nose. He rattled his big horns against Sam's antlers as if to say, "Get up, Son, you can't give in to the pain. You have too much responsibility here. Fight for your life, Son. You come from a long line of survivors and your family needs you. You gotta fight, Son. It's in your blood. Don't give up. You gotta live. The clan depends on you. You need to think of Little Sam, Star, and Grace! You gotta make it, Son. You just gotta make it!"

Later on, he had another vision about his mother and he could feel her sweet warm breath on his face. He could feel her soft muzzle nudging him as if to help him up. Her encouragement and love seemed so real and so strong that Sam found himself struggling to crawl up on the sandbar. Hours passed. Well into the night, Sam mustered strength enough to rise on his feet. The bleeding had almost stopped but the soreness and weakness was unbearable. He knew that the hunters would most likely be back in the area at daybreak and that his life depended on moving now.

Daybreak found Sam struggling along the last few yards of the path leading to his family's bedding area. Grace blew several times at his approach but quickly realized it was Sam and that he was coming home. Little Sam and Star had bounded away from the area when their mother blew, but quickly made their way back in.

Once the traditional scenting and grooming was finished, Sam said, "You won't believe where I've been and what happened to me yesterday...."

Several days passed with Sam being able to do little more than just rest. The shoulder was busted up pretty badly but no bones were broken. He would heal and live but it would take some time. Remembering his mom, he thought, *Sam you gotta be patient!*

The following Friday evening, word came to Sam that Nasty Pete had moved his bunch into the western part of the territory and that Pete himself had been seen on the Wyche farm. Sam was furious again! No doubt word had spread of his injuries and Sam knew Nasty Pete would take advantage of the situation. He thought deep into the night. About 2:30 in the morning, he got to his feet. Little Sam, Star and Grace were there when he exclaimed that he was going after Nasty Pete. Fear ran through the group as Grace, in disgust, screamed, "Sam, you're in no shape to fight! You're lucky to be alive! You have half your strength and you don't stand a chance against that big sneaky brute!"

"I'm going," Sam said, "and I'm taking Little Sam and Star with me. I want you to stay here and keep peace in the Park. Tell our crowd that I'm fine and that I'll be back midday tomorrow, Saturday. Tell them that after tomorrow, we won't be bothered by Nasty Pete ever again."

With that, Sam summoned Little Sam and Star. He led the way down the trail and headed west. Not much was said as Sam, Little Sam and Star made their way toward the O'Neal cutover. Sam was moving with a purpose and it was difficult for Little Sam and Star to keep up!

After a steady march of about an hour, they reached the R&R Creek. They were just past the Old Stage Coach Road. Sam was aware of their location. After fording the creek, Sam stopped to rest and to explain their mission. With a rare tone of fear in his voice, he told Little Sam and Star his intentions. The reason they were brought along was simple. If anything happened to him, Star was to take an accurate account back to their mother. Little Sam's purpose for being there was to locate Nasty Pete and bring him to Sam. Sam wanted to meet Nasty Pete on grounds of his choosing and not deep in Nasty Pete's own range.

Little Sam was to move into Pete's territory and put the word out that Sam wanted to talk about making peace. He was also supposed to put the word out that Sam was injured and wanted to put an end to the feud. Sam told Little Sam to arrange a meeting along their borders and he specified the back neck of the Wyche farm pastures as good ground. Little Sam seemed surprised at this talk of peace. He had never known his dad, or his granddad before him, to concede anything. He thought his dad might be hurt worse than he appeared. Maybe he was going to die and was trying to make peace for the family before his death.

Little Sam thought, *No need to ask questions, just do as you are told and hope Dad survives this thing! Hope Dad survives, but what about Star and me? What if Nasty Pete decides to whip up on me before I get him back here? What if Pete refuses to talk peace and brings a bunch of his thugs along. Dad has little chance as it is.*

Don't think, just do as you are told, he decided.

Moving up the slope of planted pines west of R&R Creek, they crossed Sam's scrape line. The scrape line had been made along the firebreak that separated the back of Sam's range and Nasty Pete's territory. It was well before dawn and Sam stopped to give last minute instructions. He was specific. He said, "Little Sam, follow the fire break to the Wyche farm corner. Stay on your side of the creek and it'll take you to a neck in the Wyche pasture. That's where I want to meet Pete.

"There's a high ridge between there and Highway 219. By the time you reach that high ridge in the pasture, Nasty Pete will know you've crossed the line and he'll know you are there. He may come to you or he may send some of his thugs."

"But what if he won't come back with me?" Little Sam asked.

"He's a coward, Son," said Sam. "If I was healthy, you couldn't drag him back here, but he's a coward and he'll not let this chance slip by. Just remember, I want to meet him between daylight and sunup. That's so important, between daylight and sunup. Star and I will be waiting in the neck of the Wyche pasture and remember, should things get frantic this morning and should a chase result, stay downwind and use caution. This is my business and the last thing in the world I want to happen is for y'all to get hurt over this."

Little Sam looked at his dad. Sam appeared so frail. The wounded shoulder was dripping some blood now from the trip. Sam looked like he had lost 75 pounds. In fact, his always-impressive antlers looked simply huge on a body that was so puny and weak!

Little Sam thought, *What if Dad's efforts to talk reason with Pete fail? What if Nasty Pete kills him? What will Star and I tell Mom? What'll happen to the territory? Can I defend it?*

All this and more ran through the young buck's mind as he started down the firebreak toward the Wyche farm pasture. Sam and Star followed at a good distance and the sky was beginning to show light in the east.

Little Sam followed the barbed-wire fence of the Wyche farm until he could see the high knoll. He could hear the traffic on Highway 219 and could see the lights of cars and trucks. He remembered briefly the stories told about his grandfather, Big Sam. He said a prayer and inched his way up the fescue slopes until he reached the top of the ridge. From there he could see forever. Across Highway 219 and to the northwest he could see the vast cutover timber all the way to O'Neal Road. In the darkness along the fence line he had just walked, he could make out the images of two deer.

As these two images grew larger, Little Sam realized they were coming closer. Soon Little Sam knew he was looking at two of the biggest animals he had ever seen in the woods! He thought, *Should I wait, or should I meet them?*

Then a lesson his dad had taught him came to mind. *Always negotiate from strength not weakness.* With that thought, he started in their direction. *If this theory of negotiation from strength rather than weakness is true, why does Dad want to talk peace when he's at half strength?* Little Sam wondered. *Don't think. Just do as you are told!*

The distance between Little Sam and the other deer closed quickly. As he approached the two strangers, he realized what his dad meant when he talked about "basket-racked half-breeds." The three deer met in the darkness with hair standing on end. Little Sam thought that a fight was unavoidable right then and there. But just before horns met in combat, Nasty Pete burst on the scene! Like his dad had always said, Pete was a dirty fighter and always let someone front for him.

Before Little Sam could begin to relay his message, Nasty Pete broke in, "Sam's hurt, ain't he? He's down and now he wants to negotiate. Let me tell you something – I'll talk to him but we're moving east. I'm moving my whole clan across R&R Creek and maybe into the Park. Where is he?"

Little Sam couldn't believe the sheer size of Pete. He was rippling with muscle and his ugly 9-point rack was broken and most disgusting. It looked like he had scraped his velvet off in a rock pile. Pete was the biggest, ugliest, most unbecoming individual Little Sam had ever seen. As they started off toward the neck of the Wyche pasture, Little Sam could see daylight breaking in the east.

Sam and Star could barely be seen in the darkness as Little Sam, Pete and his two thugs approached. Little Sam thought, *How in the world is Dad going to open up a settlement conversation with this roughneck who is so cocky and looking for a one-sided fight?*

At first light, the two big bucks stepped to front stage. Sam was weak and still bleeding from the shoulder. Pete was big and strong and fully expected Sam to open with subordinate gestures and offer concessions for peace. They summed each other up with circles that brought them closer and closer together. Little Sam kept waiting for his dad to get to high ground but he didn't. As the two big bucks got within a few feet of each other, Sam erupted; not in a subordinate manner, but with a bold and dominate bellow!

Every hair was standing out on his body and he was at full alert.

His massive rack was high in the air and his swollen neck was bulging. He screamed, "Pete you're a counterfeit, good-for-nothing faggot! You've brought shame to your herd and you're nothing but a basket-racked asshole. Now fight you two-faced bastard!"

With that, Pete gave a great snort-wheeze and slammed Sam's weakened body with 300 pounds of fury. His ugly rack gored Sam's wounded shoulder and you could hear the breath leave Sam. Sam went to his knees and the blood flowed. Pete came on again and again. It was terrifying! Sam was down, and when he got back to his feet, he lunged toward the trail home. Pete was goring him in the rump every third step.

Star was in tears. "I thought you told me Dad was a fighter, Little Sam. I'm embarrassed. My dad's a coward! He's running. I'm ashamed! I can't believe my dad's a coward!"

"Shut your mouth, Star," screamed Little Sam. "This fight ain't over. Dad may be lots of things, but he ain't a coward! I'm telling you, this fight ain't over and you just shut your mouth and remember what Dad said about following downwind and being cautious."

Little Sam was in shock. He thought Sam was there to talk peace. Instead, Sam had provoked the damndest deer fight he had ever seen. What in the devil was going on? Daylight was evident and the sun was rising in the east.

The fight and chase continued up the firebreak and across Sam's scrape line. Sam was weak. He would fight and run, fight and run. There was no question who was winning this battle. Across R&R Creek they fought – limbs breaking, horns clashing – with moans, groans and grunts. Star and Little Sam followed downwind. The two other half-breeds from Pete's bunch watched at a distance. As they fought up the Stage Coach Road, Sam broke into a run with Pete in hot pursuit.

All of a sudden, Sam cut sharply into the cover and Nasty Pete continued at full speed up Stage Coach Road! At that second, the whole territory erupted in the loudest BOOM ever heard by a deer. Sam stood in the thick cover and watched Nasty Pete fold up like a rag doll! He had been shot through the heart on the dead run!

The woods became deathly quiet! Not a sound could be heard anywhere. It was the most eerie feeling. No sound at all, nothing but silence. No birds chirping, no squirrels running, no crows calling, nothing – nothing but silence!

Shock prevailed in Little Sam and Star! Time passed and nothing moved. Little Sam whispered to Star, "I told you Dad wasn't a coward! Remember what he always says about a cool, intelligent head being beneficial! Remember what he says about fighting for what is rightfully ours? Remember all that stuff? Well, you just saw it all in action!"

The silence was broken when a bearded man with only one eye appeared. He was wearing an orange vest. As soon as he showed up, Sam broke and ran through the thicket and into the planted pines. He was headed home. Little Sam and Star stood frozen in time. The hunter approached Nasty Pete, reached down, lifted up the deer's gnarly horns, and smiled.

"What a day!" he exclaimed. Then the big man sat on a log, opened up a fresh pack of Levi Garrett chewing tobacco and admired Nasty Pete.

After some time, a second hunter appeared. He had white hair, funny looking teeth and a white mustache. He looked very much like a Southern Baptist preacher. He wore thick goofy-looking glasses and his movements were slow and deliberate, as if he were afraid of tripping over something.

The big guy said in a low voice, "So this is the deer you missed last Saturday?"

"No, hell, no," said the white-haired guy. "The son of a gun I missed had a set of horns like I've never seen. This deer here is huge, but he's the ugliest, nastiest looking bastard I've ever seen. Look at those horns. He looks like he's been fighting chain saws all of his life. Bet you five dollars he's one of those O'Neal Road freaks with bad genetics. I hope they ain't moving this way!"

The big guy said, "Nope, I just have a feeling that this put a stop to any moving of that bunch. I just have that feeling!"

Both hunters looked up and were alerted to the sound of a truck bouncing down the Old Stage Coach Road. The old road was washed out in places. It was full of gullies and nearly impassable. Both hunters were laughing and the big guy said, "Here he comes! He had to have heard me shoot and I'll bet he saw some of that fight. He was hunting on the swamp stand! Those two bucks fought all the way up that firebreak west of him. They probably went right by the creek stand!"

The ol' yellow truck came to a bouncing stop and the Italian looking driver got out. "Who shot?" he asked.

"I did," the big, one-eyed guy said.

"Which one did you shoot? I hope you killed that ugly son of a gun! He was whipping the ever-loving shit out of that big horned, good-looking deer! You know that other deer was hurt, don't you? Yeah, he had a hole in his shoulder big as a quarter and the biggest set of horns I've ever seen except for that big buck we ran over on Highway 18 several years ago. You know what? He looked a lot like that deer."

The white-haired hunter with thick glasses broke in. "I told y'all I hit that big deer! That had to be another deer that jumped up while we were looking for the one I shot last Saturday. I knew I hit him with that first shot! I just knew I did. Let me tell you one thing, he's gotta be smart! I'll bet he let us walk right by him in that creek. I never looked in the creek again after that other deer got up. He made a monkey out of us, boys!"

"Yeah," said the big guy, "that's how they grow them big balls. They tell me that the smarter they are, the bigger their balls. You ever heard that?"

"No," said the white-haired guy. "But if that deer brought this ugly one in here to get his ass shot off, then I'll guarantee you, he's got a syrup-bucket-full of balls to go along with that head full of horns of his!"

The Italian was getting a kick out of all the discussion and said, "It's time to toast this ugly old bastard and get back to camp."

They did, and after counting, "One, two, three," they threw Nasty Pete into the bed of the old yellow truck. He hit with a thud and mashed the springs down pretty good but no horns could be seen above the fender walls. The old truck turned around. Little Sam and Star saw the wrecked fender and the single headlight.

"You know, Star," said Little Sam, "Dad has always talked about an old yellow truck that ran over granddaddy, Big Sam, years ago. Could that possibly be the same truck? Could those men possibly be the same hunters?"

"No," said Star. "That ain't possible! Big Sam was killed way over yonder on Highway 18 near Flat Shoals Creek. Ain't no way. Hey, we better check on Dad. He's had time to get home by now."

Little Sam and Star bounded off, took a short cut home, and hit the logging road just past the big pipe crossing. They slipped into their sanctuary of thick, short, pines and honeysuckle. There, in a deep cover of pine straw, they bedded down for the day with their mother, Grace, and their tired, tired daddy, Sam.

After time had passed and after they had rested a bit, Little Sam turned to his dad and said, "Dad, tell me the truth. Did you plan everything that happened today? Did you provoke that fight to lure Pete into that ambush?"

After a few minutes of deep thought, Sam replied, "Little Sam, that's one thing you'll never know! What you need to know and remember from today's experience is to always fight for what is rightfully yours, and cultivate patience and humility. Strength alone will lead you down a lonely path. There ain't no fool like an old fool and most importantly, a cool, intelligent head is always more beneficial than having an over abundance of testosterone!"

Then, Sam got up, stretched long and hard, twitched his great tail several times and limped toward his favorite feeding spot in the Park.

CHAPTER 3

Life is always a gamble, and whether or not Sam schemed to draw Nasty Pete into an ambush will never be known. However, when one lives in the woods and loves the characters that dwell there, a great respect for an animal's intellect and instinct grows. The little ol' man and his two sons who hunted in the Park certainly respected this intellect and had a great appreciation for the deer they hunted. Sam had a mutual respect for them and often observed them from afar.

They were different in their approach to hunting, and although Sam feared them, he also felt a sense of harmony and peace. In fact, Sam had developed somewhat of a trust for them. He always kept his distance and his keen sense of smell alerted him of their presence.

"I know you'll not harm my does or younger bucks but it's my responsibility to keep my distance and stay out of your sight," Sam said to himself as if he were carrying on a conversation with the little ol' man. "You're a class act but I'm a trophy deer. If I make a mistake, it's my fault. If you make one, I learn from it and live another day. You learn fast when your life depends on it. The more you have at stake, the faster you learn.

"Bucks like me don't get to be king of the woods by being careless. They get to be king of the woods by being smart and cautions. Deer coolers all over Georgia are full because of dumb acts committed by careless bucks and most of them fill up during the rut. The rut brings on crazy behavior. It brings out the dumb ass in the best of us. That's what happened to Big Elrod some years ago and we believe that it was you, the ol' man, who killed him. Big Elrod was king of these woods in those days. He had everything going for him. He was huge and impressive. He had whipped every buck around and had no competition. In fact, he had it so good that he lost respect for caution.

"That's what happens when things get really good and we feel we can do no wrong or that we are invincible. That's when bad things happen. Big Elrod had plenty of does. He had so many that he couldn't service them all and he wouldn't think of letting another buck help him. No, he had to nail 'em all, and on the morning you put a hole in him, that was his intent. Yes, breed 'em all!

"He had 10 hot does in his area and his intent was to serve every one of them and probably would have if it hadn't been for you. Big Elrod walked right into an ambush. If he hadn't been so selfish, it never would have happened. But that's how it was. He had sex on the brain and it cost him a hole through his boiler room! His ol' carcass wasn't even cool in the freezer before two young bucks moved in and took care of *his* unfinished business. When things get too easy for us – look out – disaster could be lurking around the corner!"

***

Sam's wounds from his battle with Nasty Pete eventually healed. By springtime, he was well and strong. He had shed his magnificent antlers somewhere on the Curtis Avery farm and now he was a huge, slick-headed buck. Food was plentiful and life was easy. The does were fat and everyone anticipated the spring birth of fawns and new antler growth for the bucks.

A different kind of hunter was in the woods now. These hunters ignored deer, but seemed to be insanely foolish about turkeys. They moved around a lot and hooted like owls in the early morning darkness. They were strange characters, to say the least! One morning, just after daybreak, Star, Little Sam, Grace and Sam were browsing across the clear cut near the Wyche farm. Turkeys were gobbling and cackling all over the place.

One freestanding dogwood tree stood alone in the clear cut field. It was in full bloom and beautiful. The four deer were moving toward it. Thick undergrowth grew near the tree and it was the only cover within 300 yards. The deer were within five yards of the tree when the wind changed.

"It's the ol' man!" Grace snorted. "I've never smelled him so strong!"

With that, all four deer leaped into the dense cover under the dogwood tree. When they did, they literally leaped into the little ol' man's lap. He was set up in camouflage and it was him who had been cackling like a turkey. Grace skirted him on the right side, Sam leaped right over his head, Star brushed by his shoulder and Little Sam ran right over him. It was hard to determine who was startled the most – the four deer or the ol' man!

It was the closest they had ever been to him, and as they looked over their shoulders, they saw him cleaning out his pants and shaking his head. They had seen him many times and he had watched them constantly. However, they had never been elbow-to-elbow in such close quarters. He didn't seem like such a bad guy – for a hunter, that is. In fact, it happened so fast that once it was over, the four deer couldn't believe it.

They stood for a long two minutes and questioned each other to see if it really had happened.

Grace finally raised her long white tail and the others followed suit. Still in shock, the four deer jogged on toward R&R Creek for a drink and a late morning nap. However, try as they might, they couldn't get the startled expression on the little ol' man's face out of their thoughts. That look was etched in their memories forever. What a day!

CHAPTER 4

The little ol' man had lost a step. Age was showing in his face and he didn't move like he once did. His hunting tactics changed quite a bit and the two young boys were seldom seen with him. They were seen little if any. The boys were becoming men and their lives had changed. They were away at college. They loved hunting with their dad and did whenever the opportunity arose, but those golden days of hunting the Park daily were gone forever! The little ole' man sorely missed them, but he understood life was that way.

He understood that life changes constantly and that the key to happiness is enjoying every moment you have with family and friends. He cherished every hunt he and the boys shared and often smiled and laughed while sitting on his deer stand. He thought of them daily and he was really proud of the fine young men they had come to be.

He took pride in knowing the boys had learned many valuable lessons about life while hunting. But now it was just the little ol' man hunting alone and going about his business in the woods. He seemed to enjoy every second of it and savored every experience. It was as if he belonged there. He truly loved the deer and had a passion for hunting!

It's almost like he's one of us, Sam thought one day as he rested with the other deer. *It's like we somehow share the Park. However, we know our distance and we have to make sure that we keep it. He seems harmless enough, yet, we all remember the stories told about Big Elrod and that's enough to keep us wary of him. It's obvious that he's a peaceful man, but something tells me he has an underlying purpose. Could it be that big antlers are his passion? If so, his passive attitude could easily change drastically at the sight of an opportunity to collect a set like mine!*

The month of November came in with a bang. Temperatures dropped rapidly and the warm sunny days of September and October seemed long gone. Most of the leaves from the giant oak trees in the Park had fallen and food supplies were getting short. Acorns were still in reasonable supply. However, the sweet tender grasses of the Avery farm had turned to straw and it was obvious that winter was setting in.

The rut was well under way and the little ol' man was in top form for his age. He was seen almost daily by Sam in the Park. He seemed to be intrigued by every scrape and rubbed tree that Sam and Little Sam had made. He would study and evaluate each one of them. It was almost like he could tell the size of a buck's horns by the rubs they made. Sam sometimes thought the little ol' man had lost his senses. Sam thought it very odd how the ol' man often peed in his and Little Sam's scrapes. Those thoughts went through Sam's head as he lay and chewed his cud.

"How absurd is that?"Sam said to himself. "I remember the times I actually watched him pull out that little ol' shriveled up noodle of his, look over both shoulders to see if anyone was looking, and let her fly! Then, he would bend over, shake it off two or three times and put it back in his britches. But then, just about the time he started zipping up his pants, he would start cussing out loud like a sailor! Invariably, that last spoonful always ran down his leg, and it made him mad enough to fight. I never could understand why it bothers him so much when it seems so normal for deer. All big bucks like me let it run down our legs on purpose, and we do it with pride!" Sam continued chewing his cud as he rested peacefully.

***

During the peak of the rut that year, Sam noticed several huge scrapes and markings along the southwest boundaries of his territory. Big cedar trees had been rubbed and Sam became nervous. None of his crowd had made that sign and it was obvious that he had an intruder – a big one at that! Most of the sign appeared along a line near the big beaver pond on the very back section of his range. It was an area that his clan spent very little time in and probably the reason why this unknown stranger had moved in. The little ol' man soon found this same sign as well. It was apparent that he was impressed with the markings because he began hunting that area more often.

Sam pondered the situation and his family feared that he would go on a rampage and search out the maker of those scrapes and rubs. Star was very upset and well remembered the morning that Sam and Nasty Pete had fought that deadly battle along the Pete-Wyche-farm property line.

"Dad," Star said to Sam, "don't, please don't go fighting that big sucker! He seems to be a loner and he hasn't caused us any trouble. He stays in the swamp and no one has even seen him. Let him be. Maybe he'll simply go away. It's obvious he's a renegade and he'll probably leave just as he came. Why don't we just spend the winter up in the Park and let him be. If no does welcome him, he'll leave!"

Sam showed no sign of rage or anger. He simply seemed to be in a state of shock. He, too, remembered the Nasty Pete battle and realized how very close he had come to being killed. He also reasoned that Little Sam would be involved in the next fight and he didn't think that his son was ready for such battle. So much was at stake! At his age, Sam didn't need another battle-to-the-death challenge and Little Sam wasn't ready and wouldn't be for two more years.

Sam's thoughts turned to the memory of his mother and the legacy she had left him. The love and advice she had given him during his youth suddenly sparked in his brain. "Be patient," she had always told him. "Think things out and then make a decision. When you don't know what to do, don't do anything. Wait and be cautious when you don't know. Give nature a chance to work things out. No decision is better than a bad one and bad ones are easy to make. Give yourself some time...."

Sam could remember his mother's words as if she were standing before him. "Wait when you are not sure. Let the other guy make a mistake! Be patient...."

She had urged Big Sam to do those same things when he was alive and he had paid no attention to her. Instead, he had gone out and gotten himself hit by a pick-up truck!

"Learn Sam. Learn from your dad's mistakes. A cool head is always more beneficial than an abundance of testosterone!"

Sam had learned well and he did remember. In fact, he reasoned that just maybe the little ol' man might fight this battle for him. Yes, just maybe the ol' man would like that big stranger's horns hanging on the wall over his fireplace.

Several days passed and the markings made by this unwanted invader became more numerous. He became bolder and bolder and his area of movement began to expand. Sam's concerns grew. However, he also noticed that the little ol' man was concerned as well. The ol' man spent more and more time near the scrape lines and it was obvious that his intensity had increased. It was also obvious that he was not there simply to observe. He had a different manner about him. His movements were more calculated. Sam noticed that the hunting instincts exhibited by the little ol' man were totally focused on the business at hand. He was more intense than he had ever been before.

Who is this alien buck and when will he show? the little ol' thought. *Is he a true monster?*

It was almost as if the little ol' man knew that the new scrape lines were being made by an outsider and that Sam and his clan were not a part of it. The rubs and scrapes were the largest that the wise old hunter had ever seen and he patiently waited for a look at their maker. He used every method and trick he knew. He incorporated every skill he had and stretched his imagination. He searched for a winning plan that would move this big buck's horns from the Park to his living room wall.

Without question, the ol' man was challenged. He was obsessed and his determination was absolute. After several dry years of hunting for a truly big buck, he would not be denied. He had passed up literally hundreds of opportunities to take younger bucks with lesser racks. However, they were not what he wanted. Only mature bucks with impressive antlers intrigued him. The taking of an impulsive young animal with a small rack did not interest him in the least, and he knew he had the intestinal fortitude to wait for the right one to come along.

The challenge of hunting a mature buck drove him. The chase fed his hunger. The excitement of one-on-one maneuvering kept his blood pumping and his adrenaline flowing. On several occasions, the ol' man got a glimpse of his quarry. Usually these split-second viewings came just after dusk. Sometimes they came at dawn while he was straining his eyes waiting for enough light to find the cross hairs in his scope. His only description of the deer was that it was big, dark and carried a huge rack of horns!

How big was he? The little ol' man couldn't say for sure! The buck never showed himself when there was enough light to get a true measure of his size. He had an almost ghostly presence about him. Because of that, the little ol' man's quest now turned into a full-scale crusade.

It had been 10 years since a buck of this magnitude had been seen in the Park. Not since the days of Big Elrod had scrapes and rubs of this size been found. The old gentleman was excited and his imagination ran wild. He was not getting any younger and he knew the chances of killing a really big deer were growing dimmer each year. The remaining years of his hunting life were slipping away, one season at a time. He didn't like to think about it; however, he was a realist and his body didn't lie. The morning hunts seemed a little colder and getting up those high ladder stands had become a chore. His knees ached and all the years of hard work were having an effect on his stamina. He had long ago given up using the climbing stands and had now settled into a more sedentary hunting pattern.

This predictable pattern had taken its toll on the results of his efforts. The days of seeing the really big-horned deer seemed so long ago. It seemed that every deer in the Park these days knew exactly where he was and when he would be there. That was fine for Sam and his clan. He wouldn't shoot them under any circumstance! But he hoped to hang one more big rack on his wall before Father Time forced him to hang up his rifle. He'd been a great conservationist for a long, long time, but his patience was running out. That's why he was so excited about the scrape line on the back boundary of the Park.

The little ol' man knew he was hunting a big deer that was a rambling nomad. The buck certainly was not one from Sam's bunch. He wondered if the big stranger had migrated over from the Galloway property. Those big woods lay southeast of the Park. The territory was dense and deep in undergrowth. The little ol' man had never ventured into it. The reason being, it was posted! He never violated posted property. But he had heard lots of wild stories about the big bucks that roamed there.

31

The Galloway property was unique. No hunters or local people were allowed on the trophy-rich preserve because it was reserved for the very rich and famous. The little ol' man resented that. He had seen some of those wealthy hunters' pictures in magazines and newspapers. He noted the big grins on their faces as they displayed and posed with the great bucks they had taken. Often it was the first big buck that any of these privileged "pay" hunters had ever seen. And certainly none of these well-to-do hunters ever "paid their dues" by hunting for long days at a time and successfully bringing down one of these big bucks through their own skill and determination! They didn't work at it like the more traditional dyed-in-the-wool hunters did, and they didn't have a true passion for fair chase like the little ol' man had! They didn't have the patience to work at it year after year.

There was nothing wrong with the Galloway operation or the hunters who paid to hunt there, but the little ole' man just didn't have much regard for their kind of sport. He believed that before shooting a deer, a man should be a true outdoorsman and have a real love and appreciation for the game he hunted. He felt that a hunter had responsibilities to the land and to the conservation of that land: and to the wildlife it produced. Some folks referred to him as an old codger and a dinosaur and told him that his beliefs about passing up young bucks had no merit.

They told him, "Old Man, if you don't shoot them, the guy across the fence will! You're just one guy. What can one guy do to change the world?"

But the little ol' man didn't mind the criticism. He hunted by himself, looked after himself and tended to his own business!

"Let the good young fellers who have never killed a deer have the small ones," was his philosophy. But for him, to shoot a spike or a doe would have been cheating. He had set high standards for himself and to lower them at his age made no sense! Others laughed at him for coming home empty-handed year after year, but it never bothered him. He had a strong will and a strong belief in how he viewed right and wrong and nothing was going to change.

One thing was certain: if that big vagabond from the Galloway territory crossed his scope, he most assuredly planned to make up for a lot of lost seasons. He longed for his two young sons to be part of this new adventure. But they had long since grown up and pursued other interests. *How can I get a deer as big as the one I'm hunting out of the woods alone,* he wondered?

There was a day in the past when he could've handled it all by himself, but that was many hunts ago. In years past, he and the boys could've dragged a mule out of the woods. But now, those days were gone and he seldom got to hunt with the boys.

Yes, those happy days were long, long gone! Now he was fending for himself – alone! However, he was still hunting with the same fire in his gut that he'd had as a young man. That would never change. And it was with that same fire that he plotted the ambush of the Galloway monster!

Nothing could stop him. The little ol' man was determined to be successful. He knew his time had come. All those years of waiting for a buck of a lifetime were over. All he had to do now was use his skill and hope that luck didn't prove fatal to him.

The days went by. The little ol' man hunted daily with vigor and anticipation. The big deer never showed. On occasion, new sign would be found in the vicinity of the scrape line. It seemed that the buck was playing games with him. He would leave just enough sign to keep the little ol' man's hopes up. But the big deer never showed during daylight hours.

The little ol' man was wearing down but he wasn't about to give up. No one had hunted harder or scouted with more determination. No one had been more patient than he had. Yet all of this had resulted in nothing but frustration. *The record books are full of huge deer taken purely by luck or accident,* he thought. *Stories of guys bagging Boone and Crockett bucks on their first hunt, while sitting in a stand they didn't plan to hunt out of, make me ill! Luck is so powerful when it goes your way....*

The little ol' man believed that the harder he worked, the luckier he got. Nothing in life had come easy for him. On the contrary, Luck had always been his greatest enemy. He despised it when someone said, "Good luck, old man!" He thought that was a sure-fire kiss of death. All he had ever known was hard work and luck had never been his friend. So he had put all his faith in effort and persistence.

I'll make my own luck!

***

On the night before the season's final day, the little ol' man stopped by the camp house of some of his longtime deer-hunting friends. The mood of the camp was festive. The atmosphere was one of laughter and smiles. Most of the club members had taken their buck for the year, and if there was any pressure in the camp, they didn't show it. The smell of cooking cornbread filled the house and smoke from the bar-b-cue grills hovered around the back porch. Rum was being passed around as tall tales and experiences in the woods were being shared in small groups. Jokes were being told, and the little ol' man listened with a smile to a few of the stories. He felt certain that some of the stories bordered on gross exaggerations! He chuckled to himself and thought that he may have even heard a lie or two! Rum could have played a part in the lighthearted mood of the group! The ol' man believed that was the case!

He sorely wished his season had been as good as that of most of his friends. He was reminded of what Mr. Hogg, an elderly old man, whom he liked and respected, once told him about trophy deer hunting. "Son, if you're a meat hunter and shoot everything you can, you'll never make the cover of a wildlife magazine, but you'll always have plenty of meat!"

How true those words had proven to be! The little ol' man wondered if he should lighten up a bit and not take things so seriously. *Back off,* he thought. *Have some fun and enjoy your last hunt. Shoot you a deer. Don't set your goals so high. After all, you're not a young man anymore. It's not so much bad luck as it is simply the odds. You don't have but so many hunts left. It isn't luck, it's the odds. Lighten up you ol' fool. Don't be so damned hardheaded!*

About the time that thought cleared his head, Pro Parker, one of the club's most pretentious members, spotted the little ol' man in the kitchen. Pro slithered into the room, lit a long-filtered cigarette, took a deep drag, blew the smoke out of his nostrils, and said, "Ol' timer, it's been one hell of a year! I've killed two spikes, a 56-pound doe, and let a button get by me that was bigger than any of them."

He continued his grandiose bragging. "You know I missed a big'un last weekend dontcha? Yeah, I guess I missed him… I couldn't find him anyhow… Don't know how I missed him though!

"I was in one of those little ground blinds. I had just lit a cigarette when all of a sudden there he was. I mean a great big'un! I believe it was the biggest deer I've ever missed! When I shot, he just ran off out yonder and looked at me. I reloaded and shot again, but I know I missed that time because I saw the pine bark fly. I don't know how I missed him but he was a big sucker. But that's alright. I've had a hell of a year! They don't call me 'Pro' for nothing!"

Then he paused and added, "Good luck to you tomorrow. Hey, I may just sleep in and give some of these other boys a chance…he, he, he…" With that he took another long drag from his cigarette, and then a big swallow from his Miller Light, and slid out the back door toward the skinning pole and meat cooler.

A big crowd had gathered outside. A club member who hailed from the Virgin Islands was watching as the Italian fellow skinned out a doe that the Islander had killed earlier. The Islander had an unusual Caribbean accent. It was his third doe of the day and the Italian looked tired and exhausted from dressing deer. "Where you theenk I should seet tomorra' morning?" he asked the Italian. "I gotta get some more meat. I got two more coolers to fill up before I leave for the islands. I only keeled three deer today! Thees weather is messing everything up. Why don't you guys do something about thees weather? When it gonna rain? Where you theenk I should seet tomorra'?"

Then he turned to the little ol' man and said, "Ol' man feex you a drink! Somebody gotta toast all these deer I keeled! Where you theenk I should sit tomorra' morning?" he questioned the Italian again. "If you like, you can seet in the good stand I worked all summer on; the one we spent two Saturdays cutting the shooting lanes to; you know, the one we had to build a bridge to get to. Why don't you seet in it tomorra'… We've been saving it for you the entire season."

The Italian started needling the Islander about his accent!

"But where you gonna seet?" the Islander asked.

"Aw, I'll 'seet' one of my other stands or I may just slip off over yonder and poach the Mote property," said the Italian. "You know I got caught over there last Sunday morning. The property owner's little dog trailed right up to where I was and sat there howling at me. He treed me! I've never been so embarrassed. I couldn't make him leave and when I got down out of the stand, he about chewed my pants legs off. It ruined my hunt! Don't know why I keep going over there. I just can't stop."

"But I gotta get some meat. I got two more coolers to fill up!" said the Islander.

The Italian said, "I'm putting you on the best stand we've ever had. What else do you want?"

"Weel you take me to it and what time you pick me up? How long it take you to get to me after I shoot? I gotta keel some deers!"

"I know the pressure you're under," said the Italian. "I mean, being responsible for providing meat for the entire Virgin Islands is a big load to carry. Hey, don't be afraid to put a fish or two in those empty coolers when you start back over here. Will those coolers only carry meat one way? Can't you bring some fish back with you when you come?"

"Why don't y'all just shut the fuck up about that!" the Islander yelled back. "You know how much feesh cost? When you gonna skin the rest of my deer?"

The entire camp was happy and jovial. The big one-eyed guy was doing the inside cooking and several more hunters were standing around the grills outside. The large walk-in cooler was full of freshly skinned carcasses and there was no shortage of rum. The hunter from the Virgin Islands with the strange accent had seen to that. He apparently didn't haul many fish over to the U.S., but he smuggled in lots of rum. He said, "You can't dreenk a feesh so y'all just shut the fuck up!"

The one-eyed cook brought out a rum drink for the little ol' man and said, "Haven't seen much of you this year!"

"Yeah," the ol' man said. "I've been pretty low key this season. I haven't had much to get excited about the last few years. I'm hunting more and seeing fewer good deer. It seems that the more I learn about deer, the more I realize how little I know. Hunting deer has brought me so much pleasure all these years. As you know, I've killed only a few bucks and most of them were mature bucks that needed killing. I made a mistake or two along the way but I learned a lot from them. Don't know what I'd do if I couldn't hunt 'em. They're amazing animals!"

The one-eyed guy said, "You mean you haven't seen a good deer this year?"

The little ol' man said, "In fact, it's been several years since I've had a shot at a really good one. There's a great family of deer in the Park where I hunt but I've gotten so attached to them that killing any of them is out of the question. They've become a part of my life and I know them individually.

There are two really great bucks in that family. I think that fellow over yonder peeling potatoes that looks like a Baptist preacher shot one of them several weeks back. Didn't kill him though… I see him about every week. I think you and the Italian ran over his daddy a long time ago."

"Yeah," the one-eyed man said. "That was the biggest deer I've ever seen. He did a job on that old yellow truck. We were so proud of it that we never fixed it. That fender is kind of like a trophy or something. Every time someone asks about it, I get to tell the story again. When we collided with that big son of a gun, I said, 'Did we run over a deer, or did a deer just run over us?' By God, he was huge!"

"Well," the little ol' man agreed, "he was huge, but his son and grandson are just as impressive. They're really special. I call them Sam and Little Sam. Sam was born on the Hogg place but migrated to the Park after his dad got killed and his mother died. I sure am glad that preacher-guy didn't kill Sam. Hey, didn't he used to wear real thick glasses. I mean real funny looking ones?"

"Yeah," the one-eyed man said, "but he don't need 'em no more! Last year, he was about to climb up a yellow poplar in his Summit climber when lighting hit it. He said he saw a big ball of white fire and after everything cleared up, he didn't need eye glasses no more. His vision has been 20-20 ever since! Hell, he hasn't had a beer since then either! It scared the ever-loving shit out of him. Yeah, he don't drink nothin' but Jim Beam now, and he really hasn't been the same since it happened! He says his only regret was that it didn't straighten his teeth up too!"

The ol' man chuckled out loud!

"He said he thought the reason lighting struck him was because he was swigging a Coors Silver Bullet and the can drew the lighting," the one-eyed man continued. "I don't know… I do know that it changed his life. He hunts on the ground most of the time now and he don't drink any beer at all. But he'll drain one of those whisky bottles! Even lighting couldn't stop him from that."

The little ol' man was laughing out loud at the story but the one-eyed man could sense something in the air. "Are you all right?" he asked.

The little ol' man said, "Yeah, but the season is over tomorrow and time is running out."

"Running out for what?" the big guy asked.

"Well," the little ol' man said, "I've been huntin' the sign of a really big one all season and tomorrow is my last chance. I've not even had a good look at him and I've hunted him every day for most of the season. He's coming in off the Galloway property and he's huge. He never shows himself during daylight hours but always leaves me plenty of sign to show that he's been there. He's the most frustrating deer I've ever hunted. I almost hate the big son-of-a-gun. It's like he knows my every move and stays one step ahead of me. I'll be glad when the season ends. At least I'll stop thinking about him."

The big guy said, "What you need is another rum drink! You're putting way too much pressure on yourself. Relax and enjoy the season. You're not the first guy who's been outfoxed by a big'un and you surely won't be the last!"

That was little consolation to the ol' man but he knew the one-eyed guy was probably right. He knew that failure was a part of life and that disappointment was a part of hunting. He had learned that if a man enjoyed only those hunts where he took a big deer, then most of his hunts would be disappointing! Learning to handle failure was a lesson the hunting experience taught so well. Failure in life always gave flavor to success. How could a man appreciate the sweetness of joy without first experiencing the pain of sorrow?

"You gotta enjoy each day of your life," he told himself. "If a man hunts for the right reasons, then there are no bad days or disappointing hunts. The beauty of nature and God's creations are always there. They never change. Our attitude and the selfish way we look at them brings on disappointment."

Ah, he thought. *Greed and selfishness have ruined many a day and certainly many a hunt! Go to the woods tomorrow with a mindset of, TODAY IS A BLESSED DAY AND I AM EXTREMELY BLESSED TO BE A PART OF IT!*

He left the hunting camp with those thoughts ringing in his head.

CHAPTER 5

Daylight had already come when the little ol' man parked Ole Blue on the logging road. The night before had been fun, but the rum had sent him into a most restful sleep and the early morning alarm had somehow been ignored. He was late to his spot and he knew it. While walking to his stand, he was startled by the sound of a gunshot over on the Galloway property. *Must be one of those rich so-and-sos on a doe. The deer are already moving and I'm still a ways from my stand. This is some way to end the season!* he grumbled. *Getting to your stand late and hearing close shots while you're moving on the ground is not only stupid, it's also dangerous!*

Being late was not like the ol' man. It was not like him at all! He got nervous from having to rush but once settled in his ladder stand, he began to relax. The sun was already up and lighting holes in the forest floor. He could see all the way from the back of Curtis Avery's line to the Wyche farm corner. Fog was drifting up from the beaver pond, and he thought, *this sure is a beautiful morning to end the season!*

All that was needed to cap off the year was for the Galloway Monster to appear. The morning was still young when the little ol' man got a glimpse of something that didn't belong in the beaver pond's backwater and under growth. The sun was shining on something peculiarly buried in the thick brush. He squinted and strained his eyes to see it better. He slowly raised his riflescope but couldn't focus clearly on the object that was reflecting the sun's light.

Again and again he squinted and strained his eyes. Again and again he raised his rifle and fidgeted with the scope to try to focus on the strange object. But nothing came into clear focus, even though the object was still there. After some time, the sun's angle changed and the little ol' man scoped the object again. Movement! He saw movement through the scope. Just a faint little movement and he knew it wasn't the wind moving grass!

Suddenly the object in the brush became apparent. The movement was the flicker of an ear and the object reflecting the light was the last three inches of a buck's left main beam. There he was – a very nice buck! It might even be the Galloway Monster! The deer had his nose to the wind, his back to the little ol' man and he appeared to be resting peacefully in the warm morning sun. What a sight! What an opportunity to end an otherwise frustrating season! All at once, it looked as though everything might start coming together.

The little ol' man was somewhat shocked. In his wildest dreams, he'd never envisioned seeing a big buck bedded down. He had dreamed of having the Galloway Monster charge right by him. He had envisioned the buck running a doe past his position. But he never thought of seeing the buck bedded down.

"Do you know for sure it's him?" he asked himself.

No you don't, he thought. *So, be patient, and even if it isn't the big guy, this is a very nice buck and it's the last day of the season. And like the big, one-eyed guy said last night, "Loosen up and enjoy the hunt. Take some pressure off yourself. Shoot yourself a deer!"*

It's hard to fault a hunter who shoots only the biggest buck he sees in a season. This is especially true for an old man who hadn't fired a shot in three years. The little ol' man made up his mind that he was gonna shoot this buck no matter how big his rack was. He was gonna break the drought and he might even shoot him bedded down!

All at once the big deer raised his head. The ol' man could make out 10 nice points – five on each side. Was this the big buck he had been looking for? The ol' man thought not! *He's a good buck, but there's no way this deer could have made all that big sign*, he thought.

With his head up and his nose high in the air, the buck was at full alert.

The little ol' man thought, *I haven't spooked him, and I'm downwind and the sun is in his eyes. What in the Sam Hill has him so upset?*

The buck ran his tongue out and quickly licked his nose with moisture. He was looking toward the Galloway property. Then suddenly, in one liquid motion, he was on his feet and running in the little ol' man's direction!

Well, are you gonna shoot, old man, or are you gonna let another good one walk? he thought.

Simultaneously, the gun safety was pushed off and the little ol' man's instincts went into automatic pilot. His pulse raced, his heart pounded in his chest and his palms grew sweaty. It was like a different being had moved inside his body. When one decides to kill, whether it's a deer or anything else, the body takes on a different mode. It's not natural to kill, and the body and mind must reach a point of no return before the act can be completed. The little ol' man knew this. He knew that once he decided to pull the trigger, the automatic pilot would take over and the shot would be made before his true self would be back in charge. He decided to take the buck!

When the 10-pointer reached the firebreak, he came to an abrupt stop, raised his head high in the air and winded the slight breeze. Then the buck turned his head and checked his back trail. As soon as the cross hairs in the little old man's scope settled high on the deer's shoulder, the gentle and consistent pressure on the trigger did the trick. The ol' man's gun roared and the buck hit the ground. It was a perfect shot. With only a few kicks and two quick attempts to raise its antlers off the ground, the buck lay motionless. It was over!

The buck was his and the drag would be short. The little ol' man jerked another shell into the chamber and relaxed back in the stand. He never carried more than two shells. He had learned many years ago that a clip full of shells only encouraged a hunter to be impatient. He knew that the first shot was the most important and if a man only had two shells, he would never use the first one without caution. He would never take a chance if he only had one left.

He had known good hunters to rush a shot with the assurance of four more chances in the clip. Rushed shots, he believed, accounted for lost deer. Many a good buck had been left for the buzzards and never recovered because the hunter rushed the shot. *If you don't have but two shells, you will never, never rush the first shot!* he thought to himself.

The morning was still young. As the ol' man tried to relax in the stand and regain his composure, the excitement of the previous few moments caught up with him. His lower back began to cramp up and his hands began shaking. He had felt this sensation many, many times before. It didn't matter how many times he had pulled the trigger, the cramps, the shaking hands and the wet palms were always there. They were reminders of the tremendous stress that the taking of a life brings!

The sun was casting shorter shadows when the little ol' man decided it was time to recover his deer and make the drag toward his old blue truck. As he pulled his hunter orange vest around his shoulders, he suddenly heard voices. Jerking himself to a state of alertness, he saw orange in the distance. Two hunters in orange vests were approaching the head of the beaver pond. They were stooped over and moving cautiously. As they moved closer, the little ol' man realized they were tracking something. Obviously, they were following the blood trail of a deer!

One would holler, "Here's some!" and the other would hang white tissue paper on a bush. They were moving in his direction and up the very trail his deer had traveled.

What's going on? He wondered. He sat motionless and watched the scene in front of him.

On up the trail they came toward him. They were getting close to the firebreak when one of them screamed, "There he is, and he's a big 10!"

They both ran toward the deer. The little ol' man was in shock. *Surely to goodness these two bastards aren't going to claim MY deer!* he thought.

"Hey, what the hell are you doing?" he screamed.

The two hunters nearly jumped out of their camouflage and both of them dropped their toilet paper. The little ol' man climbed down his ladder stand as fast as he could and ran stumbling toward them. "What the hell are you doing?" he repeated.

"We're tracking our deer," one of them said. "We shot him over on the Galloway property and tracked him right here to this spot."

"Well," the little ol' man said, "This ain't your deer. I shot this buck about 30 minutes ago and he fell in his tracks."

"Wait a minute," the bigger of the two hunters said. "We paid good money to book a hunt with Galloway. I shot this deer right after daybreak and we've been trailing him damn-near a mile. You can follow the toilet-paper trail right to my stand!"

"I don't give a rat's ass how much you paid or how many rolls of toilet paper you used," the little ol' man argued. "This is my deer and you can follow your paper trial back to where you came from!"

"Listen, old man," the big fellow said. "This is the biggest buck I've ever killed and ain't nobody gonna take him away from me!"

It was obvious that things were about to get nasty and the little ol' man was getting nervous. He remembered his practice of carrying only two shells. *I fired one, I have one left, and if I'm not seeing double, there are two of them*, he thought. *That makes me the loser!*

He decided his only chance to win the battle was with negotiation and reason. "If you shot the deer and I shot the deer, there must be two holes in him, right?" he asked.

"Hell no!" the big guy said. "You didn't shoot. We would have heard you!"

The little ol' man, responded, "With all the screaming and hollering y'all were doing, you wouldn't have heard a cannon go off! I'm telling you, if there ain't two holes in the deer, you don't have a claim!"

"We already checked," the little guy said. "He ain't got but one hole in him and my friend here put it there. You don't have a prayer, old man! The blood trail from this deer leads straight to the stand my buddy here shot him out of."

"Well, how do you account for the fact that he fell dead when I shot?" the ol' man exclaimed.

"I'd say that he was almost gone, and your shot shocked him and he died," the little guy answered.

"What, if my bullet went in the same hole yours did?" the little ol' man gasped.

"I'd say that's a bunch of bull shit!" the big guy said.

"Well it makes more sense than your theory of me scaring him to death," the little ol' man said.

"Look old man," the big guy said. "There's no argument here. This is my biggest deer ever and the evidence is clear. No court anywhere will deny that the blood trail leads to the original shot. This is my deer! We're takin' him with us, and if you wanna do something about it, come on!"

The little ol' man knew that he had lost the contest. He began to doubt himself. *Did I miss the deer? Are they right? Did he just collapse after I shot? No way!*

This was not his first trip to the woods. Something else had happened. He didn't know what, but something was badly wrong!

"Okay," the ol' man said. "Take the damn deer. I've been huntin' all my life and I've never experienced anything like this. Anyway, if this is the biggest deer you've ever killed, you need it more than I do. Have at it!"

"By the way," the little guy said. "How far are you parked from here?"

"Just down the logging road a ways," the little ol' man answered. "Why?"

"Would you mind....?"

"You bet your sweet ass I mind!" the ol' man interrupted. "You can drag this sucker back to where you came from along every inch of your ass-wiping paper trail and make sure you pay Galloway for the deer you stole from me! You say you shot him, I say you drag him!" The ol' man was shaking with anger and he knew that in his younger days, a fight would have been the conclusion of this confrontation! He would have fought the bastards right then and there! He obviously would have lost but it would have taken both of them to whip him! The ol' man was peaceful but when he was made mad enough to fight... stopping him was out of the question! Killing him would have been easier!

The two hunters were speechless! They had won the battle for the deer, but they had lost the war to an old man. After they had started their long drag, the ol' man overheard the little guy say, "We should've let the old fool have it. I'm exhausted already and we ain't even out of his sight yet!"

The little ol' man went back to his stand and tried to think back through the sequence of events. He had hunted hard all season without firing a single shot. His theory of always having bad luck seemed to be holding up! He always believed that you make your own luck, but somehow it didn't ever work that way for him. Now the events of the morning seemed unexplainable. *You shoot a fine buck*, he thought, *and some Yankee asshole just shows up and takes it from you. It just ain't right!* He thought about firing his last shell in the air just to see the expression on the two thieves faces! *I may need that shell though,* he thought out loud!

The woods became quiet again and the ol' man tried to focus on his surroundings. Just maybe the buck he had been hunting would show after all. It wasn't likely but it could happen.

Try as he might, however, he couldn't get the events of the morning out of his mind. Continuing to hunt was out of the question. He couldn't sit still and his fidgeting in the stand only made him nervous. He was wasting his time and he knew it. *Just go on home and forget it,* he thought. *That old buck you're hunting will be back next year and he'll be even bigger. Look at it this way... You have a giant to hunt next season. Go home and start planning for it. Get you head up. You've been successful so many times in the past. Don't let this one incident get you down!*

With those thoughts, he began to descend the the steps of his ladder stand for the second time of the day. Once on the ground, he readied himself for the walk back to his truck. As he took one last look at the spot where his buck had fallen, his temper once again raged. *How could you stand there and let them Yankee sons of bitches take your deer?* He asked himself.

As he looked down the trail used by the two men to drag his deer, he saw the bright red blood trail that the deer they were dragging had apparently left. He followed it until he reached the first piece of white tissue paper that one of the men had hung in a bush. As he looked at the blood on the bush that held the tissue, his mind suddenly went into overtime! That blood had been blown from the mouth and nostrils of a deer. It was pink and mixed with mucous. The trail of the deer he had shot was bright red from a bleeding artery!

"This is unbelievable!" he said to himself. "But I guess stranger things have happened. I shot my buck high behind the shoulder. There was only one hole in him. There has to be a second deer involved in this mystery – the deer the two hunters were tracking was blowing lung mucous. My deer that they were dragging was spilling blood from an artery!"

Blood always tells a story, he thought.

He learned early in his life that just finding blood was not good enough. Experienced hunters and mature outdoorsmen could identify the type of blood and know the part of a deer's body it was spilling from. The ol' man could study the hair and blood left by a wounded deer and predict where the animal was injured! That knowledge had benefited him many times. He had often been called to help other hunters recover deer they had shot. Nothing made him prouder that helping other hunters.

All of a sudden it hit him! He'd heard a shot fired early that morning right after he got out of his truck. He remembered hearing it and thinking how late he'd been in getting to his stand. Those two hunters were dumbasses no doubt. But, they were sincere and positive in their conviction that they had shot and trailed a deer to the exact spot where his buck had fallen. Had the deer they'd been tracking passed through the area seconds before the little ol' man got to his stand? Had his buck run along the same blood trail that a wounded deer had taken earlier? It sounded bizarre but it had to be the case! His hands began to shake again and his palms got sweaty.

I have to look for blood beyond where my deer fell, he thought. As he slowly eased up the trail from where he shot his buck, he saw freshly turned leaves in the firebreak. Then he noted that the pine straw in the planted pines appeared disturbed. He crawled on his hands and knees and strained his eyes to find any sign of blood. None could be found! *There's no blood to justify the theory of a second deer,* he reasoned.

Then, moving on out the trail and into the 20-foot-tall pines, he still found no trace of blood. His thoughts were jumbled and he began to theorize that even if there had been two deer, the chances of recovering the second one were probably very slim. But this didn't discourage him at all. What he really wanted to do was prove to himself that a second deer existed. He needed the satisfaction of knowing that he had indeed killed the buck those two hunters had taken, and finding even one small speck of blood would do the trick.

Suddenly, there it was on a sweet gum leaf! It was no bigger than a pinhead, but definitely blood and the day suddenly changed! Without question, the proof was there and the ol' man thought: *Thank you Jesus... For a while there, I thought I might be losing my marbles! And if you'll send those two faggots back up here, I'll whip both their asses!*

First a drop on a leaf, next a drop on an overturned stone, then a skid mark in the pine straw, and the chase was on. More blood, more mucous;

this time it was sprayed on the base of a pine tree. It was definitely a lung shot deer and definitely a tough trail to follow. The little ol' man checked his gun. The chamber contained his last shell. *I sure am glad I did't shoot one of them bastards*, he thought!

"I need to find more blood, more blood; please more blood," he prayed. Anything to indicate that he was on the trail would be a blessing. There… there it was on a stone! It was just a speck. He moved on with hope in his heart.

What am I trailing? he wondered.

Never had he trailed a deer whose size or sex he knew nothing about. This deer could be anything from a spike to a giant for all he knew! The hunter who shot it didn't have a clue either. All those two guys seemed to know was that one of them had shot a deer and they'd later found a blood trail.

No, no, it can't be the Galloway Monster, the little ol' man thought. *Or can it? It obviously came off the Galloway property. Who knows? It just might be him!*

Further down the trail he searched. He was moving slowly one feeble step at a time. He was looking for anything… a broken twig… a speck of blood… hair… mucous… anything… anything that would make the trail continue on. He finally saw a track. The little ol' man was in shock. There, in the mud, was the biggest deer track he had ever seen! It was huge and fresh!

The little ol' man suspected that the deer was moving ahead of him as he moved. The deer was staying far enough ahead to remain unseen. He managed to stay just out of sight. The little ol' man reasoned that the deer was becoming weaker or else he would simply vacate the area. He was hurt badly, all right, and the little ol' man began wondering where and when this chase might end.

Has my luck changed, he wondered. *Absolutely not… Ain't no such thing as luck and if there is, it's always bad! Just keep looking for blood and forget about luck.*

The little ol' man had been tracking for over an hour and he had no idea how far he'd gone. All he knew was that he was still in the planted pines and that he was still within the Park property. He looked at his watch. It was well after high noon and no deer in sight. *If that deer is just out there reacting to me and saving his strength, this could go on forever, he said to himself.*

He knew those two Galloway hunters had tracked the deer nearly a mile and now this! What should he do? Should he go home and come back with help? Should he press harder? Should he abandon the trail and continue to hunt? Should he try to find a tracking dog and come back? Should he continue as he was doing? What should he do? He didn't know!

He finally decided to continue pursuing the blood trail. He found more specks of blood and kept moving ahead. The trail was leading toward a spot he called the "Deer-Stand Hollow." A dry creek bed ran through the hollow and the woods were open. The little ol' man thought, *if I can push him out of these pines and into that hardwood hollow, I might catch sight of him. It makes sense for him to save energy by traveling downhill and his intention probably is to hit that hollow and follow it to the thickets of R&R Creek.*

The little ol' man knew that if the deer got into those thickets, it would be all she wrote. A man could get lost forever in the bramble and bush of that jungle. Suddenly he heard hooves hitting the ground just ahead and he saw a flash in the pines. It was the Galloway Monster! It had to be him because this buck was a giant! He was running, stumbling, falling, struggling, and bouncing off pine trees as he headed for the Deer-Stand Hollow.

The little ol' man broke into a run. He was dodging pine trees like a halfback avoids tacklers. The sight of that deer removed all signs of his age. The ol' man was moving like a teenager! The deer was a mere 50 yards in front of him. Just as he reached the tree line of the hollow, the big buck ran into a thicket of vines and brambles. He tried to thrash and plow his way through. Suddenly the vines and brambles got tangled around his massive rack and he started throwing his great head in every direction in an effort to escape.

The little ol' man knew it was now or never. His one remaining shell was in the chamber and he had to make it count. "Don't panic, don't rush, just do your job," he mumbled.

He raised his gun and braced against a 6-inch hickory sapling. In the scope he could see the huge rack draped with vines. *Don't shoot those damn horns; find his shoulder,* he thought.

The little ol' man was back on automatic pilot now. When the cross hairs of his scope crossed the shoulder of the big buck, the gun roared. The huge buck simply sat down on his hindquarters. The massive rack, entangled in the vines, held the buck's head up momentarily. Then it started sinking lower and lower until the little ol' man heard the deer collapse on the ground. It was over. The chase had come to an end. He thought, *What a day! What a day! Thank you sweet Jesus!*

The little ol' man had tried and used every skill and advantage that his many years in the woods had taught him. Finally, he had won the chase. The Galloway Monster would go proudly on his wall for sure! He felt his hands start to sweat and the cramps in his lower back grabbed him. He sat down and leaned against the hickory tree he had used to steady his shot and waited for his tired old body to settle down.

After a few seconds, the peace and quiet of the woods was deafening. The effect a gunshot has on the world of nature is amazing. The hunt was over and now the real work would begin. *How in the world am I gonna load that huge deer in ole Blue?* The little ol' man wondered. He'd think of something! That was the least of his problems. He just needed a few minutes to relax and settle down.

His heart was still pumping overtime and the cramps in his back were still grabbing like the jaws of a steel trap. The big deer lay peacefully in the bramble thicket and his huge rack was still tangled in vines. With his head slightly up, he almost looked alive.

What a sight! The little ol' man thought. I *don't need pictures of this! This scene will be etched in my brain forever!*

As the little ol' man relaxed and slowly regained his composure, he was brought back to reality by the sound of voices. Three men in orange vests were following the buck's blood trail. *Damn it!* he thought. *Those damned Yankees must be coming back to claim this one, too! What's going on? Guess they went back and got a third guy to help drag. I'll just be damned!*

Then he heard a familiar voice say, "It's not like him to stay out this late. His wife is worried sick!"

Someone else yelled, "Old man, can you hear me? Where are you?"

Then he heard a shrill whistle and another man yell, "Old man, answer me!"

Immediately he recognized the voices. They belonged to the two hunters who had hit Big Sam several years ago with the truck – the big one-eyed guy and the Italian. The third guy was the white-haired fellow who reminded him of a Baptist preacher. He was the one who had shot Sam. *My wife must have gone by the hunting camp and sent them after me*, the little ol' man thought.

"Hey, I'm over here!" he yelled.

The three hunters came out on the trail he'd been following. As they emerged from the dense pine thicket into the hollow, the little ol' man yelled, "What are you guys doing way over here? I thought y'all were going to Flat Shoals Creek this morning."

"Old man," the one-eyed guy said, "it ain't morning. It's after 4 o'clock in the afternoon and your wife and everyone at camp has been looking for you since lunch. From what you said last night, we figured you'd hunt that back scrape line, but when we got to your stand, we found that paper trail and the blood. We couldn't figure why in the world you'd be dragging a deer into the swamp.

"We followed the paper trail for over an hour and finally caught up to two guys dragging a big 10-pointer. Man, they were a mess! They were completely exhausted, scratched up, and dehydrated. The little one kept cussing the big guy. He kept saying something about, 'I told you to let that old fart have it. I knew it wasn't our deer. Our deer was a big bastard!'

"The big guy kept saying, 'Well, if we can't get this one out of the woods, how in hell do you think we could have dragged a bigger one out?' When we left them, they were about to fight and said they had at least half a mile more to go. Then we headed back this way and heard a shot. Tell us, please… What's goin' on?"

"I ain't got time now," the ol' man said. "Just look down yonder at what I got!"

It was then that they saw the buck he had shot. There was little doubt that this huge animal had probably been responsible for all of the oversized scrapes and rubs that had been found on the backside of the property.

The Italian muttered, "That's the biggest deer I've seen in awhile!"

"Is he as big as Big Elrod?" the white-haired guy with the mustache asked.

"No, he ain't," the little ol' man answered. "But he ain't far off!"

Later, as they loaded the big deer into the bed of the ol' man's blue truck, the Italian guy said, "Man, we saw a good buck in the logging road as we were driving back here. He was with a younger buck and two does."

"And he was limping slightly on his left front leg when he ran off," the white-haired guy said.

"That's Sam, Little Sam and their does," the ol' man said. "Y'all don't mess with them; they're my buddies... Say, what time did you say it was?"

"After 4 o'clock," the one-eyed guy answered.

"Sit down," the ol' man said as he opened the toolbox in the back of ole Blue. "Here, I've been saving this bottle for some time now. Y'all take a big draw from it while I tell what happened today...."

CHAPTER 6

The little ol' man hated to admit it – luck had played a great part in his taking of the Galloway Monster, and it had finally been good! However, he had also used all his skills to track the buck and in the end, he had adhered to his belief that a serious hunter makes his own luck. After all the smoke had cleared, and after he had time to rehash the entire scenario, he realized that the big buck probably had been living on the Galloway property and had been working the Park area only on occasion. It was almost like the big deer had tried to entice Sam into engaging in a border war. Luckily, Sam had been too smart for that. Once again, Sam's patient ways had kept him alive. Hopefully he'd be around for another year in the Park.

Obviously, Sam had become keenly aware of the little ol' man's habits. His trust and understanding of the ol' man's ways had been used to his advantage once again, and it was almost like an unwritten partnership had developed between them, borne out of a deep appreciation for each other. The little ol' man admired Sam tremendously. Sam, in return, had both admiration and fear for the ol' man! Mutual respect and admiration might best describe their relationship. Respect, knowing that the ol' man had the ability to put a bullet in Sam any time he made a mistake; admiration, knowing the little ol' man was a true trophy hunter and never killed for the joy of killing!

Sam had watched from a safe distance as the little ol' man and the others had loaded the Galloway Monster into his blue truck. He had never seen horns stick that far above a truck bed liner before. Well, yes he had – one other time on that morning long ago when Big Sam had been killed. That was the day he and his mom watched as the one-eyed guy and the Italian fellow loaded his dad onto the wrecked yellow pick-up over on Highway 18. That was a morning he would never forget and a morning that changed his life forever.

Sam had mixed feelings as the little ol' man drove up the bumpy logging road with the Galloway Monster in the bed of ole Blue. All of a sudden, those same sick feelings came back to him. He didn't really care that much about the demise of the Galloway Monster, but seeing that great deer in the bed of a truck with his giant antlers and huge body brought back sad memories of his mom and dad. It was like watching a great warrior being carried from the battlefield and watching the final seconds of a great warrior's career come to an end. Sam could feel the charisma and power of the deer and he respected his strength.

The hunting season was over. Sam and his bunch had once again survived. Food was abundant and Sam knew it was almost time to shed his horns. It wouldn't be long before the whole process of growing another set would begin anew! Late winter and early spring was always a laid-back time for Sam and his clan. Things always settled down after the hunters stopped visiting the Park. Life became much easier and danger was reduced to a minimum. Once the shedding of antlers was complete, Sam could venture out into the open fields with much less concern. Except for his sheer size, with the absence of antlers he looked like a big doe. Other bucks from around the territory often came through the Park and shared wild tales of narrow escapes.

It was a special time of year. The does stayed in family groups and Sam spent most of his time with Little Sam and the other bucks of the area. The does expected to drop their fawns in the spring and the bucks were at peace with each other. There was no competition between them and they spent much of their time bragging about the previous rutting season. The young bucks bragged aloud about their past conquests during the rut. They liked to brag about how many does they'd bred and the fights they'd won.

Sam was very reserved. He had already been there and done that. He encouraged Little Sam to listen and keep his mouth shut. He would tell Little Sam, "Listen and learn. Don't let your mouth get the best of you! Let the others brag! Talk is cheap. When you get too big for your own good, you'll end up in the bed of a pick-up truck!

"Every year they come through here bragging, and every year some in their group are missing from the year before," Sam continued. "It seems that the ones who talk the loudest and brag the most are the ones that don't come back. I often hear them talking about crossing scrape lines and taking does from other areas. Little Sam, that's how you get shot! Stay in your own territory. Stay where you know every tree in the area. Always bed where you can see and wind the roads and trails. It's much easier to track a hunter when you see him enter the territory.

"Hey, I know that little ol' man's habits better than he does. I know the kind of weather he likes to hunt in and where he'll be on every wind change. When you leave your own territory, you don't know those things. Sometimes the bucks that have a great nose for receptive does will follow them right into a shooting lane in a strange property. I know every stand the little ol' man has. I can tell within 100 yards of where he's going by where he parks that old blue truck of his. I always listen until he parks his truck, and then I slip out in the opposite direction.

"It doesn't take a smart buck to figure that out! Listen and learn, Little Sam, and remember: it ain't how many does you nailed last year that counts. It's whether you lived through the rut to do it again next year. That's important! Don't you ever forget it! Don't ever think you can do them all. There's a lot to be said for an old buck that lives long enough to die of old age. Let those bragging assholes do their thing."

"Remember what I said. Next year when we gather here, many of the loudest talkers will be absent. They may have nailed the most does, but their rewards ended up being a free ticket to a skinning-pole show! A good, sharp mind will always keep you alive longer than a smart mouth, Son!"

***

One of the loudest bucks that showed up in the Park that year was a cocky, 4-year-old. He boasted to everyone around that he was "the man" over on Flat Shoals Creek. He told the others that he could remember stories being passed down about Big Sam. He said he hadn't been around in Big Sam's time, but the legend of Big Sam still circulated in those parts. He said other big bucks he knew still marveled at the legacy that Big Sam had left behind. He said that no one really knew where Big Sam's son had gone after Big Sam died.

Neither Sam nor Little Sam gave any indication that they had ever heard of Big Sam. Instead, they just let the 4-year-old continue with his bragging. He said his name was Scrap. He bragged that he had run all the older bucks across Flat Shoals Creek and that he ruled everything in Harris County from the Mote Hole to the Hutchinson Monument. Sam couldn't help but like old Scrap because he had such a good sense of humor.

Scrap prided himself in taking chances and loved close encounters with the men who hunted him over near Flat Shoals Creek. Scrap said he liked nothing better than playing chess games with those hunters. He talked about making big scrapes and watching from afar as they moved their stands near them. He told everyone that some of those hunters had actually built houses over there. He said some of them were so tall that they could be seen for half a mile. Scrap laughed when he talked about the hunters there. He knew them all by name.

His favorite was the one everyone called "the Pro." Scrap described the Pro as being a little skinny, pale-faced, puny fellow who constantly smoked cigarettes in his stand. Scrap said he had developed affection for the guy because he always put out corn for him to eat. One day, Scrap said, he was going to get his corn when all of a sudden he noticed smoke boiling out of the big box the hunter always hunted in. The Pro had cut some holes in the box to enable him to view the corn pile. Smoke was boiling out of the holes. The box appeared to be on fire. Scrap said he finally realized that is was only an extra-long Marlboro that Pro had fired up so he dropped his caution and relaxed. Scrap said he could see the corn out in front of the box and was just about to take a chance on some of it when, out of nowhere, the game warden showed up.

Scrap said the game warden walked up behind the Pro and started knocking on his box. Scrap said the look on that hunter's face was something to remember when he crawled out and saw the game warden. Even more amusing was the hunter's explanation of how the corn had gotten there in the first place, since hunting deer over bait was highly illegal in Georgia!

Scrap laughed and said he just walked right out there in the middle of that corn pile and, while the Pro and the game warden watched, ate himself a big belly full!

Scrap told about one particular area in his territory that looked like Pearl Harbor. He said there was one little creek over behind the Prater property that had those big high hunter houses lined up like battle ships in a harbor. Scrap said there was enough fire- power along that line to do in every deer between Flat Shoals Creek and the Interstate. About once a week he would go down that creek at night making rubs and scrapes. He said that one trip would keep those houses full of hunters for three weekends running! Scrap said that at times, there would be 20 to 30 hunters in the woods, and most of the time the hunters outnumbered deer.

Scrap was an impressive individual and he was a rare character. He loved to tell stories. He said his favorite story was about an encounter that Big Sam had with a little ol' man! Scrap said another old Flat Shoals buck had told him the story. It had happened many years earlier but he could remember the buck telling it like it was yesterday. The old buck told Scrap the incident occurred over behind the four big lakes on Marshall Williams Road.

Big Sam had been out all night carousing and ended up chasing one particular doe. He'd let the time slip away, and just after daylight, as he was headed home, he ran into a big bunch of does bedded down. There must have been a dozen of them, and when he ran in on them, they scattered like wildfire. Scrap related that the does went in every direction and that Big Sam took after them at a full run and grunting loudly with every leap.

The old buck said Big Sam fell in behind the prettiest one and was hot on her trail when all of a sudden she put on her brakes and simply slid down the trail to a sudden stop! The old buck said what happened next would always be an unforgettable memory in Big Sam's life. The doe slid right up to the little ol' man's feet. He was standing in her trail. The ol' man stood motionless and the doe was frozen at his feet.

Big Sam, being hot on her heals, froze in the trail as well, and waited to see what was going to happen next! The bright morning sun was shining directly in Big Sam's eyes, and he couldn't see that the ol' man had raised his rifle and was poised to take a shot at him! The old buck said the next sound that Big Sam heard was the roar of a gun, and he knew that either he or the doe had to be dead. With the roar of the gun and the distinct clicking of the bolt that placed another shell in the chamber of the ol' man's gun, the doe leaped up and ran again.

Big Sam thought, *Well, if she ain't dead, it must be me!*

The old buck said that Big Sam looked himself over and declared, "No pain, no holes in my ass, no blood: Hell, I must be alive!" and he quickly bolted after the doe! Big Sam told the old buck that the bullet had to have passed between his brow tines and that the little ol' man simply must have gotten carried away and aimed at his horns. For whatever reason, Big Sam was still alive and he never saw that ol' man again. Sam and Little Sam never told Scrap that they knew the little ol' man or that they were well aware of who Big Sam was! They just let Scrap talk! It shocked them to learn that the little ol' man was hunting over in Big Sam's territory.

"I told you that that ol' man would shoot a buck with a good set of horns," Sam warned Little Sam! "Just because he hasn't busted you yet doesn't mean he won't! I'm telling you, trust him a little but don't ever let your guard down. Keep a safe distance from him and remember, the bigger your horns grow, the more likely you are to become a target! Even the ol' man can be tempted. If you don't believe me, just think about that Galloway buck! He busted his ass didn't he?"

Scrap loved the attention he was getting and it was obvious. Sam and Little Sam made a great audience. Scrap was much more into the talking than he was the listening and he told one story after another.

I like this Scrap, Sam thought. *He's funny and amusing. However, I'm not so sure he'd be as funny during the rut. I have no problem with him being in the Park this time of year. But, come rutting time, we'd probably be going at it with each other.*

Star and several other deer came bounding in from the Avery pastures. Scrap immediately turned his attention to the girls. His charm was impressive. He began strutting around and attempting to get a sweet sniff from the does. He especially took a liking to Star and Sam couldn't stand it. Little Sam was really ticked off as well because he thought Star was enjoying the attention. Old Scrap would lower his nose to the ground, stretch his long neck out and chase the does around in circles. The does would scatter and run off, only to venture back and tempt Scrap again.

It was the first time Star had been seriously courted by an outsider. And even though it would be next fall before she would seriously consider a mate, it was the beginning of Star's entry into the world of mature deer. Sam knew it. Little Sam knew it as well. And if he'd been equipped with larger headgear, he would have gladly taken on old Scrap and challenged him to a fight!

Outsiders fooling around with does in our territory is one thing, Little Sam thought, *but Star is my sister and it ain't gonna happen! This clown ain't running off with my sister. I don't care how funny and debonair he is. We don't even know anything about his breeding. For all we know, he could have some of that Nasty Pete blood running through his veins!*

Tensions began to mount between Little Sam and Scrap. A springtime fight was in the making and Sam decided he'd had enough of Scrap also. He reared high on his back legs and with two powerful blows from his front hooves, he all but knocked Scrap to the ground. About the time Scrap regained his balance, both Sam and Little Sam rammed him in the side with piercing jolts from their bare heads. Scrap couldn't think of anything funny to say so he gingerly tucked his tail and ambled off in the direction of the R&R pastures. He paused after a short distance and looked back. Sam noticed that his eyes were fixed on Star, and Star was gazing back in Scrap's direction.

Sam thought, *we ain't seen the end of this! He'll be back next fall or Star will be over there.*

Sam had dreaded the day that Star would come of age; however, in a way, he welcomed it now. He knew Star would choose an outsider for her mate and it was just a matter of time before it happened. Sam thought, *If Scrap is from the Flat Shoals Creek area, he has to be well bred!*

Flat Shoals was the homeland of the greatest buck Sam had ever known. Big Sam had scattered his genetics all up and down that territory and Scrap probably was a distant relative. Star could make a worse choice, and even Sam had been impressed with him! There was no way Star could choose a mate that would completely satisfy Sam. Naturally, he thought that no buck walking was good enough for his daughter. But who was he to say? Star had a mind of her own and he had raised her that way.

What's more, nobody had told him which doe to select for his mate. He had done it his way and it had been a wonderful life. He thought about the words of his mother, "Sam, go find someone to love; someone to lie down with and run with." How could Sam fault Scrap or Star? *Leave them alone and don't try to run their lives*, he thought. *Let Star make her own decisions and choose her own life. Isn't that what I did? Isn't that the way it's supposed to be?*

After thinking those thoughts, Sam glanced again in the direction Scrap had taken. Scrap was walking in broom sedge in the R&R back pasture. He was obviously headed home. Sam said to Little Sam, "Son, go get him. It's not our job to run Star's life. Anyway, we need a few laughs around here. Give them a chance, and if Star gets tired of him or if he mistreats her, we'll make him wish he had never come over here and I'll personally escort that joker back to Flat Shoals. Go get him and, hey, pass this word of advice to him: *Don't ever let your mouth overload your ass!*

"Ain't no smart-mouth clown going to hang in the Park, especially if he wants anything to do with Star. Tell him that if he wants to behave with a little class and develop some humility, he's welcome. Tell him that there's a time and place for everything. Tell him that class is a special quality. Tell him that showing class is a unique part of our breeding and if you have class, you can't hide it, but if you don't, you can't buy it. Tell him that too much bragging shows no class and it'll get him a good ass kicking! Go get him, Son!"

Old Scrap felt the pressure. He may have been a big stud over on Flat Shoals, but he wasn't nearly as big a deer in the Park. Sam was the big man on the block and Little Sam was heir apparent and Scrap was relegated to running a distant third in rank and order. Scrap couldn't accept that and it showed. His brilliant and funny manner became subdued and his outgoing personality changed. It would take some time for him to adjust.

It was difficult for Scrap to go from "the man" to Sam's "handy man." However, Stars' big, brown, sparkling eyes, and her long sleek feminine body, along with the thought of her being *his* doe, made him feel like a king! His problems would be worked out in time, and after all, who could be unhappy in the Park?

CHAPTER 7

Spring came and went. The does dropped their fawns in late spring and the bucks grew great sets of antlers. Sam was certainly in his late prime and he grew a set of horns like no one had ever seen before in the Park. He was huge and his headgear matched his gigantic body. Little Sam could have been "the man" anywhere except the Park. He often thought of moving to another area and leaving everything to his dad but Sam encouraged him to stay.

"Little Sam," he said, "I know you have the urge to run. I know you want a life of your own and you certainly deserve it but life doesn't get any better than here in the Park. All you need is to get out of here for a few days next fall and find yourself a doe. I don't mean to just go out and take care of business. I mean find the right one – one like your mother or one like Star.

"Good does are hard to find, Son. Most of them are poorly bred. It's hard to find one with nothing but Texas or Wisconsin blood and when you do, she'll probably be running with 3 or 4 yearlings. They will be nothing more than rut-crazed idiots. You can get killed trying to find the right one, Son. When I found your mother in the Park, it was simply a miracle. She just appeared, and I knew when I saw her that it was forever. You saw the look in Scrap's eyes when he saw Star. It'll be that way with you too.

"You just gotta get out of here this fall and do some looking and when you find her you'll know it! You'll feel things you've never felt before. The sun will shine a little brighter. The grass will smell sweeter and every morning you get up will seem like an adventure. It'll change your life and make a new being out of you. Just wait and see!"

Little Sam listened to all his dad had to say. Somehow it all seemed terribly complex to him. He wanted all those feelings but every doe in the Park was a relative – being either his mother, aunt, sister or a cousin. Where would he find such a doe?

"Be patient," his dad told him. "Wait until fall. Something good will happen for you. Just keep your class and style. It's hard to keep a good being down when they have class. If they refuse to accept anything but class, then class will find them. Just make sure you know what you want!

"Make sure that what you want fits your needs. Often our wants exceed our needs and that can become dangerous. If you don't set some standards, then you'll not recognize class when you find it. Sometimes the hottest thing in the woods ain't the best thing in the woods. Sometimes what everyone else is chasing may not be what's right for you. You gotta find a doe you can trust. Trust is the most important thing in the world and it has to be earned. There's a high price to be paid for trust. You'll have many friends in your life, Son, but trust goes a lot deeper than friendship.

"Family, Son! Family and trust! When you fail your family, nothing else you accomplish in life will mean very much! Remember that!"

All the wisdom and knowledge that Sam passed to Little Sam came from the lessons that Sam learned from his mother. His philosophy of life and his values in life were instilled in him by his sweet mother. Her love, tenderness and caring ways had made a greater impression on him than Big Sam's macho lifestyle. Without question, Sam had loved his great father, but his mother's stability and common sense-approach to life had left a lasting impression.

The ideals his mother had lived by were probably the reason Sam was still alive. He thought of her every day, and when tough decisions had to be made, he drew from the vast storehouse of lessons she had taught him. Those lessons had made him a better being and they were largely responsible for his personal strength. Sam had learned the value of those lessons and he tried his best to pass that legacy on to Little Sam and Star.

It was his duty. Sam knew that he was a product of both genetics and environment, but he was also a victim of his own instincts! He knew that much of his strength and physical appeal had been inherited from Big Sam. However, his inner-strength and code of values had definitely come from his sweet mother. Her quiet, reserved manner always had a strong, reassuring quality. It was never loud or boisterous. That was what bothered Sam about Scrap. Why did he have to be so boastful and self-serving? If he stayed in the Park, he would have to tone down. If he wanted Star, he would have to develop some class, or Sam would send him reeling all the way back across Flat Shoals Creek!

Scrap began to run with Sam and Little Sam daily. Slowly but surely, he was accepted by both of them. Autumn arrived and the Park was beautiful in its fall splendor. The huge oak trees were loaded with acorns as usual and food was plentiful. The does were grouped up with their fawns and the bucks were running in bachelor groups. The fawns had lost their spots and most had been weaned from their mothers. The little button-head bucks were torn between staying with their mothers and following the buck groups. Many of the yearlings had grown spike horns and bullied the button heads and young does.

Order of dominance was being established even at this early age with the young bucks and does. The older animals already had their pecking order established. Grace ruled the doe group. She set the tone for the day's activities. Grace was obviously the largest of the group and she needed only to fold her ears back and paw with her front feet to get her way with the others. When she was challenged or crossed by any of the other females, she would rear high on her hind legs, pin her ears back and with both front hooves flying, maul any and everything within reach.

Sam said it reminded him of how his mother had mauled Big Sam when he acted foolhardy and came home late! Big Sam would stay out half the night and come home looking for love. Sam said that when his dad tried to cozy up to his mom on those nights, she would respond by meeting him down the trail from the bedding area and paw him unmercifully.

She would say, "Big Sam, you like those gals so much, why don't you just go live with 'em! Don't come in here with the scent of those O'Neal Road wenches all over you and expect me to be in a loving mood!" Then she would work him over again! He must have liked it. He kept coming back for more!

CHAPTER 8

As the days grew shorter, tension in Sam's group began to build. Grace had a run-in with one of her group and mouths were wagging. Lies were being told and tempers were flaring! Sam had his own troubles as well. Scrap had again approached him about taking Star and moving back to Flat Shoal Creek. Sam didn't like that one bit because he knew the hunters over there would shoot her if given half a chance. He didn't care that much about Scrap's hide, but he did care about Star.

"Sam, there ain't nothing here for me but Star," Scrap told Sam. "If I stay here, you and I will have trouble. The rut is just around the corner and first thing you know, you and I'll be locking horns and one of us will get hurt. Let me take Star home with me. Let me take her back to my territory. After all, I have the same pride and respect over there that you have here in the Park. It's the right thing to do, Sam. It'll prevent trouble, and I promise I'll take care of her. I promise that when the rut is over, I'll bring her back and we'll stay in the Park when the fawns are born next spring. I know her mother will want her here during that time. It's the right thing to do, Sam!"

Sam hated the thought of losing Star, but he knew Scrap was right. He knew that when the rut came, trouble *would* develop and he'd probably have to kill Scrap. After agonizing over the issue several days, he discussed the matter with Star and Grace. Grace was furious! Her first thoughts were,

No, absolutely not! Star isn't going anywhere with that joker. We don't know enough about him and Star is so young..."

"Young?" Star repeated. "I'm fully 2 1/2 years old, and besides, I've probably already done some things that y'all don't know about! I'd rather leave with Scrap and have a legitimate life than stay here and get raped by a first cousin or who knows what! Scrap and I have talked. Y'all have gotta know how I feel about him and it's time you let go. I can't stay under your wing for the rest of my life! We might make some mistakes, but we'll make it. We'll make it just like you and Dad did! Besides, I like his light-hearted way! He doesn't take everything so seriously like y'all do. He makes me laugh and I need that. Don't you see that I love him?"

Star stopped with those words. Sam looked at Grace and their eyes locked in a stare. What could they say? Nothing! They couldn't say anything! A long silence was finally broken when Sam said, "Star, your mother and I want your happiness more than anything in the world and we don't have a thing against Scrap. It's just that we really don't think there's a being out there good enough for you and you'll understand how we feel someday. If you've given it plenty of thought and if you've agreed on it, then go! Go with him. You have our blessings. But remember, if he ever mistreats you or fails you in any way, you know the way home!"

Grace broke in and said, "No, Sam. That's not the way it is. No, Star, you don't come home if things don't go to suit you. You stay and try to work them out. Sam, if I'd left you every time I wanted to, we wouldn't have made it! No Star, you make a commitment and you keep it! You leave with him and you come back with him. He's not perfect, but none of them are. When the rut comes each year, you'll want to kill him, but be patient and let time heal any wounds. If you think things are going to be perfect for you two, forget it! Life is tough and it gets tougher! Just wait 'til next summer when you have two little ones to look after as well as Scrap. You'll understand things a little better then!"

"Scrap is coming by tonight," Star said. "I can't wait to see him. He's been over in his territory making ready for our coming. There are some things we need to discuss, some commitments we need to make, and some understandings we need to have. Dad and Mom, there are some things you need to know about Scrap. We've talked about them and think you need to know. I think you deserve to know! I'd rather Scrap be here when it's discussed and tomorrow probably is the best time. I think you'll understand him better after that!

"We plan to meet just after dark tonight and I'd like to talk to y'all one last time before we leave. Scrap and I will be in the Avery pastures tomorrow morning. We'll bed tonight in the big oaks in that finger woodlot. See you at daylight tomorrow!" With that said, Star eased out of the area.

CHAPTER 9

Sam, Little Sam and Grace browsed together all night long. The moon was full and as they grazed across the Avery farm pastures, they cast full, life-like shadows. All night long Sam kept mumbling, "What in the world could they be waiting to tell us? What could Scrap and Star be harboring that's so important? Why haven't they told us before now?"

Grace told Sam to just be patient and wait. "We'll find out in due time," she said. "Wait 'til we meet them at daylight."

The moon disappeared in the western horizon and a night that had been so bright was suddenly very, very dark. The three deer bedded down in the finger for some late-hour sleep. The finger of woods divided the Avery pastures from the Park and was a favorite bedding area. Sam and Grace lay silently. Both knew the other's thoughts. Tomorrow, Star would be leaving the Park and they were both very worried.

At first light, Sam scrambled to his feet. "I haven't slept a wink; let's go," he said to Grace and Little Sam. As they galloped through the big oaks and reached high ground, Sam saw Star and Scrap in the lush Avery pastures.

Grace said, "There they are, Sam, right where they said they'd be!"

Scrap and Star were grazing toward them and they appeared to be happy and relaxed.

Sam just looked at them with admiration Grace said, "You tell me if they're happy! They look just like we did at that age! In fact, Sam, you were standing in this exact spot the first time I saw you! I came grazing over that hill, just like Star and Scrap are doing now and I saw you standing here.

"Sam," she continued, "you looked so lonely and lost. I thought you were the most handsome deer I had ever seen... also the loneliest. I knew you had everything that I needed except for love and I was about to teach you about love! Isn't that right Sam?"

Sam said nothing. He twitched his tail twice and started stepping off the distance to Star. As they approached, Scrap suddenly threw his head high in the air and took on a protective posture.

"Relax Scrap," Star said. "It's just Mom and Dad! Why are you so nervous all of a sudden?"

"You know why I'm nervous," Scrap exclaimed.

"Just relax and everything will be okay," answered Star.

Sam got right down to business. His first words were, "Let's hear it. I've not slept a wink. What's going on? What do you have to tell us that's so all-fired important?"

Star started to speak when Scrap interrupted. "Let me tell it, Star!"

Scrap began by explaining how truly grateful he was for being accepted in the Park and how much he admired Sam and his family. Eventually he alluded to the fact that he knew Sam was worried about his background and his genetics, especially since he had asked for Star.

Sam grew more anxious and said, "Get to the point, Scrap. Stop beating around the bush. I knew it all the time... Go on and tell me... You're from that bunch of weak-kneed, half-breeds down on O'Neal Road, aren't you? Go on, tell us. You've got ol' Nasty Pete's blood running in your veins, don't you?"

"No Sam," Scrap answered with a slight grin. "That's not it at all. You see, I'm so proud of Star. I think she's the most beautiful thing in the world and I know you want the very best for her and that you've been leery of me since I've been here. Sam, what I'm about to tell you, well, you aren't going to believe it. I have trouble believing it myself at times. You see, Sam, things haven't exactly been easy for me. My arrogant attitude and personality come from the way I was raised. It's a long story, Sam."

Sam said, "I don't care how long it is. If you plan on taking Star away from here, you'd better tell it all and get started pretty quick!"

"Sam, I've heard you speak of the little ol' man who you see often in the Park," Scrap began. "I've listened to you describe him and your relationship and your respect for him and how well you know him...."

Sam interrupted, "Scrap, that ain't got one thing to do with your heritage, now get on to the point!"

Scrap began again. "You see, Sam, I was raised an orphan. My mom was killed when I was two days old."

"Your mother died when you were two days old and you lived?" Sam asked in amazement.

"Yes," Scrap said.

"Then who in the devil raised you?" Sam asked.

Scrap took a long, deep breath, looked Sam squarely in the eyes, and said, "I told you, you wouldn't believe it... The little ol' man raised me!"

Sam nearly fell over. He was in shock. His first impulse was to fight. How could anyone tell him a lie that big right to his face?

"The little ol' man raised you?" exclaimed Sam. "Do you expect us to believe that? Star, how can you be in love with this counterfeit?"

Star said, "It's the truth, Dad. Please, please just let him finish. Let him finish."

Sam said, "I'm sorry I ever let him start! I knew I should have run him off the first day I ever laid eyes on him. What a fool I've been. I've let a lying, loudmouthed bastard stay in the Park and I almost let him run off with my only daughter! Tell me it ain't so, Star! Say it ain't so!"

"Dad, it is so!" Star insisted. "Please let him finish! It's all the truth and you haven't heard the half of it yet!"

Scrap said, "Sam, I know it's a shock to you. That's why I wanted to tell you. I didn't want you to hear it from some of those tongue-wagging wenches over on Flat Shoals Creek."

"Everyone over on Flat Shoals knows about it?" Sam asked. "Wait, Scrap, you want me to believe that your mother died when you were two days old and that the ol' man is your daddy? No, Scrap, that's a little much for me to believe!"

"Sam, I didn't say he was my daddy," Scrap said firmly. "I said he took care of me and raised me. Sam, he raised me like my mom would have! Just listen, Sam! Just listen and believe me!"

"Scrap, I'll listen but I'm not promising that I'll believe any of it," Sam replied.

Scrap decided to start his story from the beginning and he opened by saying that he was born in the fescue pasture on the Steve Morgan farm. When Scrap said that, Sam had a fit.

"What?" Sam screamed. "You're telling me you were born in the Park? The Morgan farm is part of the Park, you know."

"Yes," Scrap answered, "I was born in a briar patch right in the middle of Steve Morgan's fescue pasture."

Even Grace and Little Sam were beginning to doubt Scrap now. Little Sam said, "Scrap, you told us you were 'the man' over on Flat Shoals Creek. Now you're telling us you were born in the Park?"

"It's true!" screamed Star. "Will y'all please just be quiet and listen to his story. It's the most incredible tale I've ever heard and all of it's true. Does anyone here have the courtesy to just listen?"

"Out of respect for you, Star, and respect for the family, we'll listen," Sam said. "I promise you we'll listen. But, if this is a lie, we'll also kick his ass and run him off! I can promise you that, too!"

Scrap again picked up where he'd left off. "It was early June five years ago when my mom gave me life," he said. "My mom birthed me and we were safe as could be in a big briar patch of the Morgan farm fescue pasture. We could see for a long distance in every direction. Whenever danger from dogs or coyotes came, Mom would jump up and run. I would scoot down in our bed and become almost invisible. The dogs would see Mom and she would lure them away from me."

Sam screamed. "Scrap, we know all about how that works. We've managed to survive as well. Give us some credit. We want to know how in the devil you got to Flat Shoals Creek!"

Scrap took another deep breath. "The evening of our second day, we heard a tractor and bush-hog running. Mr. Morgan was mowing our field."

Sam interrupted again. "Scrap, they don't ever mow those pastures!"

"They did that year, Sam. I'm telling you they did! I'm telling you they went 'round and 'round that field until nothing was left but the briar patch! Mom had jumped and run and I was there all alone. When the tractor got so close that I could stand it no longer, I jumped up to my feet and took off. I didn't know where I was going, but I wasn't going to be chopped up like ragweed. I ran as fast as I could, but it wasn't fast enough. Before I knew it, Mr. Morgan's wife had me cornered and was all over me. She had come to the field to bring Mr. Morgan a drink when she saw me. I'm telling you, that woman can run!

"Mr. Morgan finished cutting the briar patch and the two of them loaded me in the back of their truck and hauled me to their house. Mrs. Morgan told her husband that I must belong to the doe that had just been killed out on the road. My heart was broken. I knew that Mom ran away to draw attention to herself and I knew that she probably had crossed highway 219 without looking.

"What was I going to do? My mom was dead and there I was, alone in the world. We were in the Morgan's back yard and they were discussing what they should do with me when a miracle occurred! An old blue pick-up truck came chugging up the field road from the Park and stopped. A little ol' man got out and hollered, 'What have y'all got there?'

"'It's a deer!' the wife hollered back. 'It's a little buck fawn.'

"'Well, turn him loose!' the little ol' man yelled.

"'We can't,' Mrs. Morgan said. 'His mom just got hit by a car. What're we going to do with him? He'll starve without his mother.'

"The ol' man had gotten to us by then. He took one look at me and you could see the wheels turning in his mind. 'Ain't he something!' he said.

"'Yeah, he is,' Mr. Morgan agreed. 'But what in the heck are we gonna do with him?'

"With all the confidence in the world, the little ol' man said, 'Let me have him. I know what to do with him. I'll take him home and raise him myself. I've got bottles and milk and my little girl will take care of him. Let me have him.'"

Scrap looked around to see if Sam and the rest of the group looked as though they might believe him. The entire group was standing spellbound. Mouths were hanging open in total disbelief.

"Well don't stop now," Sam said. "Let's hear the rest!"

"It's gotta be the truth," said Little Sam. "No one could make up a lie that big!"

Scrap shrugged, took another deep breath and continued. "The ol' man took me in his arms and we got into the truck," Scrap said. "The Morgan's closed the pasture gate after we passed through and down the highway we went. We turned west at the crossroads and headed toward Flat Shoals Creek. We took another left on a bumpy road and it seemed we had traveled forever. I was squirming and trying to break free from the little ol' man's grip, but he held me tight. I was exhausted when we finally stopped at his house. We must have traveled a good 5 miles in 10 minutes."

"Ain't no way!" said Little Sam.

"I'm telling you," Scrap said. "The little ol' man let the hammer down on ol' Blue and we were there in no time!"

"Tell me," said Sam, "did you pass a big tall silo?"

"Did we pass it?" Scrap answered. "The ol' man lives right near it!"

"That's where I spent the early part of my life!" Sam said to Grace. "That silo is near the Hogg place. That's near the spot where Mom and I were bedded the night Big Sam was killed. That silo will be in my mind forever. We used it as a reference point all those years."

Grace broke into the conversation. "Let's get back to you, Scrap. What happened when you reached the ol' man's house?"

"Well, it's difficult to describe," Scrap said. "The little ol' man gathered me up in his arms and carried me inside."

"No," Sam said. "You didn't go into the little ol' man's house. No way! You're making every bit of this up and it's all a huge lie! There's no way a white-tailed deer has ever been inside the little ol' man's house!"

"I'm telling you, Sam, not only did he take me inside, but I lived in there for three weeks," said Scrap. "He fed me from a bottle and I slept in the corner behind his kitchen table. I ran all over his house and played with his dog, Punkin! I chased Punkin up and down his stairs and slipped and slid on his kitchen floor."

"Scrap, where did you... you know.. go?" Little Sam asked. "I know the ol' man didn't let you leave droppings all over his house."

"In my corner," answered Scrap. "The little ol' man fixed a special place for me. I slept in one corner and left my droppings in another. I never made a mess. He put towels on the floor for me."

Grace interrupted again. "Scrap, does the little ol' man have a wife? Where was she when you were running all over her house?"

"She was there," Scrap answered. "When the ol' man brought me in the house that first day, she almost fainted! She told him she didn't care whose momma got hit by a car, no deer was gonna stay in her house! After a while, though, she kinda fell in love with me, especially after she realized I didn't smell bad and wouldn't make a mess everywhere. It was something else living in that place. There were no bugs, no flies, no coyotes and no hunters!"

"No hunters?" Sam questioned. "What about the little ol' man? You better believe he's a hunter! Why, if he saw you today, he'd shoot your ass so fast you wouldn't know what hit you!"

"Maybe so," Scrap said. "But not if he recognized me."

"Well, go on with the story," Grace said.

Scrap said, "Sam, I've heard y'all talk about Big Elrod… You said once you thought the little ol' man killed him. Well, he did!"

"How do you know that, Scrap?" Sam asked.

"Because I've seen him!" answered Scrap.

"What?" Sam said. "You've seen Big Elrod? Big Elrod has been dead for years!"

"I'm telling you, I used to lay in my corner and look at him on the den wall," Scrap answered. "Sam, Ole Elrod was something else! Big 10-pointer, he was, and something special! I used to stare up at him and hope someday I could be as impressive as he was."

"How big was he, Scrap?" Little Sam asked.

"He ain't as big as your daddy and probably couldn't hold a candle to Big Sam, but he was impressive," said Scrap. "He had dark, long tines and heavy mass. I used to lay at night in the dim light and shadows of that room and think, *Nothing can happen to me with Ole Elrod watching over me!*

"That security probably kept me going. That and Punkin! Punkin was a dog, but she was my friend. We played together daily and she shared her food with me.

"What?" Sam declared. "You ate dog food?"

"It beats acorns any day!" said Scrap. "Don't knock dog food until you've tried it!"

"Go on with your tale," Grace said. "How did you get out of the house? Obviously, you don't still live with the ol' man!"

"I'm so ashamed," Scrap said. "I know what y'all must be thinking of me. You probably hate the little ol' man and all other hunters like him. However, I loved him and it just ain't right for a deer to have feelings for a hunter!"

"Forget it, Scrap," said Sam. "You're alive, aren't you? Forget it and go on with the story."

"Well the summer weeks passed quickly and the little ol' man started letting me and Punkin go outside to play. At the same time, he started putting shelled corn out around his yard and pastures. Me and Punkin would romp and play all over the yard and pastures. At night, the little ol' man would fasten us up in Punkin's pen and, in the wee hours of the night, 'Mother' would bring my two sisters to the pasture edge to eat corn."

"What?" Sam screamed. "You told us your mother was hit by a car over here near the Park!"

"She was Sam. My *real* mom was, that is. But the doe I'm talking about became the only real 'Mother' I ever knew. The little ol' man was smart. He knew that if he fed corn near my pen, other deer would come to eat it, and just maybe he would attract a doe with young fawns. That's exactly what happened. Mother was scared to death of me at first. She couldn't believe a young buck like me was living in harmony with a cocker spaniel dog, in a pen, eating dog food and wearing a big red ribbon around his neck!

"Late at night she would bring my two little sisters into the yard and, as Punkin slept, we would rub noses through the wire fence. She even started hanging around the pastures late in the evenings. The little ol' man was pleased, and he started letting me out every time he saw Mother! Finally, one evening, I decided to invite myself to join their group!

"That particular evening, Mother had her sister and her two fawns with her and also a big worrisome spike buck. The spike was worrying Mother to the point of being a real nuisance. I was hidden in the fencerow out in front of the little ol' man's house. When the group got close enough for me to wind them, I jumped out of my hiding place and charged toward them. Mother wasn't surprised, but her sister and that nerd of a spike turned inside out. They had never seen a deer with a three-inch red ribbon around his neck and a big bow, to boot! The spike literally ran through the little ol' man's fence and disappeared through the woods.

"We never saw him again. I chased Mother all over those pastures until she finally stopped. She gave me a nudge with her nose and made a sound that only moms can make and I knew my life was about to change. She shared her goodness between me and her two fawns. I don't think her girls were very happy about it, but I was overjoyed. It got to be a habit. The little ol' man would turn me and Punkin out in late evening, his little girl, Bess, would give me a bottle of milk and then she would feed me dog food – one acorn-size piece at a time. Just before dark, Mother and my sisters would appear and I would run with them until time for bed. When Mother and the girls had eaten their corn and began browsing away from the pastures, I would head back home.

"Punkin would always bark when I came home and the little ol' man would come out and put us to bed in the pen. This went on all summer and I started staying out later and later with Mother! Mother didn't like me traveling with them very much because of the ribbon around my neck. The little ol' man said it was to keep me from getting shot. Mother said it caused me to be a social outcast and I could never have any true friends until I got rid of it! One evening, as I was crawling through the barbed wire fence, and chasing Punkin, my ribbon got caught in the fence. After a terrible struggle, the ribbon slipped over my nose and stayed hung in the fence.

"The little ol' man saw it but never put it back on me. I was free! I looked like all the other deer and Mother was so proud. After that, she started letting me travel with her and the girls and I stayed out later and later. The little ol' man missed me. He didn't like me being gone so much. On several nights, he called me and I would go to his warm bottle of milk. I was getting big and that became a problem. I had knots on my head where my horns would someday grow and I had started smelling like a deer. My impatience had grown and when the little ol' man offered me my milk, I'd stand on my hind feet and paw at him while I nursed the bottle. He got to where he would slap my big ears whenever I did that. Don't think he can't punch you out, Sam."

"Scrap, this is the most incredible story I've ever heard," Sam said. "I almost feel like a fool even listening to it."

"It's the truth, Sam," Scrap insisted. "I know it must be hard for you to believe, but it's the truth!"

"Go on," Grace said. "I want to hear the rest of it."

"When the fall of the year came, and the days were getting shorter and shorter," Scrap continued, the leaves on the trees around the pasture were turning beautiful colors and I hadn't seen the little ol' man in several days. Punkin often rambled in the woods and I ran and chased her when she did. Late one night, I had the urge to see the ol' man one last time. I ventured from the pastures to his back porch. Punkin and I had played chase on that porch so many times. Just being there made me hungry. The little ol' man had fed me so many nights on that porch. The lights were on in the house, but he didn't come out. I reared up on my hind legs and pawed at his back door.

"All of a sudden, floodlights came on and the little ol' man stepped out. He rubbed my head and scratched my button horns. It felt so good. I reared on my hind legs and pawed with my front feet. He immediately slapped me with an open hand and said, "Scrap!" That was the first time I ever heard the name.

"'Scrap,' he said, 'it's time for you to make it on your own! I love you and Punkin will miss you, but it's time for you to *scrap* for yourself. You go on, now. It's not fair for me to continue to take care of you. You've gotta learn to fend for yourself. You've gotta learn to be a real deer. I've done all I can for you. You've brought me so much pleasure. It's been a thrill to watch you grow up and though we love you and will miss you, it's time for you to be with your own kind. You've gotta learn the ways of your kind and you've gotta learn that all humans out there are not like me.

"'You'll be okay, Scrap,' he continued. 'I just hope that some day I can see you all grown up with a family of your own. Life hasn't been so kind to you. You'll be laughed at because of being raised here in a pen with Punkin. However, you can prove yourself. You need to remember all the good times and fun we've had, but you also need to remember that this way of life is not *your* life. Your life should be your own. You've been raised like a dog, but you'll become a great buck some day, and you need to be proud of your heritage.'

"He told me I came from outstanding stock and that I would someday have great influence and that my presence would be felt in the area. Well, Sam, everything he told me has come true. I've had to scrap for everything that I've ever done. From the time I wore that red ribbon until today, I've had to fight and fend for myself. It hasn't been easy, but the little ol' man never said it would be! He knew what he was doing when he named me Scrap!"

At that point, Sam stopped the story. "Scrap, what can I say? I never thought about my daughter running off with a pen-raised buck, but I couldn't be prouder. I'm just ashamed that you kept this from us all summer long."

"Well," Scrap said, "I know how you feel about who you are! I know how strongly y'all feel about family tree and heritage. I'm embarrassed about the fact that I don't even know who my real mother was and the only daddy I've ever known is the ol' man."

"Scrap, there's something strange about your mom's death," Sam said. "I think that if a prominent doe like her had been killed by a car in our area, we'd have heard about it. Something just doesn't seem to add up. But if you say that's what happened, then okay. Five years ago is a long time. I wish I could remember more about it."

Sam thought for a moment. "You know, Scrap, if you were born in the Park, then we're most likely related. I'm trying to remember your mom and the doe that took you in. Who was that doe, Scrap? What did your surrogate mother look like?"

"Sam, she was huge, and the sweetest thing in the world!" Scrap answered. "She nursed me and both of her little doe fawns and we all did well. She had a muzzle as long as a mule and ears like a jackrabbit. She was huge Sam, and her age had just about done her in. She died right after she weaned us. She got shot over near the Mote Road.

"That was her area," Scrap continued. "That's where she bedded and raised us. She ate corn at the little ol' man's place and at night browsed on the Hogg place. Her area was about a mile square and it usually took us three days to make the cycle. The little ol' man made sure we never went hungry, but he never hunted us. He only wanted to watch and observe. I've seen Mother crawl through his fence and eat a belly full of corn with him standing in the yard with her. He was sick when she got killed. He always remembered her for taking care of me. You couldn't mistake Mother! She was so big and she had an unmistakable gray face.

"Sam," Scrap continued, there's no telling how many little'ns she raised! I loved her like she was my own mother and will forever be grateful to her. She was one-of-a-kind and a true lady in every respect."

"Were you with her the day she was killed?" Sam asked.

"Yes I was," said Scrap. "Mother had lost a lot of her survival instincts. I guess hanging out around the little ol' man's place made her less afraid of hunters. We were bedded in Troup County, just northeast of the Mote place when Mother decided it was time to browse toward the Hogg property. I smelled the hunter before she did but she ignored my blowing and stomping. She acted like she was determined to know where he was and who he was.

"We were standing in a growth of pines in plain view! I can't imagine why Mother was so relaxed. I saw the hunter and I don't know why she didn't recognize the danger. She was so hardheaded that I'll never know if she was surprised or just determined to take the hunter's attention away from me and her girls. Anyway, a gun roared and Mother went down without even a struggle. She was dead before she hit the ground. I looked around and the two girls were bounding toward Flat Shoals Creek. I followed them for a step or two, then turned around and saw the hunter going toward Mother!"

"What did he look like?" Sam asked.

"Well, he was different looking. Didn't look anything like most of the hunters we see from around these parts. He acted kind of nervous and jittery and wore camouflage bib overalls. He had beady eyes, black hair and dark skin and was real skinny. He wasn't from around these parts. I don't believe he hunted over there very much. It was the first time we'd ever seen him. He favored another hunter that poached the Mote place a lot. They looked so much alike they could have been brothers. The other guy is the one who swings from trees. We called him the "monkey man" because he always hunted out of a peculiar looking saddle harness that hung from the limb of a tree. You were never safe with him around and he was liable to show up anywhere. Neither one of them could sit still for very long. The monkey man was always on the move. Both of these hunters were Italian looking and I would swear that they were brothers."

"What kind of truck did he drive?" Sam asked.

"It was different too," Scrap said. "It had a flat bed on it with short side panels. When you saw him in it you didn't know whether he was hunting, delivering refrigerators, or both! I don't know how he got Mother on the truck or even had room for her because the bed was loaded down with all kinds of junk!"

Sam said, "I don't think we've ever seen him in the Park. I'd remember a truck like that. However, I believe that hunter you call 'monkey man' is one of the hunters that helped the ol' man load up the Galloway buck. You know what? I believe he was there the morning that Nasty Pete went down as well! You didn't see a beat up old yellow truck, did you?"

"No, just the one that looked like a delivery truck," Scrap answered.

Grace was getting anxious. "Sam, this conversation could go on forever," she said. "If these two are headed out this morning, they need to get moving. It's already past sunrise and we both know hunters are due in the woods any day now." Grace turned to Star and said, "Take good care of him and both of you take good care of each other."

Scrap looked at Little Sam and said, "Big boy, when you get to where you think you can handle some of that Flat Shoals Creek stuff, just grunt your way on over!"

Little Sam grinned and Scrap laughed out loud.

"There you go, running your mouth again, Scrap!" Sam said. "Just about the time I start liking you — and believe me I've had to try — you get all cocky. You better look out for Star because if anything happens to her, I'll bury you in Flat Shoals Creek! Do you understand me? I don't know where you got your attitude. I don't ever remember any of the bucks acting like that when I ran the Flat Shoals territory.

Scrap grinned and said, "Yeah, Sam, but they haven't eaten as much high-protein Purina dog chow as I have!"

"No, and I don't remember any of them wearing red ribbons with bows around their necks either!" Sam fired back.

Star screamed, "Y'all stop it! The last thing I need is you two fighting."

"Yeah, Sam, leave him alone," Grace said. "He's been through enough already. Can't you see he has enough of a problem being accepted as it is? He doesn't need you provoking him on his last day in the Park."

"There y'all go again – taking sides against me!" Sam said. "I can't do anything right around here anymore."

Grace said, "That's not it, Sam. It's just that you talk too much yourself at times!"

Sam could handle any buck in the woods – he wasn't afraid of any of them – he was fearless, yet Grace could bring him to his knees with words! Sam once said that the only adversaries he had were those he loved and those who loved him! If he didn't love them, they couldn't hurt him!

Little Sam's mind was somewhere else. All he could say was, "Scrap, are you serious about those Flat Shoals Creek females?"

Scrap grinned again and said, "They're just like Purina dog food, Son! Don't knock 'em until you've tried 'em!"

All at once, the hair on Sam's back stood straight up! His ears went back against his neck, his front legs grew stiff, and he gave a loud snort-wheeze. Then he lunged at Scrap. Scrap leaped backwards and went to his knees. Sam locked horns with him and drove him to the ground. When Scrap regained his feet, Sam rammed him in the hindquarters with tremendous force. Sam then thrust his great horns up in the air and Scrap went flying tail over antlers. When he hit the ground, all four legs were moving and he was headed in the direction of Flat Shoals Creek with Sam hot on his trail! Star ran out in front of them with her long, white, tail flared up and waving in the morning sun like a flag.

Grace and Little Sam stood watching in shock! Sam chased them for a few more yards and then turned back toward Grace and Little Sam. He yelled, "I've put that off long enough! Scrap needs to develop some humility and I'm gonna help him with it!"

"You ran them off!" Grace said. "What's gotten into you?"

Sam twitched his tail and dropped his nose to the ground. He turned and winded the direction in which the two had run. "They'll be back, and Scrap will be better from the scare I gave him. As long as I live, I'm running this show and we ain't putting up with a smart mouth around here. He'll come back humble or he won't come back at all. And I can assure you that Star will be back as well! She'll be back in the Park and she'll run with us again. Scrap will work the Flat Shoals area until the rut is over and then he'll come back too. That is, unless he takes a load of buckshot in his backside! There is always the possibility of that over there!

"Those guys who hunt the Flat Shoals will hang him by the heels. The ol' man can't take care of him now! You know what? Remember what he said? Remember him saying that the little ol' man wanted to see him all grown up with a family of his own? I can assure you that the pastures behind the little ol' man's house are where they're headed!

"Scrap will keep them there until Star is bred and then she'll come home. Scrap may be a cocky clown, but he ain't no fool. Just because I kicked his ass don't mean I'll dislike him forever! Remember what Mom told me years ago? Sometimes a good ass kicking is what we need to get our thinking straight! I certainly remember it and Scrap will, too – sooner than he thinks!"

CHAPTER 10

Grace stood still and stared ahead. Little Sam appeared to be perplexed. Six weeks had passed since Sam had embarrassed Star by chasing Scrap out of the Park. Sam's behavior became more and more aggressive and now he was strutting with his long white tail all flared out. He was obviously nervous and anxious! Turning to Grace and Little Sam, he said, "Haven't you heard? The rut is in! Two does were bred on the Avery farm last night and the rut is in full swing! Don't expect me to behave like a saint! I apologize for embarrassing Star a few weeks ago, but the rut has arrived, and that probably won't be the only stupid thing I do in the coming weeks."

Over on some adjoining property, the loud roar of a rifle shook the morning air.

"You're right, Sam, the rut *is* in," Grace agreed. "But that also means that hunting season is here! You don't need to do but one stupid thing... One stupid mistake and you'll be hanging over someone's fireplace for eternity! Granted, the little ol' man has been kind to you, but you know as well as I do that poachers are working the Park's perimeter and you're a prime candidate for one of those vultures.

"There was lots of shooting all around us last year. The only safe place is here in the Park and if you let your attitude and desires get the best of you, you'll meet the same demise that Big Sam did, or even worse, Big Elrod!"

"I know you're right," Sam said in a much-more-humble tone. "I jumped Scrap all the time about lack of humility and here I am acting like a juvenile. I guess I always need to remember Mom's advice to Dad: 'A cool and intelligent head is always more beneficial than a brain floating in testosterone! Sometimes it is easier to control these woods than it is to control myself!'"

"Sam, run your scrape lines inside the Park," Grace said. "Don't go hanging out in the Avery pastures during daylight hours or rambling through the policeman's property. Just stay in the Park. If you do that, you'll have more business than you can take care of and you won't get yourself killed. Promise me that! Promise me, Sam!"

"It's a promise," Sam said. He dropped his big antlers to the ground so that Grace could groom his neck and shoulders. Little Sam browsed on out of hearing distance and Sam said, "What's up with Little Sam? You'd think he would be more interested in the does than he is! I'm beginning to worry about him. When I was that age, I was chasing and checking everything that moved. He doesn't appear to even know what the rut is all about. You don't think he's *funny* do you?"

"No, Sam, he ain't funny!" Grace answered. "He is as normal as you are and just because he is not a carbon copy of you don't mean he is funny!

"Give him time, Sam! After all, you've been so dominant in his life that he hasn't had much of a chance. He probably feels suppressed by you and needs some breathing room. You may need to give him some space and let him grow up. If you don't, it ain't gonna be funny!"

"There you go again," Sam said, "blaming everything on me!"

"Well, just think about it," Grace said. "How can he establish any relationships of his own if he's always running in your shadow? If you remember, you left the Flat Shoals area to establish a life of your own. Maybe Little Sam needs to do the same thing!"

"What?" Sam countered. "And leave the sanctuary of the Park to get his ass shot off!"

"That's right!" Grace said. "You did it, and if he keeps hanging around here, the two of you will end up fighting! Then what do you think will happen?"

"Do you think I should run him off?" Sam asked.

"I think it's time for him to mature and move on with his life," Grace answered. "Now, that's a *boy thing* with you two and you know how to handle it better than I do. Sometimes you just have to do what you have to do. It wasn't easy for me to wean Star and Little Sam, but I did it! Now it's time for you to do what you have to do. Star took that first step six weeks ago when she left with Scrap! That's all I'm going to say."

With that, Grace twitched her tail and wandered off through the big oaks toward the big Pipe Crossing. She had planted a seed in Sam's head! Females know how to do that!

Sam bedded down by a huge fallen log and drifted off into a mid-morning doze. The bright sun warmed his back. As he chewed his cud, his mind started wandering. How could he bring himself to tell Little Sam he didn't want him in the Park anymore? After all, Little Sam was not only his son, but his best friend as well.

As he rested, the silence was broken by a loud crashing sound in the brush just beyond the spot where Little Sam had disappeared a few minutes earlier. Sam could see movement. Then he heard several grunts and the sound of antlers crashing together. All of a sudden a beautiful doe charged out of the thicket with three juvenile bucks hot on her trail. One of the bucks was Little Sam.

This is it! Sam thought. *This is a wonderful time to teach my son some lessons and send him on his way at the same time!*

The three young bucks chased the doe by the little ol' man's ladder stand that was set in the corner of the woods and on the edge of the Avery pastures. Sam watched from the logging road and winded the doe as she ran circles in the pastures. Sam knew she was not quite ready for mating and that her three pursuers were burning energy and wasting their time. Up through the big oaks they ran, chasing the doe. Sam quietly stood up and waited patiently with his nose high in the air. It was all he could do to control his own urges. He wanted to join in the chase. But this was not his first rodeo.

He knew that when a receptive doe tired of the chase, she would submit to the buck that was most dominant. The three adolescents ran until their tongues were hanging out. The doe was tiring also. Sam walked to the nearest bush and began thrashing it with his great horns. As he broke limbs and pawed the ground and grunted, he saw the group headed in his direction from the Avery pasture. When they crossed the fence, they were only a mere 20 yards away.

The doe came to an abrupt halt. When she stopped, Sam bolted in the direction of the younger bucks and with all his strength, tore into the three juvenile bucks! He sent them scattering in every direction, Little Sam included! Little Sam couldn't believe what was happening to him. Sam was all over him, grunting, snort-wheezing and kicking his ass!

The doe stood motionless while Sam sent hair flying. The battle lasted only minutes but the results were far-reaching. Two of the young bucks bounded off toward the Steve Morgan farm but Little Sam lingered behind.

"Remember what Scrap said about those Flat Shoals Creek females?" Sam asked. "Maybe this is a good time for you to go over there and try nailing some of them! There ain't room enough for both of us here in the Park any more, Son! Take care of yourself while you're gone and come back in the spring! And, hey, bring Scrap back with you when you come!"

With that, Sam fell in behind the hot doe and the two of them disappeared down the logging road at a slow gallop. Little Sam watched them disappear. His heart was broken. How could this be happening to him? He was in shock. His own dad had just expelled him from the Park. It was a hard lesson to swallow, but one that had to be learned. Little Sam was related to virtually every doe in the Park and Sam knew he needed to move to another area.

Sam knew that the pain of learning a valuable lesson was short lived, and that his son would be back in the Park when the rut was over. He also knew that the battles Little Sam was destined to fight would be crucial to his future. Sam remembered all the struggles he'd had on his way up the ladder to becoming a dominant buck. He felt sympathy for Little Sam, but he knew that those battles had to be fought by Little Sam. Only through survival of the fittest could Little Sam grow. He had to earn his respect in the herd and that was that!

Little Sam gazed in the direction his dad had gone. He had the urge to follow but his instincts told him no! He dropped his nose to the ground, twitched his tail in resignation and slowly moved down the trail the other two young bucks had taken. It was a new beginning for Little Sam. Where would his instincts lead him?

CHAPTER 11

(O)ne time a young man asked for some advice from a wise and older gentleman. "Should I go away to pursue my career or stay closer to home?" The young man asked.

The old gentleman answered, "Ain't no way you can ever outdo your dad, so I guess you'd better move on."

This aptly summarized the situation with Sam and Little Sam. Leaving home can be a traumatic experience. At best, it's a drastic, life-changing experience. In Little Sam's case, it was extremely drastic. His dad had prepared him for almost everything. However, he was totally unprepared for the emotional shock of being kicked out of his home range by his father.

Many emotions filled his head, including a never-before-felt, love-hate sensation regarding his dad. At one moment, he loved his dad unconditionally. The next, he hated him in the worst way. How could his dad kick him out! How could Sam do this to him? He understood the situation with old Scrap. But how could Sam run off his own flesh and blood?

As Little Sam wandered down trails that led away from the Park, he kept looking back! He hoped to see Sam and his mom moving down the trail behind him. He hoped that Sam had changed his mind. But it was not to be. Little Sam was definitely on his own! His future depended totally on his own instincts and abilities. He knew he couldn't depend on his mom and dad ever again. It was time to grow up and he would either make it or he wouldn't!

Little Sam moved in a northwestward direction. As he traveled, the countryside became increasingly strange and unfamiliar with many new and foreign odors. Darkness was upon him and he had no idea where he was going. Insecurity and doubt often lead to fear, and for the first time in his life, Little Sam was afraid. He couldn't go back, and he knew nothing about what lay ahead. He was a stranger in a strange land!

For hours, Little Sam wandered down unknown trails. When the trails would split, he would take the one he thought most traveled. A bright moon broke through a cloudy sky and the landscape became more defined. In the far distance, he saw a bright light and a quaint little white structure. It was a church and it was surrounded by several huge oak trees.

Little Sam was famished. He had not eaten for hours and he wondered if the big oaks could possibly offer a midnight snack. He crossed a large pasture where a new lake was under construction. Big earth-moving equipment shimmered ghost-like in the moonlight. He moved cautiously as he traveled the length of the newly constructed dam and thought about how sweet the freshly turned earth smelled.

As he approached the little white church, he found himself walking among huge flat rocks with inscriptions carved on them. Although he didn't know it, he was in the middle of a small cemetery. One of the big flat rocks caught his eye and he studied it briefly. The inscription read: *Susan Elise Oliver, Forever Seventeen!* Suddenly he felt a strange rush of emotions. Although he didn't understand it, Little Sam knew he was in the presence of something very special. He sensed a strange aura all around him and he was perplexed. His emotions seemed to flow with both pain and joy. It was a spiritual moment.

How could this be? How could this strange place emit so much sorrow, yet foster such a feeling of hope and solitude. How could this be? Little Sam was confused, but he definitely felt a kinship with this sacred place. He definitely felt a oneness with his surroundings. Other stones were engraved with the names of Avery, Morgan, Paul, Williams, Hogg, Marlowe, Parmer and McKeen! He thought: *All life is so sacred…What a peaceful place….*

Little Sam found literally bushels of acorns under the huge white oak trees! He ate until his sides bulged and he could hold no more. *Why haven't the other deer found this abundant food?* he wondered.

Just then, from behind the church, the biggest dog he had ever seen snorted, barked and lunged toward him. It didn't take long to figure out why the acorns had been left alone. Little Sam leaped into full speed. Before he knew it, he had bounded across highway 219 and was running headlong into a pasture behind a huge junkyard. Old, abandoned cars were parked out in the woods. Some had trees growing up through them. The big churchyard dog was still hot on his heels. Little Sam made a dash for the junkyard. He was zigzagging between cars, trucks, tractors, and plows.

He managed to stay just out of the dog's jaws as he ran. Several times he leaped over the hoods of old vehicles. The dog remained in hot pursuit. Then Little Sam suddenly heard snarls and barks coming from a different direction. The junkyard apparently had its own guard dog, and that dog wanted no intruders.

Sure enough, the junkyard dog lunged out from under an old pick-up truck and sent the churchyard dog reeling. Hair flew and Little Sam had never seen such a fight. About that time, floodlights came on and a shotgun cut loose with three loads of No. 4 shot. Windshields caved in and shot ricocheted off fenders, hoods and hubcaps. Then he heard someone scream, "Come outa' there with your hands up!"

Little Sam was standing behind a rusty old 1960 Ford Crown Victoria when a little black man crawled out of a nearby Cadillac and hollered, "Mr. Paul, don't shoot! It just me, Ole Tennis Shoes! I swear I ain't stealin' nothin'! I was just cetchen' a little nap out of da' cold!"

"What's goin' on out there?" a voice cried back.

"I don't know!" yelled the black man. "I was asleep when this huge buck deer done come a-runnin' in here jumpin' over cars and such. That churchyard dog be chasin' him. Your ol' guard dog jumped him and about that time I started hearin' a lota' shootin'! Ain't never seen nothin' like it! Just let me slide on outa' here, Mr. Paul, and I promise I'll sleep somewhere else from now on!"

With that, the floodlights went out and Little Sam eased out of the junkyard and continued on his way. As he moved on, he could hear the black man mumbling, "Can't get no sleep nowhere these days! Dat dang big deer dun' stirred up a mess and caused me to luse my apartment lease! He jest about got me kilt too!"

CHAPTER 12

Little Sam had no idea where he was, but instinct told him he couldn't be far from the Flat Shoals Creek area. At daylight, he could see a building made of stone near a crossroads. Antique plows and other items lay on the front porch of the building. Little Sam vaguely remembered Scrap talking about his trip as a fawn with the little ol' man from the Morgan farm to the ol' man's house. He knew this crossroads intersection must have been the spot where the little ol' man turned left to take Scrap to his house.

All day long Little Sam explored the area. He crossed branches. He crossed fields and he climbed hills. As the sun set in the western sky, Little Sam reached a high knoll in a fescue pasture where he could see the outline of a huge silo. The setting sun behind the silo created a beautiful view.

It can't be! Little Sam thought. *This can't be the same silo that Scrap had talked about.* Yet something told him that it was and that he was now in Scrap's territory. Four beautiful lakes could be seen just ahead. All of a sudden Little Sam recalled the story Scrap had told about Big Sam's encounter with the little ol' man. He remembered that the ol' man had fired a shot at Big Sam in the woods behind some lakes. This had to be the place!

Oh, my gosh, he thought. Hunters! Scrap said they were everywhere over here!

About that time the ground exploded in front of him and the loud roar of a gun deafened his ears. Little Sam was standing in the middle of a pasture and all he could do was run for his life. There was no cover nearby. Another shot was fired, and he heard the death yielding hot lead whistle right over his head. Then he heard another shot and he felt a burning sensation in his ear. The bullet had cut a notch in his left ear, and blood began to trickle down his neck.

Little Sam had never been shot at, much less hit, and he was scared to death. He had felt more pain when Sam had gored him, but nevertheless, it was a scary proposition to be hit by a bullet. He well remembered that morning when he witnessed Nasty Pete take that slug through the heart, and now it sent adrenalin pouring through his veins. Little Sam never ran so fast in all his life. With nothing but wide open space ahead, he knew his only defense was speed and distance.

More shots sounded. It seemed that lead was being sent toward him from every direction. He stumbled and fell to his knees as another bullet whistle over his head.

Had I not fallen, he thought, *I would have taken one through the neck!*

He now realized that the shooters – he couldn't call them hunters – were stationed behind the big round hay bales in the field. It seemed that every bale had a gun behind it and bullets were flying everywhere.

If I can't get to cover quickly, it'll be all she wrote! he thought.

A thick, brushy area straight ahead near the upper end of a spring-fed lake seemed to be his only hope. The head of the lake grew thick with cattails, alder bushes and swamp grass. *It seems like the perfect place for a deer to hide,* he thought. *However, it looks awfully small when shooters have scopes trained on you!*

Still, it was the only cover around, and Little Sam wasted little time baling into the thickest part of it. To his utter amazement, two startled deer jumped up from their hidden beds. They stood looking at him in sheer shock and disbelief. One was a big buck, the other a beautiful doe. Little Sam couldn't believe his eyes! Scrap and Star were as bewildered as he was!

"Little Sam, what in hell are you doing over here?" Scrap screamed. "You idiot – you're' gonna get us all killed!"

Little Sam was exhausted and shaking. Blood trickled down his neck and shoulder from the wounded ear.

Star screamed, "Little Sam, you've been shot!"

Scrap looked at Little Sam and muttered, "It's just a nick in his big floppy ear. He'll be okay. I'm surprised he didn't get his ass shot off!"

"What should we do, Scrap?" asked Little Sam.

"We gotta get ourselves outta here, and fast!" Scrap yelled. "Don't think for a minute those guys are out of shells. Yesterday, I saw them shoot two boxes of shells at an armadillo. No telling what they have saved up for us."

"Well let's go, then," Little Sam said.

"No, wait," Scrap said. "Let's wait 'til we hear them crank their big red truck. Those ol' boys are really lazy – too lazy to do any walking. When we hear their truck crank, we'll haul ass across Rivers Road and get on the ol' man's place. He lives right over yonder, you know."

"You can see his house from here," Star said.

"That's right, you can see it, but you can also get killed trying to get there from here," Scrap said.

Just then, they heard the truck crank and start moving. It was now or never. The three deer had to break for better cover and the only way to reach the little ol' man's property was to cross several open fields.

"Star, you break first," Scrap said. "They haven't seen you and, being a doe, they're not likely to try to shoot you. Instead, they'll wait for Little Sam or me. You run the ridge along the pasture edge and Little Sam and I will skirt the low side downwind from you!"

Star made her break and the red truck slammed to a stop. One of the boys sitting in the truck's bed jumped up. Using the cab to steady his rifle, he started blasting away. Scrap was furious. He screamed, "Those jackasses! They saw you, Little Sam, and they knew for sure that a buck was in here, yet they're shooting at Star and does are out of season!"

"Let me tell you something, Scrap," Little Sam yelled. "If anything happens to Star, you won't have to worry about those guns… *Dad* will kill your ass!"

"Star and I were doing just fine until you showed up, Little Sam," Scrap said. "We've been bedding near the head of this lake for a week. Those assholes come in the same way, at the same time, every day. We watch them hide behind those hay bales until dark every night. Then, after they leave, we have all these lush fields to browse in all night long.

"So – don't be blaming anything on me, Little Sam," Scrap continued. "You're the one that screwed things up today. This ain't the Park. This is the *real world* over here and it's full of danger. Every day is an adventure, and there are no free lunches. You earn every day you live. One simple mistake and you're dead meat riding in the bed of a pick-up truck or hanging off the back of someone's 4-wheeler. This is true life, Little Sam! The ol' man has everyone spoiled over in the Park."

Scrap finally stopped scolding Little Sam and got down to business. "Little Sam, I'm about to break out of here and run the ridge toward the Harrell farm over yonder. You stay put until you hear the first shot fired at me, and then you break in the direction Star went! They probably think there's only one buck in here. When they see me and start shooting, you should be able to make it across Rivers Road. Stay downwind from Star. She knows where she's going, and I'll meet you at the lake behind the little ol' man's house. Don't expect me until after dark!"

With that said, Scrap broke at full speed across the ridge toward the Harrell farm. Little Sam held tight waiting for shots to be fired. He didn't have to wait long. No question about those boys seeing Old Scrap! It sounded like fireworks going off. Scrap was running low to the ground. He had his long neck extended, his big rack tilted back around his shoulders, and his nose to the horizon. His tail was cropped tightly against his hindquarters and his profile was so low to the ground that he almost looked like he was crawling.

Scrap ran for all he was worth as bullets whistled around him. Some kicked up dirt in front of him and some sang high-pitched songs over his head. It was obvious that Scrap had been in this situation before. He was bobbing, weaving, changing speed and changing directions. He knew what to do!

Little Sam moved after the first shots. He slipped unnoticed around the ridge and across Rivers Road. As he cleared the fence near the little ol' man's cattle catch pen, he glanced back to check on Scrap. He saw Scrap's long white tail go up in the air as he cleared the Harrell farm fence. Then he vanished into the thick cover. Scrap had made it to safety. Little Sam thought, *Scrap just risked his life for me!*

Star was standing on the dam of the lake as Little Sam made his way across the fields. She hoped that her brother was alright and wondered where Scrap had gone. As Little Sam approached, she asked, "Are you hit? Where is that crazy ole Scrap?"

"I'm fine," Little Sam said, "just a bloody ear and a few bumps and bruises. Scrap drew their fire and he's over the fence line on the Harrell place. He told me to hang with you; that you'd know where to go."

"Are you sure he wasn't hit?" Star asked. "There must have been two dozen shots fired. It sounded like a war."

"I'm telling you Star, he's fine. You'd have been proud of him. I've never seen a deer cover that much ground in such a short time. He was stretched out low to the ground and all you could see was a blur. When he cleared the Harrell farm fence, he raised his tail high for me to see the direction he was headed and to signal me that he was okay. Why are we standing out here in the wide open for everyone to see?"

"Don't worry," Star said. "We're safe here. Nobody shoots on the little ol' man's place! In fact, there's the ol' man on his back porch now! See him? I'll guarantee you he watched this whole episode. See his binoculars? He looks out for us and always knows what's going on."

"Star, where is that dog pen Scrap told us about?" Little Sam asked.

"Right up there," said Star. "Can't you see it, right behind the house? Scrap still goes up there at night. He always waits until the little ol' man's dogs are asleep and he slips up there and reminisces. He knows that the ol' man saved his life and he'll never forget it. He'll tell you straight out that he loves the ol' man!"

Darkness was approaching and lights were coming on in the ol' man's house. "Come on, Little Sam," Star said. "Scrap will wait 'til after dark and he'll cross Rivers Road and be looking for us in our bedding area behind the pond. I sure hope he's okay. He'll come in here starving to death and want to head for the persimmon trees. We've been eating ripe persimmons for a week now and I'm tired of them. But Scrap could eat them every day for the rest of his life. Me, I'm sick of them!"

"Anything sounds good to me!" Little Sam said. "I'm famished. I think I could even eat some of the ol' man's dog food!"

"That won't happen," said Star. "Since Punkin, his cocker spaniel, died, the little ol' man has filled his pen up with wiener dogs and they eat everything in sight. You'll probably have to settle for persimmons or maybe some rye grass. Scrap decides the menu around here and you can be sure we'll stay close to home this night. We won't be going back to the lakes area. We really dodged some bullets this evening."

The brother and sister deer meandered around the little ol' man's pond for some time, and then drifted down the hollow behind the lake. The little ol' man stood on his back porch and watched until the last bit of light brought in their blurry images through his binoculars. At the last possible second for viewing, he saw Scrap making his way across his pasture to meet Star and Little Sam. His rack was huge and the white tips of his antler tines were all the little ol' man could make out. He knew it was Scrap, though. He had watched him from his porch before. Although he couldn't prove it, he was certain this was the same deer he had raised on a bottle and that the deer had returned to make the little farm his sanctuary.

The ol' man started wondering! *That other buck and doe looks so familiar,* he thought. *I'm sure I've seen them in the Park. No, it can't be, it can't be, or can it? I swear they look a lot like Little Sam and Star!* The ol' man felt a surge of excitement. It made sense as he began to put things together. *The rut is in and Sam probably ran them out of the Park,* he thought. *If that's so, then Scrap would have naturally brought them back here.*

Little Sam and Star bedded in a thicket not far from the pond. Scrap came slipping in about an hour after dark. Star jumped to her feet blowing and stomping. Scrap stood motionless and allowed his scent to drift. When Star picked it up, she licked her nose and raised her nostrils into the air. No doubt about it! It was Scrap and slowly she lowered her flared tail. Little Sam waited until the red-alert signals from Star were gone and he slowly got to his feet.

"What a day!" Scrap said. "Are you guys okay?"

"Yes," Star answered. "We're fine except for Little Sam's floppy ear. But it's stopped bleeding!"

"It's just another battle scar," Scrap said. "We're known by our scars. Life leaves us with scars. Scars, both inward and outward, tell our life stories. If you go through life without any scars, you probably haven't done very much. The key to healing injuries, both inward and outward, is to heal but let the scars remain. We learn from injury and if we're smart, the scars will remind us not to make the same mistake again. Know what I mean, Little Sam?"

"Yes sir!" Little Sam answered. "You got one thing right. This ain't the Park and this big hole in my ear will be a constant reminder!"

"We were lucky today," Scrap said. "We could have been killed. We could have all been killed. It just wasn't our day to go!"

CHAPTER 13

The night passed quickly! Little Sam, Star and Scrap browsed on rye grass and persimmons. They even picked at some tasty beans the little ol' man had planted in his garden. The little wiener dogs in their pen were sound asleep and the night was quiet and peaceful. An hour before daylight, Scrap said, "It's time to make our way back behind the pond. The ol' man will be up any minute now and we need to be going. He won't shoot us for grazing in his fields, but he'll bust our ass for eating his beans!"

The three deer made their way across the little ol' man's pasture and settled down to rest behind his lake. They bedded down in thick cover. As they chewed their cud, Scrap said, "Little Sam, which trail did you travel coming over here from the Park?"

"I really don't know," Little Sam answered. "I crossed a bunch of fields, went through a church yard, and about got killed in a junk yard. Two dogs – a churchyard dog and a junkyard dog – all but did me in."

"Is that junkyard dog still alive?" Scrap asked.

"He sure is!" Little Sam answered. "Why do you ask?"

"Well, when Star and I came that way he was tied to a 50-foot piece of chain," Scrap said. "One end of the chain was fastened to the bumper of an old Cadillac and the other end was snug around his neck. We were slipping through the junkyard when Star heard some loud snoring. In fact, you could hear snoring inside the old car and the junkyard dog was asleep and snoring under the car.

I tried to get Star to sneak out of there, but she had to know what was making all that noise. So we slipped up and stood really close for a while! It sounded like an army of hibernating bears in there! We waited. The night was perfectly quiet except for all that loud snoring. All of a sudden, the old car started shaking and the ugliest black man we'd ever seen – he goes by the name of ol' Tennis Shoes – sat straight up in the back seat. Star blew with a great nasal explosion and the junkyard dog came out from under that Cadillac at full speed.

He was snarling, growling, and his teeth were shining in the moonlight. We wheeled around and took off with him breathing down our necks. We were running for our lives when that old dog hit the end of his chain. That's why I asked you if he was still alive. We thought he might be dead!"

"You mean choked to death by that chain?" Little Sam asked.

"No", laughed Scrap. "He was going so fast when he hit the end of the chain he turned wrong-side-out! And we thought that his asshole may have choked him to death!"

"Danged if you don't beat all, Scrap!" Little Sam said. "We almost got ourselves killed here today, and you're trying to be funny! You ain't changed a bit. It's a good thing Dad ain't here. He'd be steady kicking your ass for running your mouth!"

"How is old Sam?" Scrap asked.

"I guess he's fine," Little Sam answered. "Except he and I got into it!"

"You two had a fight?" Scrap asked.

"Yeah, we sure did," Little Sam said. "We fought big time!"

"No question about who won, either, I suppose," Scrap said. "And I'll bet it was over a doe, wasn't it?"

"Yep!" said Little Sam. "It was a hot doe at that! You know how Dad is. There's enough of everything in the Park to go around, except young hot does, and Dad thinks they all belong to him. He's never been good at sharing!"

"I know," Scrap agreed. "And that's why Star and I are here! I ain't going back over there until spring. I know Star will want to be with her mother when the fawns come."

"When the fawns come?" Little Sam exclaimed. "You mean… Star is gonna have…?"

"Yep!" said Scrap. We are pregnant and this place is too covered up with coyotes and wild dogs. I don't want Star to go through birthing them over here. We'll hang out here with the little ol' man until spring and then head back to the Park."

Star slowly got to her feet, stretched long and hard and lay back down. None of the conversation seemed relevant to her. She was thinking about warm weather, spring, and two little fawns nursing and twitching their tails.

The three deer lay silently, dozing, resting and chewing their cud. One would doze off while the other two kept a close watch for danger. It was an age-old arrangement. At no time did all three deer doze off at once, then or ever. It was a survival ritual that had become a way of life.

Big Sam had said it best years ago. "The only way to stay alive is to stay awake! A sleeping deer will soon become a dead deer. It's okay to doze, but don't ever close! Never let your guard down! There's safety in numbers. Four eyes are better that two, but all eyes looking in the same direction are no better than one looking in that direction.

"If you want to die young," Big Sam had emphasized, "then get into the habit of looking at what everyone else is looking at!" Big Sam believed that what you could see could seldom harm you! "It's what you don't see that puts holes in your ass!" he liked to say. "Believe what you see – heed what you hear, but always trust your nose. The nose never lies!

"Your eyes can deceive you, your ears can fail you, but your nose can save you. No matter what it looks like, or sounds like, make sure it smells right before you put your life on it."

Big Sam had preached all of these things, yet during the rut, he threw all caution out the window and it ended up getting him killed! Both Sam and Little Sam were well aware of that fact. Big Sam's philosophy must have been, *Do as I say, not do as I do,* Little Sam thought. Grace reminded them of it often! However, they were descendants of the great "Big Sam," and it's difficult to deny genetics! Blood runs deep and apples fall near the tree! In most cases, the blood never lies! The blood will tell!"

Little Sam was very much aware of the importance of purity in genetics. He had heard many stories about how Big Sam fought all his life to keep inferior bucks from breeding his does. He also remembered his dad, Sam, battling Nasty Pete, and he knew that one day, the task would fall on his shoulders to defend the Park.

The night continued to pass peacefully for the three deer. Now and then, one would stand, stretch, move around a bit and test the air for possible danger. When all seemed well, they would bed down again and continue taking turns dozing and chewing their cud. At one point, Little Sam asked Scrap, "Do you know that black man who was in that ol' Cadillac?"

Scrap grinned. "You mean ol' Tennis Shoes? Yes, he used to haul hay for Mr. Harold Parmer. They used to be over here at the little ol' man's place all the time. Yes sir, ol' Tennis Shoes is a mess! He had a bad habit of clearing out his sinuses all the time. And whenever he sucked on those sinuses of his, why you could hear him half a mile away! Louder than any deer snorting!

"And whenever he did it, Mr. Harold would cuss him like a sailor. Tennis Shoes would always apologize and say, 'You right Mr. Harold, you right! I won't do it no mo'. Say, reckon you could spare one of those short Millers in the cooler yonder? It sho' is hot out here today and it might jus' keep me from suckin' my nose so much!'

"Harold would cuss him again and say, 'Tennis, you done drank up all your pay for the day and it ain't even 4 o'clock yet. Guess you'll have to pump gas for me tonight to pay back all you done drank up!'

"'Yes sir, Mr. Harold, yes sir,' Tennis Shoes would say.

"You see, Mr. Harold ran that little country store up at the crossroads and Tennis Shoes was his gopher. He pumped gas and took out the trash. Mostly what he did was keep Mr. Harold company and drink up all his short Millers! The little ol' man could tell Tennis Shoes' stories forever. I use to hear those stories when I lived with him. The ol' man loved Harold and Tennis Shoes," said Scrap.

"Whatever happened to Mr. Harold?" Little Sam asked.

"Mr. Harold passed away and the old store closed up," Scrap said. "I hadn't seen Tennis Shoes in a 'coon's age until he woke up in that ol' Cadillac. I reckon he's still hauling hay and drinking pony Millers for somebody around these parts. What a pair those two were! I know the little ol' man misses them!"

***

Daylight was approaching and the eastern sky was showing a gleam of light. "What's that?" Little Sam asked. "What's that noise I hear?"

"It's those hunters going to the woods," answered Scrap. "Those are the 4-wheelers I told you about. They're right on time coming down Rivers Road!"

Little Sam could see headlights moving down the road; four, maybe five, sets of headlights all moving at a steady pace. The three deer could hear the low hum of the engines. The 4-wheelers passed the silo on Rivers Road and headed south.

"Where're they going?" Little Sam asked.

"They're headed out to shoot deer. And you can be sure that before lunch, one of 'em will come back down that same road with a friend of ours stretched across the luggage rack! Mostly they kill little bucks and does, but there are a couple of hunters in that bunch that'll wait all season long for a chance at a hide like yours, Little Sam!

"They'd love a shot at you! You can bet on that! I'm telling you, this ain't the Park and you can't be *too* cautious around this place. I've lost so many friends here. It seems that every week one of our clan makes a mistake and gets put down by a rifle slug."

"Well why do you stay here, then?" Little Sam asked with a puzzled look.

"It's home, that's why!" Scrap said. "It's whatever you get accustomed to! I've gotten used to the challenge! You know what I mean? Every day is an adventure and when you wake up in the morning and know that it could be your last day, you appreciate living a lot more! You're more alert and more sensitive to everything around you. You're always at your best. I can't imagine a day without danger... It gives me the feeling of truly being alive!"

"Well, I sure can!" Little Sam responded. "I think I'd rather fight my dad over a doe every day. And at least know who I was fighting. I rather do that than spend the rest of my life over here worrying night and day about getting shot!"

"But Little Sam," Scrap said, "You don't understand."

"Don't understand what?" Little Sam asked.

"The girls, man! The girls! They're everywhere. There are does galore over here. Some of the finest does in the world live around here and there ain't many mature bucks. Those hunters you saw have killed most of the bucks so you can have your pick with the does! All you have to do is keep your nose clean, don't travel during daylight hours, and be careful crossing Highway 18."

"What do you mean by keeping my nose clean?" Little Sam asked.

"I mean you can't take anything for granted. You gotta trust your nose and don't put it where it don't belong. When I said there were only a few mature bucks over here, I didn't say there were none. There are a few big ones left and they're tough and they don't play games. So what you do is stay out of their way! There are plenty of does to go around, so we don't need to fight over them."

"I just sleep all day here on the little ol' man's place and work the edges after dark. Just wait 'til tonight and I'll show you what I'm talking about. An hour after dark and after all those hunters have called it quits, these pastures will be full of does. I've seen as many as 15 at a time standing under the night light by the old silo. I don't know what it is about that silo but the does seem to love the rye grass that grows around it. They can't resist it. They gather out there and feed for hours. And with that far-reaching night-light turned on, you can see them for a mile."

"The little ol' man watches them through his binoculars every night. Sometimes a buck will be with them, but usually they're alone. Then, after they've eaten their fill, they head over to the ol' man's cattle mineral feeder. It's out there in his pasture, you know, and when they show up, that's when the fun starts!"

"Little Sam, you can just pick and choose! And they all know that I hang out here behind the lake. Whenever one of them is ready for a little action, this is where they come! I've had as many as three come by in one night. Sometimes they'll come in here teasing and want me to follow them off to another farm, but that's how you get your ass killed. Son, you can chase them all night long, but if daylight catches you way off over yonder somewhere, you'll end up getting blasted by those hunters.

"No, Little Sam, I don't follow them anywhere. And if there's one in the bunch that's ready to dally – I mean one that's serious about her business – she'll trail off away from the others and come back by here.

"That's when you know you got 'em! When they come back you know you got 'em! You're working on your own terms then! You don't have to contend with the juvenile gals and there ain't no stupid little spikes worrying the fool out of you. That's the way I do it, Little Sam!"

"Scrap," Little Sam asked, "what does Star think about all of this? Isn't she jealous?"

"Well, Little Sam, it's just the way it is and the way it's always been with our kind! Star was jealous in the beginning but since she got pregnant, she kind of understands. I think she knows that you can't keep a great man all to yourself, and as great as I am, I need to spread some of my greatness around!"

"Scrap, you old fool, there you go again, bragging and running your mouth!" Little Sam yelled. "When're you ever going to learn? I don't know how Star stands you sometimes. Get some humility, man! You didn't seem so great back when Dad turned you upside-down over in the Park. You weren't so cocky then!"

"I guess my attitude kinda comes and goes," Scrap said. "You see, Little Sam, I ain't near as big a buck over there as I am over here!"

Little Sam chuckled. Scrap grinned, and they were friends again.

CHAPTER 14

A day or two passed and Little Sam got to thinking. He asked Scrap if he remembered the offer he had made him about helping him out with the does in the Flat Shoals area. "Scrap, do you remember that day in the Park when you said, 'Little Sam, why don't you go home with me and try on some of those Flat Shoals does?"

"Vaguely," replied Scrap.

"Vaguely?" repeated Little Sam. "You know damn well you said it, and I'm holding you to it. I've come all the way over here, risked my life every step of the way, and you say you vaguely remember our deal?"

"Little Sam, let me give you some advise," Scrap said. "Don't be so anxious and try to be a little patient! I might try to fix you up when the time is right, but you gotta realize, good looking does don't fall out of the sky. You gotta be in the right place at the right time and even then, it don't always work out. Sometimes you gotta get lucky; however, if you stay around all winter, I'll see to it that you get your bell rung at least once."

Little Sam was not at all happy with that response but there was little he could do about it. He was a long way from home and he had no other place to go. He'd just have to make the best of it. At least, his odds of exerting his manhood were better here than in the Park. He knew that if he were in the Park, his dad would hammer him if he even looked at a cute doe.

Scrap, Little Sam and Star ran together almost every night and spent the days bedded down on the little ol' man's place or behind the lake. The

109

peak of the rut was passing quickly and Little Sam had not even scented a doe in heat. Scrap had a habit of disappearing periodically and Little Sam finally figured out what was going on. Scrap was leaving him to take care of Star while he was out carousing!

"Little Sam," Star finally said. "Scrap is a rutting buck and you have to understand that he's just like all the rest. He's not gonna tell you all he knows. And when it comes to chasing does, he's *certainly* not gonna set you up! If he did, it would be with a doe he didn't want, and think about it... he's never been accused of turning down anything! If you want a doe for yourself, you'll have to get her yourself and no big buck I know is gonna help you out! If I were you, and if it was that important to me, I'd break out of here and go find one for myself!"

"But where?" asked Little Sam.

"The Hogg place, for one," Star said. "All those does Scrap talks about bed on the Hogg place."

"Where's that?" asked Little Sam.

"Across from the big silo," Star said. "There aren't many hunters over there and you might have a chance. Sometimes they come over this way after dark but they usually stay on the Hogg Place!"

"Are they pretty, Star?" Little Sam asked.

"They're as pretty as anything in the Park," Star answered.

"You know, Star, all I really want is someone special that I can call my own. I've been very lonely since leaving the Park! You guys have been great to me and all that, but, deep down inside, I'm lonely! I mean, you have Scrap, Dad and Mom have each other, and it seems that everyone in the family is happy and secure except me.

"To be honest with you, it's not about numbers with me. What I really want is one single doe to love; a very special one that understands me and will stay with me through thick and thin. One that I can take back and show Mom. One that Mom will be proud of. I want a doe that I respect like Dad respects Mom. I can't really explain it, Star! Do you know what I mean?"

"Yes," Star said. "You're of that age and it happens to all of us. I know you guys, I mean, you *bucks*, are gonna run, but I also know that when your horns fall off in the spring, you'll need love and care and that's what family is about. Why don't you slip off to the Hogg place tonight and see what happens? I'll keep Scrap off your trail and you just stay over there 'til you find what you're looking for. It may take a while. Don't sell yourself short and shop around! You'll know when the right one shows up. There'll be no question about it!"

"How will I know?" Little Sam asked.

"Your heart will tell you," Star said. "Follow your heart. Remember what the old doe always told Big Sam, 'a sharp mind and a little humility is always more beneficial than a river of testosterone!' Follow your heart and nose!"

***

Taking Star's advice, Little Sam slipped away from the little ol' man's farm at sundown. He worked his way down through the big pines and headed for the Hogg place. As he crossed the western corner of the 13-acre field, he could see the big silo. It was standing like a national monument. The last rays of the evening sun gave it an unforgettable brilliance and Little Sam stood for a few minutes and marveled at the beauty of the moment. Then he thought about what Scrap had said. The silo was a familiar landmark that every deer in the Flat Shoals area recognized and you could see it for miles. *If I ever get lost, this silo will guide me back to the ol' man's place*, Little Sam thought.

Little Sam jumped the fence going into the Hogg property. He headed across the grassy fields and kept his nose to the ground. The well-traveled trails that led through the grass and broom sedge told him that does were in the vicinity. Then, suddenly, the scent on one particular trail told him that a doe in heat had passed that way a short time earlier! Little Sam stopped and the adrenaline in his body began to pump.

Across the field, he saw the image of a deer. It stood motionless against the background of pine trees and brush. Its head was raised high in the air and its ears were up and alert. Little Sam was stunned at the sight before him! He remembered what Big Sam had said about "using your eyes, believing your ears but trusting your nose." He raised his head and turned his nose to the sky. He licked his nose and nostrils several times and slowly but surely the sweet scent of the opposite sex settled in.

As he watched, the doe raised her own nose high, and her huge white tail straightened out behind her. Without question, she saw him and had

111

picked up his scent as well. The two deer stood dead still staring at each other for a full minute. Suddenly, with one quick motion, as if something had stuck her, the doe lowered her rear end and urinated on the ground. She twitched her tail a few times, and took several steps down the tree line before disappearing over the horizon.

Little Sam waited for several minutes. Then he slowly made his way in the direction that his nose took him. He could smell the urine she had posted on the ground. It was a definite calling card and he wondered, *What do I do now?*

Except for the one he had chased back in the Park with the two other young bucks, he had never been in the presence of a hot doe! Little Sam wasn't sure what to do. His natural instincts soon took over, however, and before he knew it, he had pawed up the earth all around the spot where the doe had stood. Then, without even thinking, he stood over the spot, flexed his hind legs up under him and allowed his urine to trickle down his back legs and over his tarsal glands as he rubbed them together. The strong-smelling urine finally found its way to the pawed earth below.

When he had finished, he made his way over to the tree line and began mouthing a low-hanging tree branch. He soon worked himself into a state of frenzy! He began thrashing his big antlers in the limbs above. He rubbed his forehead glands and his preorbital glands on everything he could reach and touch with his head.

Without knowing why, he felt like a different being. He had just marked his territory for the very first time! He wasn't afraid of anything or anybody and his neck felt huge. As he raised his head and scented the air again, he suddenly saw the doe standing along the tree line further down the field's edge.

He took a step in her direction and she dropped low again and urinated. Little Sam was getting excited! He took several quick steps toward her as she dropped her head low to the ground and hopped into the pine thicket and disappeared! He slowly made his way to the spot where she'd been standing and he was shocked to see that she had urinated in a fresh scrape!

Little Sam's adrenaline went into orbit! *Whoa, here!* he thought. *I wonder who made this scrape? It sure as hell wasn't me!*

Little Sam could hear the doe bounding off through the piney woods.

His first impulse was to chase her as fast as he could and try to breed her right then and there. But he remembered what Scrap had told him about the remaining bucks in the area being really tough customers to deal with. He also remembered Scrap saying, "Don't chase 'em, boy... That'll just get you killed. Be patient and wait. They'll always come back, and when they do, you gotta be sure you get 'em on your own ground! You can do things your way then. If they're ready, they'll come back. If you chase 'em before they're ready, they'll get you killed!"

With that thought in his mind, Little Sam walked right up to the fresh scrape and urinated in it. The foam gathered up in the fresh earth and Little Sam was pleased with his work. Something seemed to be missing though, so he raised his tail high and deposited the remainder of his last night's meal in the open scrape. He was in his element now. He even felt a little cocky. His uneasy feelings had been replaced with an air of supreme confidence.

He walked over to a nearby cedar sapling and attacked it with his antlers. He dug his brow tines into the bark, and rubbed his head and neck against the tree until he smelled strongly of cedar. The sap and bark that remained on his antlers stained them a dark brown color. All of a sudden, Little Sam didn't feel like the little brother anymore. He felt a new confidence that he had never experienced. *This little spot of earth is mine and I dare anything or any deer to deny it*, he thought. *This is my territory! It's all mine! This is home and where I should be. It's where I belong!*

Little Sam created several more rubs on pine trees and scrub oaks. Then he wandered off into a patch of thick honeysuckle and began browsing the tender growth and fresh shoots. The night was cool and as the moon began to rise, Little Sam found a soft spot in the honeysuckle and bedded down. Soon he was chewing his cud and thinking about the doe. He lay there chewing and relaxing for some time. He was virtually invisible in his surroundings. All that could be seen of him was his large rack and long ears.

Even the ear that had been wounded stood straight up. The moon was high enough now so that it cast shadows in the woods and Little Sam could see his own shadow move as he chewed his cud and flicked his ears to monitor the sounds of the night. It was a most peaceful and happy time.

For the first time in his life, he felt normal and he understood some of the ways of his dad. He thought, *Mom and Dad would be proud of me!*

Moments later, Little Sam's peace was interrupted by the sound of a twig breaking and he saw movement in the pine trees. He could see the silhouette of another deer in the moonlight. Through the shadows of the pine saplings, he saw a doe moving slowly and meticulously with her nose to the ground. She stopped often to wind the night air. She gave every indication that she knew Little Sam was nearby, but she didn't seem to know quite where he was. Little Sam lay motionless.

The only movement that could be detected was the slow, steady grinding of his jaws as he chewed his cud. As he swallowed, he had the urge to stand up for a better look but a little voice inside told him to just wait and watch! The doe stopped in one spot for 20 minutes. She strained her eyes and ears in an attempt to identify what her nose told her was out there somewhere. Finally, she twitched her tail and took several steps in Little Sam's direction.

She raised her head high to see if her movement triggered any movement ahead. It didn't, so she continued on. Little Sam watched and made no sound. The doe stretched her long body and raised her tail as she had done earlier. Then she twitched it several times and deposited droppings on the ground as she walked.

All of a sudden, she stopped, dropped her rear end down and urinated. She was definitely showing signs of being ready to breed and it was all Little Sam could do to remain still. He was confused as to what he should do. Should he stand up and move toward her or just stay where he was?

What would Scrap do? he wondered. *I guess I should stay here and see what happens.*

The doe eased through the piney woods and cautiously made her way over to the edge of the field. When she got to the scrape that Little Sam had taken over, she stopped. Little Sam watched as she jumped back after getting the first whiff of the calling card he had deposited in the scrape. She was fully alert now.

Wow! That stuff really is powerful, he thought. *It really got her attention.* Then, much like his friend Scrap might do, he started feeling a little arrogant. *It's probably not the smell so much, but the sheer volume. She probably thinks a mule has passed through here! Ain't no buck ever left that much piss in a scrape before!*

The doe started pawing in the scrape. Just after she had deposited more urine, Little Sam, enthralled with watching her, suddenly heard branches cracking over in the pines. Then it sounded like two Volkswagens had collided! As he and the doe both watched, two big mature bucks locked horns and a vicious battle began. The bucks fought like bulls and Little Sam could hear the sounds of raw strength and agony. Hair flew in the moonlight, and the sharp claps of their antlers banging together and the thuds of their bodies crashing into each other were deafening.

The doe silently stepped out of the pines and eased toward Little Sam. When she reached the honeysuckle patch where he was bedded, their eyes met. She jumped straight up and started to blow. Little Sam didn't move. The doe turned her head back toward the ensuing battle and then back to Little Sam. She appeared to be on the verge of panic and Little Sam just knew that she was going to break and run. That's the last thing he wanted! Fortunately she seemed to calm down somewhat. Finally she settled down on all fours and lay within nose reach of him.

The two deer watched the fearsome battle without even making a sound. In truth, they were both afraid. The moans and groans of the two rapidly tiring gladiators and the sounds of breaking limbs and flying brush continued to fill the night air. Little Sam thought about what Scrap had said about the local hunters killing most of the big bucks in the area. He marveled, *they sure as hell missed these two!*

Little Sam couldn't believe what he was witnessing! Two monster bucks were fighting over a doe that lay next to him! He remembered what Scrap had said about being in the right place at the right time and patience. *Sometimes, you just get lucky!* Little Sam thought!

The two bucks were nearly exhausted. Their energy was spent and they were greatly weakened. The awesome fight had quickly been reduced to a pushing contest. One would fall down and the other would gore and gouge until the other stumbled to his feet. Then the pushing and blowing would begin again. Both of the bucks were too worn out to do much damage.

Little Sam could see their silhouettes moving through the pines and the bright moon highlighted the heavy mist coming from their nostrils in the cool air. He had never witnessed such a fight! Why hadn't one of them called it quits? What was so great about this particular doe that had inspired such a fierce struggle? Amazingly, the two bucks continued to fight. The gasping for breath, the moans and groans and the bellows they emitted were horrifying.

Little Sam looked at the doe and he realized that she had long since stopped watching the fight. Instead, she was watching him! Her big brown eyes sparkled in the moonlight and the scent she carried was the sweetest he had ever smelled. It reminded him of Star and his mom.

Her looks, her scent, the moonlit night, the new confidence Little Sam had gained and his determination to find the right mate all seemed to suddenly come together! At that moment, a great surge of energy engulfed him. He sprang to his feet and every hair on his body stood straight out. All of a sudden, he looked fully 1/3 bigger than he actually was and his color turned almost black in the darkness. The doe was startled!

Without hesitation or fear, Little Sam bounded from the honeysuckle patch and headed for the battle at a full gallop. The doe could see his rack shining in the moonlight and it looked huge. He ran through the shadows like a ghost, and when he reached the field of battle, Little Sam plowed his horns into both deer; first one and then the other. Flinging and gouging his mighty antlers in every direction, Little Sam grunted and snort-wheezed with every breath. His work didn't take long!

One of the bucks was limping badly from an injured rear leg and the other was bleeding from his nostrils and mouth. With his strongest and most intimidating charge yet, Little Sam sent both animals running and stumbling down the trail they had followed the doe in on. Both bucks quickly disappeared into the night. As he stood victorious, Little Sam threw his head high in the air and held his tail straight out. The combination of his imposing antlers, the moonlight shining through his bristled hair, and his youthful strength made the doe's heart start to beat out of control!

Though the circumstances had been unusual and in his favor, Little Sam had won his first big battle. He wondered what would have happened if he had not listened to that little voice inside. If he had followed the doe like his initial impulses wanted him to do, he would have run headlong into those two big jokers in their full strength.

Without question, they would have shown no pity; they might have even killed him! Patience and luck had played a big part in his victory. What's more, Little Sam had made a great impression on the doe. When he glanced back at the honeysuckle patch, she was standing up watching him. What a beautiful reward for a job well done! Little Sam was her hero!

The two older bucks had aggravated her and hung around her for days. She was young and they were old; she had no interest in them. Now their selfish desires had gotten the best of them and they had lost the prize. *The guy with the humility came away the winner,* little Sam thought happily.

He dropped his nose to the ground and drew in the musky scents left by the two bucks. He took one long last look in the direction they had fled. Then, with a newfound confidence and much pride, he trotted back to the doe.

CHAPTER 15

Her name was Sally and she was the prettiest doe Little Sam had ever seen. She was every bit the equal of his mom and no doubt about it, she was well bred. She had never been with a buck and was as naive about courtship as Little Sam. However, she was eager to learn! She nuzzled Little Sam and walked around him with her tail up high. Little Sam knew he was supposed to do something, but wasn't sure what, so he just followed her around in circles, sniffing everything within reach.

Before he knew it, Sally walked around and tried to mount him from behind. *Wait a second*, he thought. *I'm supposed to be the one doing that!*

Then they walked around in circles smelling each other and attempting to mount each other. Whenever Little Sam would rear up on her, she would scoot out from under him for several steps and stop. His patience was soon being tested. Sally would run off several yards, make a few quick circles around him, then turn her back to him and sniff the ground. When Little Sam would approach her again, she would lay her ears back and paw at him with her front feet.

What's going on? He wondered. *Scrap said that when a doe comes back, everything after that is a piece of cake.*

Little Sam knew he was in the right place, but he had some serious doubts about the timing, so he decided to wait. *Just be patient and see what happens!* he thought.

He decided to ignore Sally and give her the silent treatment. He went about his business browsing, rubbing trees and doing all the things that a big buck does. It was killing him, but he pretended to have no interest in her whatsoever. It didn't take but a few minutes of this behavior before Sally changed her tune. She quickly decided that this buck was not into playing games, and that she had better pay attention to him or else he'd be gone! She ambled up to him and began grooming Little Sam! She licked his face, his neck and his muscular shoulders. His thick winter coat was beautiful and shined in the moonlight.

Little Sam started having feelings he'd never had before. His adrenaline was flowing again, and now parts of his anatomy started doing things they'd never done before. Sally urged that on with a little nudge here and there. Before Little Sam knew it, he was contemplating action! In what seemed like a semi-conscience state of mind, Little Sam mounted Sally!

It was all like a hazy dream, and then the lights went out. Just as he finished the task at hand, Little Sam literally fell backward off of Sally flat on his back. His feet were sticking straight up in the air as if he'd just been shot. *Perhaps lightning just struck me!* he thought.

Little Sam's eyes rolled back in his head and he emitted an uncontrollable bellowing sound. Then he went into a trembling seizure! When he finally regained his senses, he realized what had happened and he started looking for Sally. She was browsing in the honeysuckle. She had a slight bow in her back and a cheerful expression of exultation on her face. Without question, she was happy and content.

Little Sam was totally embarrassed. He looked around sheepishly to see if any other creatures in the woods had seen him. He felt like such a fool. *How much of this love making and courtship thing will I be able to handle?* he wondered. Then, with wobbly knees, he eased up to Sally. Her brown eyes were sparkling. Without even thinking, he asked, "Was it as good for you as it was for me?"

"Heavens to Betsy, no!" she answered. "You've been unconscious for five whole minutes. I thought you were dead!"

"Well, I ain't," Little Sam said. "Not even close! In fact, I may be more alive right now than I've ever been in my entire life!"

"Me too," Sally responded. "And now we'd better get out of here before those two fighting fools get their strength back. You know that you're a marked buck now, don't you? Nobody whips those two big old warriors and gets away with it. You just raised the mark around here and you'll find no peace ever again. They will always want to get even with you. They'll hunt you down like a dog, even if it takes both of them, and they won't rest 'til they pay you back. We can't stay here any longer."

"They can't hurt us in the place we're going," Little Sam said confidently. "I'm taking you back to the Park and I can assure you, it'll be a mistake for them to follow us there."

"Where is The Park?" Sally questioned. "Where is that?"

"It's a long way from here," Little Sam told her. "But it's the greatest place in the world. It has huge oak trees, lush pastures, dense pine thickets, persimmon trees and plenty of minerals and fresh water. It's almost like heaven, Sally. And it's totally safe!"

"If it's so great, Sally asked, "Why aren't a bunch of deer already there?"

"Oh, other deer are there," Little Sam said. "Plenty of them and they're mostly my family – my mom, my dad, Star, Scrap and all my young cousins."

"Did you say Scrap?" Sally asked with a funny look.

"Yeah," answered Little Sam. "Scrap took up with my sister some time ago. She left the Park with him and came over here. They stay over on the little ol' man's place."

"How well do you know Scrap?" Sally asked.

"Well enough to know that he runs his mouth too much," Little Sam said. "Well enough to know that he's funny and that my sister loves him. Well enough to know that he fears my dad! And if he ever gets out of line in the Park, Sam will straighten him out and kick his ass! Why do you ask?"

"Well," Sally said, "when I was growing up, there was a lot of talk about Scrap. Nobody really knew where he came from. He just kind of showed up over here one day. There are those who believe he belonged to the little ol' man who lives in the house near the silo. There are others who believe he was brought in here from somewhere else."

"Well I can tell you that everything you said is true," Little Sam said. "Scrap was brought in here from somewhere else, and he was raised by the little ol' man!"

Little Sam and Sally slowly worked their way across the Hogg place. Daylight found them browsing in the big timber just west of the little ol' man's pasture. Little Sam said to Sally, "I can't wait for you to meet my sister, Star. She and Scrap will be bedding down about now and I'm sure they'll be glad to meet you! They are wonderful family and I love them but you sometimes have to take the good with the bad with old Scrap! You know how brother-in-laws can be! His personality is kinda strange, and you need to know his background to fully understand him."

"I suppose that's true with most of us," Sally said. "If you only consider the bad in us, few of us are worth a cuss!"

Little Sam grinned!

***

Scrap checked the wind. He could smell other deer, but he couldn't possibly know their location or direction. He blew several times and stomped his foot. Star threw her head up, dropped her tail down between her legs and stood motionless. Slowly they appeared, Sally in the lead, followed a short distance behind by Little Sam. They came off a high ridge near the little ol' man's deer stand that he called "Ole Gran'dad." They crossed a lazy stream and made their way up through the heavy timber. Scrap and Star watched as they jumped the logging road and continued up the slope toward them.

Sally came to an abrupt halt. Little Sam took the clue and froze in his tracks. The four deer, Scrap, Star, Sally and Little Sam stood carefully studying each other for several minutes. Finally, Little Sam dropped his tail and eased up beside Sally. "That's them," he whispered. "That's Scrap and Star!"

Star moved toward them in a stiff-legged gait as if she were walking on egg shells. She recognized Little Sam but she was leery of this strange doe. Star walked cautiously around Sally. Then, when the two deer were almost touching noses, she suddenly reared up on her hind legs and started pawing at Sally.

Scrap kept his distance. Little Sam just watched. The two does skirmished briefly, and then Little Sam came running into the action. Both does scampered aside and Little Sam threw his head up in Scrap's direction as if to say, "That's enough of this! We all know each other here or, at least, we should! And if we don't, we will!"

Scrap headed in Sally's direction but Little Sam cut him off. "No!" Little Sam said defiantly. "It ain't gonna happen! This is Sally; she's mine, so just keep your distance! Whatever you are thinking is wrong and if need be, we'll just throw down right here and now!"

He backed up his words by dropping his nose to the ground and charging Scrap. Scrap dodged to one side and ran around for a few seconds with his nose to the ground. Then he stopped, threw his head up and said, "Congratulations, Little Sam, she ain't bad... No, she really ain't bad at all!"

"For once we agree on something," said Little Sam with a grin.

"Where did you get her?" asked Scrap. "She ain't one of those Hogg does is she? She ain't bad at all. Surely to goodness you ain't been over there! Have you been on that Hogg place?"

"Maybe," muttered Little Sam.

"No you haven't," Scrap said. "No way! If you had, you wouldn't have come back in one piece!"

With that the two does broke and ran. The early morning sun was shining through the flared hair of their tails and they looked almost like they were on fire. Little Sam and Scrap followed and they made their way to the bedding area.

CHAPTER 16

"Little Sam," Scrap said, "tell me it ain't so. Tell me that you didn't go doe hunting over on the Hogg place!"

"Why shouldn't I have gone over there?" Little Sam asked.

"Because it's just plain suicide to go over there, that's why!" Scrap said. "Yeah, there're lots of does over there, but two big war-lord bucks rule that place. They don't ever leave, and if you want one of their does, you gotta fight 'em for her. They always run together and they love a battle! In fact, I've been told they were born fighting!"

"Thanks for warning me!" Little Sam said. "You said all the big bucks had been killed out of these parts."

"No, I said *most* of them had been killed out!" Scrap replied.

"But you didn't bother to tell me about those two monsters and I went over there right in the middle of their range," Little Sam said.

"Well," Scrap responded, "there's a whole lot about chasing *poontang* that I didn't tell you about. You've just gotta learn some things on your own. Sometimes it's a tough way to go, but nobody can do it for you. Ya' just gotta do it for yourself! Poontang is a strange thing! It's hard to describe and hard to put a finger on! Yet, once you get a taste of it, it kinda grabs you and won't let go! I've heard that chasing poontang can become addictive and can be the ruin of many a good being."

"I know," said Little Sam. "And, you should have warned me!"

Sally was listening to the conversation with perked ears. Her eyes were full of pride.

"Tell me, Little Sam, did you run into John and Melvin over there?" Scrap asked.

"Who are John and Melvin?" Little Sam said.

"If you'd run into them, you'd know who they are!" Scrap said.

"He *did* run into them!" Sally said, butting in. "And he sent them packing with their tails between their legs! The last time we saw them, they were hightailing it toward the Mote place."

"He did what?" Scrap exclaimed. "There's no way he got away with that! John and Melvin always work in tandem and there's no way Little Sam could have walked away if he'd been in a fight with those two! They are seasoned hard-asses and the two toughest bucks this side of the Alabama State line!"

"I witnessed the whole thing!" Sally said. "Little Sam fought magnificently and it was something to behold! I'm so proud of him! He's really something! He'll always be my hero!"

"Yeah, he's something, alright!" Scrap agreed. "But I don't buy any story about him whipping those two outlaws and then bringing you back over here! John and Melvin have been fighting their entire lives! I wouldn't take either of them on alone, much less both of them together!"

"We know that, Scrap, but you're *not* Little Sam!" Sally said. Then she winked at Little Sam.

Scrap's hair stood on end as he bowed up! By the look on his face, it was obvious that he didn't like being on the receiving end of a joke. His pride was clearly shaken.

"Just settle down, Scrap," Star said. "You asked for that and you got what you deserved. Usually, you're the one making those kinds of comments, so just grin and bare it. Relax, Scrap, and tell us what you know about John and Melvin."

"Well," said Scrap. "They're a little older than me and they're very strange! They've ruled that little Hogg kingdom forever. They've been fighting each other since most of the local deer can remember. In fact, whenever they see or even smell a doe, they go at it! I guarantee you that any doe could go over there this very minute and the first time they saw her, they'd start a battle. They'd fight even in the summertime! The rut has nothing to do with it!"

"Why?" Star asked. "That *is* very strange."

"They say it's because of their upbringing," Scrap answered.

"Are they related?" Little Sam asked.

"Related?" exclaimed Scrap. "Why they're brothers. They fell out of the same womb the same day and they've been fighting since they were two weeks old! They're fine until they smell a doe... Then just like that, they go into a knock-down, drag-out fight!"

"I wonder why," Sally said. "It doesn't make sense."

"The story goes that when they were two weeks old, their mom got tangled up in barbed wire and some big bramble in a thorn thicket. Wild dogs were hot on her trail and she had no time to lose. During the mad scramble and panic, she caught her milk bag on a long thorn vine and cut up it pretty badly. It was damaged and sore for days. As a result, she was left with only one teat that could be nursed. Every time little John or Melvin tried to nurse the teats that got cut up in the bramble, she'd kick the living shit out of them! She couldn't stand for them to touch her injured teats.

"After that, it didn't take long for the two fawns to learn that the one who latched onto the healthy teat first was the only one that was going to eat that day. The odd man out knew he was going to get his ears kicked off trying to suck a sore teat! The story goes on that their mom would hide them while she went off to browse, and at the first sight of her coming to them, those two little bastards would jump up and start fighting. As they got older, the simple scent of her would trigger a fight. They never grew out of it. Even up to this very day, the scent of a doe sends them into a savage battle!"

"Well, I do declare!" Little Sam said. "That's the strangest tale I've ever heard, that is, beside the one you told about the little ol' man raising you! Do you expect us to believe you, Scrap?"

"Little Sam," said Scrap, "I've been known to exaggerate, but I always own up to it! And whenever I tell outright lies, most of time they're about me. When it comes to my excursions with poontang, I've always exaggerated! It seems like the older I get, the better I was! I do apologize to you for not warning you about John and Melvin. Every hunter in the Flat Shoals Creek area has dreamed about hanging one of them on the wall. But so far, they've managed to outsmart every one of those guys.

"I guess they'll finally end up killing each other some day. That is, if they don't die of old age! They appear to be eccentric but they have savvy and they know how to survive. They can make it when things get tough and they stick together. They're brothers, but they love each other like father and son, and sometimes they're their own worst enemy!

"One thing I've learned, Little Sam, is don't beat yourself," Scrap continued. "No telling how many does they've missed because of their emotional hang-ups! That's the way life is though…Some bucks would rather fight than frig. I guess a fellow needs to decide whether he's going to be a fighter or a frigger! Me? I've come to the conclusion that if a fellow is going to be a breeder, he's gonna have to do a little fighting! If he won't fight, he probably won't breed!"

"I couldn't agree more!" said Little Sam. "I found that out last night on the Hogg place and yes, I did fight John and Melvin! And yes, I did whip their ass but I did it with patience. I'll tell you about it someday when I've got more time and things aren't so pressing. Everything you see and hear ain't necessary as it appears! Often, what you don't see may be more important than what you are looking at!"

"Pressing?" Scrap asked. "What's pressing?"

"Sally and I are heading back to the Park today," Little Sam answered. "John and Melvin will be looking for my hide soon as they rest up. I was very fortunate last night and I know it. I am not real smart but I learn fast and I've decided that I'd rather be a lover than a fighter! If they want to follow me to the Park, well, okay, let 'em come. Dad will have a say in what happens over there.

"Anyway, I want Sally to go home with me and there's no need to stay over here any longer. I got what I came for. I can't handle the hunting pressure and I surely don't need to fight John and Melvin again!"

"Sam will be after Sally," said Scrap. "You know that.…"

"No he won't," answered Little Sam. "This is family business now! I've fought Dad before but never over family business! It's different now. Mom will see to that and if I have to, I'll fight for what's mine. It'll work out. It's got to work out. Say, what are you and Star planning to do?"

"Don't really have any plans," answered Scrap! "The rut is all but over and I haven't seen a doe that needed an escort in two days. They've all bunched up it seems. Winter is coming on fast and I've got a feeling it's going to be a tough one. There are few acorns left over here, Little Sam. About the only thing left over here is pine trees. Those near-sighted timber people have cut all the oak trees, and without acorns, the winters get awfully tough in these parts."

"Don't you think I know that?" Little Sam asked.

"Yeah," said Scrap, "but you've never seen this place when the woods were full of acorns and honeysuckle. It was almost like the Park around here. We had everything and life was good."

"You can't look back, Scrap," Little Sam said. "You can't look back and you can't control what has happened around here. Don't worry about the things you have no control over. What you can do, though, is *adjust*! You can adjust and look to the future! What I mean is – you and Star can go back with us!"

"Ain't no way!" exclaimed Scrap. "Your daddy would be waiting for me! Don't you remember the day we left? Don't you remember?"

"I remember that he told you to come back in the spring," Little Sam answered.

"Well, it ain't yet spring and the rut may still be in over there for a while longer," Scrap said.

"The rut should be the least of your worries!" said Little Sam. "The hunting season is in and the woods are filled with meat-hunting hunters over here. Without question, they'll fill you full of lead! You'd better get Star back to the Park before she gets killed! Besides, if you go back over there with us and show some simple humility, Dad will leave you alone."

"You're one to talk!" Scrap said. "He ran you off too! He ran you off and you're his own son! If he kicked your ass, what do you think he will do to mine?"

"You may want to strike a low profile for a while," Little Sam said. "Just run with us and stay away from Dad. And if the rut is still going on, just let Dad take care of things. It ain't like you've been deprived, and the rut can't last much longer. The leaves are off all the trees now and that's a sure sign the rut is coming to a close. You know how it is… When the leaves are gone and the woods open up, the girls all bunch up and hide, and there ain't much going on. What do you say, Scrap?"

"When are you leaving?" Scrap asked.

"Now... We're leaving right now," Little Sam said.

"You can't leave now and travel during the daylight," Scrap said. "It's too dangerous. It's too far and there are too many hunters between here and the Park. Wait 'til tonight. Wait 'til all those 4-wheelers have passed through here after dark, then go."

"If we wait, will y'all go with us?" Little Sam asked.

"We might," answered Scrap. "We might. I need to discuss it with Star."

***

The four deer spent the rest of the day lounging behind the little ol' man's lake. About mid-afternoon, they heard the 4-wheelers coming down Rivers Road.

"Look at 'em – here they come!" Scrap said. "There must be at least 10 of 'em, all lined up in a row."

The engines purred, and to the four deer, the sound was menacing, like an ominous song of death! As soon as the 4-wheelers were gone, the big red truck appeared rumbling down the road. Inside were the two boys that had slung lead at Little Sam and Scrap. The truck was headed toward the big lakes.

Scrap said, "Little Sam, there must be 20 guns out there now. You and Sally would have been dead meat if you'd left earlier. Ain't you glad you waited?"

"I sure am," answered Little Sam. "I sure am! It never hurts to be patient!"

CHAPTER 17

The afternoon passed quickly. The four deer relaxed. From their vantage point, they watched the little ol' man cut his grass and feed his cows. Just at dusk dark, floodlights came on at the house and they observed him feeding his wiener dogs and putting them in their pens for the night.

"You could set your clock by the little ol' man's habits," Scrap sighed. "He turns those lights on and feeds those dogs at the same time every night. It's the same time he used to feed me and put me in the dog pen. I've slept many a night in that pen."

"What was the little ol' man really like?" Star asked.

"He was a good man," Scrap answered. "He loved ole Punkin! And he had a taste for Jim Beam whiskey! I never saw him drink too much or get tipsy, but he always enjoyed his little nip around suppertime. It seemed like he talked to me and Punkin more after he'd had him a little snort."

"What was his wife like?" asked Star.

Scrap's eyes lit up and a peaceful look came to his face. He swallowed his cud, and after another big wad traveled up his esophagus and into his mouth, he began chewing again and thinking. Finally, he said, "His wife was a special lady. Why, in all the days I was there, I never once saw her lose her temper. She really was the little ol' man's strength. She was always there for him and showed him lots of love and affection.

"She was also good looking you know! They say when she was younger she was the best-looking thing around. Age hasn't taken much away from her though and the little ol' man still worships her. He always seemed to know when to straighten up his act when she was around. About the only two things she ever really crawled on him about were his drinking whiskey and his hunting. She didn't put up with him doing too much of either. However, the little ol' man had a way of doing just about everything he really wanted to do!

"They both were strong willed and determined. The little ole lady fussed about him spending too much time with his cows and wasting money on them. The cattle were his passion and she often referred to him as the 'Cow Whisperer.' Why, he could put his hands on all 150 of them and with a feed bucket, he could lead them about anywhere.

"He loved that little ole lady. She knew it too! To answer your question a little better, I'd say she was just about perfect. She took the best care of their kids that you ever saw and she was so down to earth in every way. She was a lot smarter than the little ol' man but he was smart enough to know it. He depended on her. He never did anything of consequence without discussing it with her first.

"How he talked her into letting me live in that house with them I'll never know. She would go along with the ol' man on just about anything if she thought it was really important to him. She was wonderful, Star, not only to me and the little ol' man, but to everyone she knew."

"Sounds just like my mother!" Star said.

"Yeah," said Scrap, "the little ol' man's wife was special. She wasn't very big. In fact, she was a little lady with a big smile and beautiful natural features. She was living proof that strength doesn't necessarily come in big packages. When things got tough in that house, it was always the little lady who held things together.

"The ol' man could lose his temper and say things he didn't really mean, but the little lady just took things in stride and prayed a lot! She could make his eyes sparkle when she wanted to. She just had a way about her. Just the way she went about things amused me. She never seemed to get in a hurry, but always got everything done. She often fed me when the little ol' man was away, and it always tasted better coming from her. Punkin was always jealous when the little lady took too much time with me!"

"Dang!" said Little Sam. "Star asked you a simple question and you gave your life history! Let's talk about something else like going home and seeing my mother."

***

By now it was dark. Headlights started popping up down on Rivers Road and the hunters were headed back to camp. Slowly the 4-wheelers turned at the big silo and made their way past the little ol' man's house. When they were out of sight, Little Sam said, "They're finally gone! Let's get started toward the Park."

"Not so fast!" Scrap said. "That red truck ain't come by yet. We gotta wait on it!"

"But it's dark," Little Sam said. "They can't shoot us at night. It's late already and we've got a long way to go."

"All right," Scrap said. "But I've got a feeling that red truck is still over there. Those boys don't follow all the rules and you can't ever predict what they might do!"

The four deer bounded across the little ol' man's pasture. An old black cow threw her head up and watched as they jumped the fence and crossed Rivers Road. Just as they reached the slopes above the big lakes, a bright light suddenly popped on and it lit up the pasture!

"Don't look!" Scrap screamed. "Don't look at that light! For heaven's sake, don't look and haul ass!"

"Why?" Little Sam asked as he stopped.

"Because they'll shoot you full of holes!" screamed Scrap.

Little Sam stood gazing at the mysterious light.

"Don't look and haul ass!" Scrap screamed again.

Little Sam was in a trance. The light had him mesmerized. He couldn't take his eyes off it. It was almost like he was being hypnotized. He looked down at the ground and saw his shadow and jumped in disbelief! The does turned and bounded over a ridge.

Scrap was shaking in his tracks. He knew the cross hairs of rifle scopes were being focused on Little Sam. He'd seen it all before. He'd heard the roar of big-caliber guns in the night. They always sounded different in the night air! They were louder and their roar lasted longer! Scrap had lost a buddy on a night just like this one the very year before.

133

"Come on, Little Sam!" Scrap begged. "Pleased don't look at that light – just come on!"

Little Sam threw his head high in the air. His huge antlers shined as white as snow in the bright light. Scrap momentarily thought about how big and strong Little Sam looked with his thick neck bulging and his muscles flexed!

"Come on! Come on, you big fool! You're gonna get yourself killed!" Scrap yelled.

But there was no way Scrap could make Little Sam aware of the danger. Little Sam had never seen a spotlight before and the mystery of that bright beam took all his senses away. Scrap was literally dancing now. He was jumping around and blowing. But Little Sam stood motionless as he gazed at the light!

All at once the still night air erupted with the roar of a large caliber rifle. It was deafening. The sound rang over the hills and echoed down the hollows below the big lake. Geese and ducks on the pond flapped their wings and made their way across the water to get airborne. Frogs hushed in mid-croak as the echoes from the shot drifted further and further away.

Tensing up, Scrap watched and waited for Little Sam to fold and fall. It had been that way with his buddy! He had watched helplessly as his friend bolted backwards. And then, with his head high in the air, the buck had crumbled into a heap on the cold, frozen ground!

Little Sam still refused to move. Scrap was frantic. Suddenly he heard the ominous *clack, clack, clack, and clack*, the familiar sound of a bolt-action rifle chambering a new cartridge. As Little Sam continued to stare at the light, Scrap's instincts took over. He blew loudly and plowed right into Little Sam, sending him reeling. The rifle discharged again, and hot lead from its barrel sent dirt and sparks flying from the rocky soil in the spot where Little Sam had been standing.

"Are you a complete fool?" Scrap screamed. "Get out of here now! Get the hell out of here before we both get killed!"

The light changed direction and now both deer were fully illuminated. Scrap broke and ran. Little Sam finally regained his senses after the third shot whistled over Scrap's head. They dodged their shadows as they zigzagged across the slope and jumped into a dense thicket on the Leo

Harrell farm. Sally and Star had been watching from the fence line. After the two big bucks leaped over the fence, the two does joined them and watched as the two would-be poachers made their way to the spot where Little Sam and Scrap had been standing.

In the still of the night, the deer could clearly hear the conversation as one of the boys said, "Damn! You missed them both! I told you to shoot sooner! I told you he wasn't gonna stand there all night. How in hell could you miss a deer that big? I know what you did… You got all worked up and shot at the horns! You had that whole deer to shoot at and you screwed up and shot at his horns!"

"Well why didn't you shoot him?" said the other boy.

"Because…."

"Because why?"

"Because I was busy watching those headlights coming down the lane!"

Two sets of lights were moving quickly in their direction. When the vehicles stopped, a red light came on and several men began fanning out in every direction.

"It's the game warden!" said one of the boys. "Let's get out of here!"

"Ain't no way!" the second boy yelled. "We don't have anywhere to hide. We're caught!"

The boys looked toward the little ol' man's house and saw the floodlights go off.

"He called the law on us, didn't he?" one of the poachers said.

"Who knows?" said the other.

"Who knows? We can't prove it, but you know how that old man is about these deer. He watches out for them and now we're in deep shit!"

The four deer stood and watched as the taillights from three different trucks disappeared over the ridge toward Rivers Road.

"I wonder what happened!" Star said.

"Probably nothing," Scrap answered. "The little ol' man has tried for years to stop the shining and night hunting over here but it still goes on. And there are plenty of deer bones and hides strewn all up and down these roads to prove it."

"That's why we're going to the *Park*!" Little Sam said. "You can have this place and all the poontang in it!"

CHAPTER 18

Every light was on when he drove his old blue truck into the camp house parking lot. He'd never seen so many new trucks. The ol' man thought to himself, *these boys must sure make a better living than I do.*

As he slammed the door of ol' Blue, somebody hollered, "Hey old man, did you see anything today? I know you didn't shoot, you never do, but did you see a big deer?"

"May have," he answered. "Maybe I did, maybe I didn't! You can't prove it either way! How did y'all do?"

"Camp meat!" was the answer. "We just gathered us some camp meat. Come on in, ain't you about ready?"

"Ready for what!" the little ol' man answered.

"Aren't you ready for one of these Harris County, mood changing, lie enhancing, ego building, make-the-hair-stand-up-on-your-neck, liquid concoctions?"

"Just a little one!" said the little ol' man. "Make me just a little one!"

He knew good and well that what they were going to bring him would jump-start a Yamaha! All the hunters were gathered on the front porch. It seemed as though they were all talking at the same time. The little ol' man reasoned that he had never seen all of them in such a great mood. Laughter rang out from every corner and one wild tale was being told after another. The Pro had missed another deer that morning and just about everybody had seen deer.

Several of the guys were questioning as to how invisible deer could eat so much corn, leave so many tracks and get shot at over across the creek!

A big guy who spent most of his time in the kitchen and did most of his hunting in an area he called the car hoods, said he wasn't going to feed any more deer. He said he hadn't seen a deer in a week's worth of hunting! Yet all the deer brought into camp were full of *his* corn! Said he was tired of feeding somebody else's deer.

The Pro spoke up and said, "Y'all know that ain't against the law, don't ya!"

"What ain't against the law?" asked the big cook as he finished off a quart size plastic cup of grapefruit juice and mad Russian vodka!

"Feeding somebody else's deer ain't against the law! You just can't feed your own!" said the Pro.

"Well, how in hell do you know which ones are yours?" asked the cook as he rattled the ice in his empty cup!

"That's the tricky part!" the Pro answered. "That's why they call me 'the Pro.' Just hang around and someday I'll show you! It ain't an easy thing to do, you know! But once you figure it out, ain't nothing to it. It took me years to learn it, though!"

"Come on now," said one of the younger guys in the crowd! "Ain't no way you can tell your deer from my deer!"

"It's as easy as gettin' your nubbin greased up at the Legion," said the Pro. "And by the way, there's a whole lot I ain't taught y'all yet! You need to hang out at the Legion with me some Saturday night!"

The hunter who looked like a Baptist preacher spoke up and said, "I hate to change the subject but… Ol' Man, was that you shooting over at the lakes last night?"

"No!" answered the ol' man. "It was those boys who hunt over there, I guess. That's one reason I dropped by tonight. The game wardens were over there. I just wanted everybody to know that they're working this area pretty heavy. I've called them several times about night poachers."

The big, one-eyed hunter spoke up and said, "We welcome them. Ain't none of us broken no laws. I wish they'd come more often!" Then he added, "Well, they did nail the Pro several years ago for illegal baiting but apparently he's got that figured out now!"

About that time, the Italian showed up with the ol' man's drink and said, "Yeah, we were all in the bed last night when those shots were fired. Hell, we had to wake some of the guys up just to toast it. You know, it don't take much around here to cause a toast! Back in the fall, there was a dove shoot on the Irvington farm, and we about drank ourselves blind. Every time they shot, somebody here would say, 'let's toast that one!' Hell, we didn't even cook supper that night!"

"Have you seen any deer over at your place?" asked the big, one-eyed hunter. "I mean, at your house?"

"Yeah, I have," answered the little ol' man. "I truly believe the buck I raised has been coming around lately. I've seen him several times. He's running with a doe and I've seen him with another big buck. Y'all probably think I'm crazy, but I swear that other buck looks like Little Sam!"

"You mean *Little Sam* from over in the Park?" the big, one-eyed guy asked.

"Yeah, that deer looks just like him."

"What did you call that deer you raised?" asked the Italian.

"Scrap," the little ol' man answered. "And the doe he's running with has got to be Star!"

"You mean Star, the doe you always talk about from over in the Park?" asked the big, one-eyed guy.

"Yes," said the little ol' man. "And the *Little Sam* buck had a doe with him last night. I saw the four of them while I was cutting my grass. I recognized that doe too. She's that big young doe I've seen over at the silo at night. I know she comes off the Hogg place and how in the world that Little Sam stole her from over there I'll never know. Those two big bucks y'all call Melvin and John are still over there."

"How do you know?" someone asked.

"I saw 'em," the little ol' man replied. "I was taking my dogs for a ride two nights ago and they crossed the road right in front of me. They're huge. One of them is thin and extremely tall. The other is stout and full of muscle. Both of them are big time shooters!"

"Where were they?" asked the Preacher.

"They crossed off the Mote property onto the Hogg place," the little ol' man said. "If they're ranging that far back, y'all might get lucky and see them."

"That's interesting," said the big, one-eyed hunter. "I've got a stand not far from there. You know where it is. It's the one I call 'Chicken Shit!'"

"What a name for a deer stand!" said the ol' man. "How in the world did you come up with a name like that?"

"Well," said the big man, "we have this one guy from the Virgin Islands – you know, the one who talks funny – who hunts with us, and he's always afraid he'll get lost. I put that stand right on the edge of a logging road and told him that if he was afraid to hunt it he was *chicken shit!*"

Everybody laughed and the little ol' man was amused. "Chicken Shit," he mumbled. "I'll have to remember that! How do you tell your wife that you sat all morning in Chicken Shit?"

"Don't take it lightly," remarked the big guy. "I've seen some good ones over there!"

"Anyway," the little ol' man continued, "last night, just at dark, I saw those four deer. The ones I'm talking about crossed over into the big lake pastures. I'm sure the shots you heard were fired at them. When they crossed my place, they appeared to know where they were going. It's hard to believe it, but I think those deer are ranging all the way from the Park to here!"

"That's over five miles!" the Italian remarked.

"I know it," said the ol' man. "But with Scrap being born over there, and raised at my place, he may have sneaked Star out of the Park and Little Sam probably followed them!"

"That's hard to believe!" one of the young guys said.

"I know it," the little ol' man agreed, "but I'm telling you, I've seen them in the Park and there's no doubt they've been in my pastures this week! I always hoped Scrap would come back. He's grown into one hellacious deer, you know, and that Little Sam buck, why he's something to see as well! He's just like his daddy, only he's probably gonna be bigger. Something tells me that with the rut tailing off and all the huntin' pressure over here they were headed home to the Park last night. I'm going over there Saturday morning and I'll just bet you I see them!"

"How's that drink?" someone asked.

"What drink?" the little ol' man asked. "The one I had when I got here was really good, but it's been so long ago that I can hardly remember how it tasted!"

"Fix him up!" the big, one-eyed hunter ordered. "His wife is probably already in the bed and we need to tell some more lies!"

"Now wait a minute, here," the Pro said with an air of self-importance. "We may stretch the truth every once in a while, but ain't nobody here ever just out-and-out lied! Maybe some of us have expanded our property lines just a wee bit, but we never deny the truth! There is a big difference in stretching the truth and just lying!"

"No, I can't stay," the little ol' man said. "I really gotta go! I appreciate the drink offer, but the little lady is liable to be waiting on me. I'd rather slap a hornet's nest than have her mad with me!"

"Is she that tough on you?" one of the younger hunters asked with a laugh.

"No," said the ol' man. "It's just that she's so damn good to me that I can't stand to disappoint her. But don't think for one minute that she ain't tough. If she can't out-talk me, she'll give me that silent treatment. You know what I mean… I'm immune to a lot of things, but the silent treatment ain't one of them.

"Why, I remember one time when I had messed up real bad and she was on my case, I said to her, 'Ol' woman, cuss me, slap me, shoot me, put my testicles in a vise: anything, but just say something! This silent treatment is killin' me!'"

"Well, how'd you get her out of it?" the Pro asked.

"I came in one evening and told her that some of the neighbors had accused me of running around on her and wondered if she'd heard anything about it. You better believe she went to talkin' 90-miles-an-hour right away! That cured the silent treatment but I ain't sure it was worth it! She started talkin', and the first words she said in dang-near three days were, 'You been doing what? You been running around with who? While I've been here washin' your dirty drawers, you been doing what? Who in the world said that? Why… you've always been sorry! Your mother told me so! How in the world could you do that to me? I should have known it… I'm packing up, and from now on, you can wash your own drawers and hang up your own clothes!'

"She stopped for a full minute and then a big grin crossed her face and she said, 'you old goat, you almost had me!' and that's the way it ended. That woman can get mad quicker, stay mad longer and get over it faster than anybody I've ever seen! I wouldn't trade her for nothin', though, and I ain't worried about her ever leavin' me."

"Why's that?" the Pro asked.

"Because if she starts out the door, I'm gonna be right behind her! There ain't no doubt about who runs our house. It's the little ole lady and she's a good'un!"

With that, the ol' man cranked his truck, turned around in the dirt road and headed home. One of the hunters commented, "He's as full of crap as ever, ain't he?"

"Yeah," agreed the big, one-eyed hunter. "But he's telling the truth about one thing: He's a fool about that little ole lady!"

***

As the ol' man's taillights faded into the night, the big, one-eyed hunter looked in the Pro's direction and gave him a head jerk that said follow me. The two hunters, with their drinks in hand, ambled out back of the camp house. They were making small talk when the Pro said, "What do you want to tell me that you don't want the bunch inside to hear?"

"Well, I've been thinkin' about what you said about feedin' your own deer and feedin' someone else's," the big guy said. "You see a lot of deer, and God knows you've missed some big'ns. I believe most everything you say around here, but dang if I believe you can tell your deer from mine! You don't have to tell me if you don't want to, but it's about to drive me crazy! I've read every magazine and watched every tape on the market and nobody has a corner on that technique. If you'd just tell me how you do it, we might make some money... I mean some good money!"

"It would have to be a bunch of money because it's taken me a lot of years to learn it," the Pro said. "Tell you what, you let me sit the Chicken Shit stand tomorrow morning and I'll think about it. How's that, you let me hunt Chicken Shit and I might just tell you!"

"Hell," said the big, one-eyed guy. "You heard the little ol' man talking about seeing Big John and Melvin over there. You're liable to get a shot at either one of them off my stand!"

"Well," said the Pro, "I guess you don't want to know bad enough!"

"Alright," the big, one-eyed man said. "You can hunt it but just this one time, and if all this trash you're talking don't amount to nothin', well, we'll just see!"

The Pro chuckled, took a big drag from his cigarette, blew the smoke out of his nose and said, "It's so simple you won't believe it when I tell you!"

***

The following morning was absolutely beautiful! A heavy frost covered the landscape and the pasture fields were white as snow. Smoke from the cabin's fireplace rose undisturbed from the chimney. Well before dawn, all of the camp-house gang was up and moving. Fresh coffee brewing gave the camp a special atmosphere and several of the boys were in the kitchen making biscuits and frying bacon. Someone asked, "What's the temperature?"

"Just right!" answered the Pro. "That's what it says on the thermometer."

"I mean, what's the outside temperature?" asked the Preacher.

"All that thermometer says is, 'A little hot, too hot; a little cold, too cold; and just right,'" the Pro answered. "Boys, today she's registering dead in the middle of, 'just right!' It's gonna be a good'n this morning!"

The Italian wandered into the kitchen from one of the back rooms. He was wearing boxer shorts and a tool belt! As he rubbed his eyes and tried to wake up he said, "Gonna be a good'n boys," and then he cursed as the claw hammer in his tool belt struck his knee. He adjusted the belt so that his wire pliers and tin snips hung to the side rather than in the back and tugged at the steel wire brush that hung in his front!

"Damn, son!" remarked one of the young hunters. "Do you sleep in that outfit?"

"Hell yes!" he answered. "With the bunch I bunk with, you can't be safe enough, especially if one of 'em is from the Virgin Islands!"

Everybody in the kitchen roared in laughter as the Italian threw his tool belt in the corner and wandered outside toward the outhouse! With everyone seated at the table and with everyone holding a biscuits, the

Islander asked, "Where you guys gonna seet thees morning? I'm seeting on Chicken Shit!"

Everything got quiet. It got really quiet. It was so quiet you could hear the termites in the old wooden floor. You could even hear electricity in the wires. No one spoke or moved; there was nothing but silence. Then the Islander looked around and said, "What the matter with you suckers? What deed I say? All I said was 'I'm seeting Chicken Shit.' Why you all shut up? What deed I say? What the matter with you guys anymore?"

The big, one-eyed guy piped up and said, "Well, I guess I kind of told the Pro he could sit that stand today. I figured you would probably wanna go back to Flat Shoals Creek and I kind of got a deal with him, if you know what I mean."

"Yeah," said the Pro. "What he means is, if you sit Chicken Shit, there's gonna be *two* of us in it!"

"Now wait a freegin' minute!" The Islander said. "Seence when do he getto pick first around here? I go home next Saturday and I gotta have meat to take with me!"

"Get your meat over yonder on Flat Shoals Creek 'cause I'm sitting in Chicken Shit this morning!" the Pro said in no uncertain terms.

The big, one-eyed guy tried to smooth things over and get everything back to normal. He had a way of doing that. About the time things simmered down, the Pro leaned back away from the table, lit a smoke and said to the Islander, "Hell, I'm liable to shoot both of them big bastards this morning... I know I could if you'd loan me some of that kinky smelling cologne you wear!"

Infuriated, the Islander said, "No more rum for you tonight! No more rum for you *ever*!"

The big, one-eyed guy brought the argument to a halt when he said, "Look, I made a deal with the Pro, and it's about to get daylight. Are we gonna sit here and argue over Chicken Shit or, are we gonna hunt?"

With that, everyone got up from the table and started grabbing gear. Hunters were off in every direction. Four-wheelers headed out into the morning darkness and without question, every hunter in the club just knew that this would be his best day ever in the woods! The Pro and the big, one-eyed guy were the last to leave the house. As they stepped off the front porch, the big, one-eyed guy said, "Now, remember, a deal's a deal!"

The Pro chuckled. "I really got him, didn't I? He can't stand being teased about his perfume… He, he… I really nailed him, and I don't even drink rum! That did me good…Did you see the look on his face? I been waiting to piss him off for the longest and I really got him this morning! He, he, he…."

CHAPTER 19

When the Pro got to his stand, he couldn't believe it. Chicken Shit was a little, sawed off, wooden tripod with metal supports, sitting on the side of a logging road with absolutely nothing of much interest to look at. *So this is Chicken Shit!* he thought. *I wish I'd let that sweet smelling, rum running old fart have it!*

As daylight came, The Pro strained to see into the pine thickets. After an hour of boredom, he lit up a smoke and his mind began to wander. He thought about the Legion Hall and all the great parties back home, and he wondered if he'd missed anything over the weekend. He imagined hearing the music and the different conversations around the bar. All of a sudden, he realized that he really was hearing music and he really was hearing conversation!

That's the Today Show on TV, I'm hearing, he realized. *Good gosh, that's Mr. Hogg's television!*

Ol' Mr. Hogg was hard of hearing and always kept his TV volume very loud. The Pro was fit to be tied! No one had told him that Chicken Shit was directly across the road from old Mr. Hogg's house, not more than 75 yards from his front door.

Well, here I am in the middle of a pine thicket with nothing to look at but pulpwood and nothing to listen to but the Today Show, the Pro thought. *I could have stayed in camp and watched CNN instead! Oh well... Ain't nothin' goin' on so I may as well have some breakfast....*

He reached in his coat pocket and pulled out a tall Budweiser. As he popped the top and watched the familiar fizz and foam gather on the can, he said, "Yes sir, breakfast of champions, breakfast of champions!"

Just as he brought the can to his mouth, a doe came charging through the pines and startled him to such a degree that he almost fell off the tripod. His gun was resting by his side. He had a cigarette in one hand and a Budweiser in the other. The doe came to a sliding stop right in front of him and threw her head up. She was looking straight into his eyes. The cigarette had burned down to the filter and was giving off a terrible odor. Foam was dripping from the beer. The Pro couldn't move and his heart was about to jump out of his chest.

Then he heard more deer coming! He looked up, and two of the biggest bucks he had ever seen in his life were moving toward him. *What do I do now?* he wondered. *If I move, the doe will spook and the bucks will follow her. What should I do?*

Desperation sometimes brings out the best in all people and the Pro was certainly in a desperate situation. Without thinking, he reared back and threw his Budweiser at the doe. Then he quickly reached for his gun!

Startled, the doe jumped to one side as the Budweiser sailed by! She could not comprehend what was happening! She had been shot at with arrows, slugs, buckshot and BBs, but never had she dodged a beer can! In all her days, no hunter had ever thrown a beer at her!

As she stood in amazement, the two big bucks suddenly spotted her. As if on cue, they eyed each other maliciously and broke into the most savage, antler-clashing fight the Pro had ever witnessed! He was in shock. *Good gosh, those two have to be Melvin and John!* he thought.

The bucks' antlers came together with such tremendous force that the unbelievable sounds drowned out the Today Show. The two deer went at it with horns, hooves, heads and snort wheezes! The Pro tried to get his gun into shooting position. All he could see in the scope was a blur of gray and white. The bucks went around and around in a circle as the Pro tried to follow them with his rifle. Finally, his level of excitement reached a fever pitch and he just started shooting. Before he could regain control of his emotions, he had emptied his gun and the two bucks had disappeared!

***

About lunchtime, hunters began gathering back at the camp house. Conversations drifted back and forth about who had seen what and who had heard shots. The big, one-eyed hunter asked, "Did anyone hear any shots from Chicken Shit?"

The one eyed guy's son stuck his head out of the kitchen and said, "Did we hear shots? Hell yes! It sounded like the Pro set off a whole case of M-80s over there!"

"Is he back in camp yet?"

"No," someone answered.

"Well," said the Preacher, "Looks like we're in for some entertainment when he does get in!"

Everyone ate lunch and all the hunters began to slip off to their favorite napping places. Everyone except the Pro, that is. He was nowhere to be seen. "Reckon we 'oughta go look for him?" someone asked.

"Naw," answered The one-eyed hunter's son. "He's probably over there making up the tale he's gonna tell us. Either that or he stopped to holler at Mr. Hogg. Y'all know Mr. Hogg's hearing has gotten so bad lately that you can't very well talk to him. You gotta holler!"

"Did anyone smell smoke this morning?" the big, one-eyed guy asked.

"I did," the Italian answered. "I sure did. In fact, I started smelling it right after I heard those five shots!"

"Me too!" the big, one-eyed guy responded. "It smelled like the pulpwood company was doing some burning."

"I though that's what it was, but you know they don't ever burn during the huntin' season," the big cook said.

"Aw, Mr. Hogg was probably burning trash," the Preacher said.

"Yeah," someone agreed, and they all settled down for a midday nap.

***

About 2 o'clock, someone said, "The Pro ain't back yet, boys. We better go check on him. He may have both those big deer down over there."

"Yeah," someone said, and several of the men began to shuffle around the camp house.

About that time, a cloud of dust boiled up outside, and Mr. Hogg's old Ford truck came sliding into the parking lot. The Pro jumped out from behind the steering wheel, and old Mr. Hogg, who'd been riding shotgun, sort of stumbled out the passenger side. They were both covered in ash and the Pro's coat was smoking. It was obvious he had used it to fight a fire.

"Where you been?" asked the Italian.

"Where have I been?" answered the Pro. "The question is, 'Where have you bastards been?' Mr. Hogg and I have been fightin' a fire for two hours over yonder! We damn-near got burned up while y'all been over here resting!"

"Well, do you need any help?" the big, one-eyed guy asked.

"Not now! Hell no! Not now! Maybe two frigging hours ago, but not now!" the Pro screamed.

Old Mr. Hogg cranked his truck and headed back home. The Pro was steaming and it took him a good 10 minutes to calm down. No one in camp had the courage to ask what had happened.

Finally, the Italian said, "I think we need to toast them shots we heard!"

"Hell no!" the Pro screamed. "We ain't toasting nothin' now!" And with that, he stomped off toward the shower. His old hunting coat was still smoking and the back of his pants were torn so that his under-drawers were showing.

"You borrow theem funnee-looking drawers from Mr. Hogg?" the Islander asked. "I know theem not yours and there ain't nobody in camp wear drawers like theem there!"

Everyone howled with laughter and that only infuriated the Pro more. As he disappeared into the shower, one of the young hunters hollered, "That Chicken Shit must have been really hot this morning!"

Then, above the sound of running water, came those famous words, "Go to Hell! Every one you just go to hell!"

CHAPTER 20

The Pro didn't have much to say for the remainder of the day. Everyone in camp was about to go crazy to find out what had happened to him on the morning hunt. About 30 minutes after dark, the little ol' man walked into the camp house kitchen where several of the club members were busy chopping carrots and making salad. The big, one-eyed guy paused at his chores and said, "Mix you one… You know where everything is."

"Why is everything so quiet around here tonight?" the ol' man asked.

"We don't know," the one eyed hunter answered. "The Pro blew in here about 2 o'clock this evening in Mr. Hogg's ole truck and said he and Mr. Hogg had been fightin' fire all morning. He ain't said a word to nobody since. He sat the Chicken Shit stand and we all heard him shoot but he won't talk about it."

About that time, the Pro slithered into the kitchen and pulled up a chair next to the big table. Without question, his face showed great stress.

"Talk to us," said the little ol' man. "Did you see those two big bucks this morning and what was Mr. Hogg doing bringing you home? Where's your 4-wheeler?"

"Give me a frigging minute…" The Pro said. "One thing at a time… Lemme take one thing at a time." He lit a smoke, leaned back in his chair and said, "Y'all really don't want to hear this shit!"

By that time, the kitchen was full of hunters and everyone was anxious to hear his story. The big, one-eyed guy said, "I know you must've had

151

a terrible morning, and I was just kiddin' about your being able to hunt Chicken Shit just the one time. Hell, you know how I am. You can hunt it again tomorrow if it'll help your feelings. Hell, you can hunt it all week long as far as that goes!"

"There ain't no Chicken Shit," the Pro said solemnly. "There ain't no Chicken Shit, no more, not after this morning! Chicken Shit is gone!"

"Can't be," the big, one-eyed hunter said. "It was there last week and I know nobody stole it. In fact, I hunted it last week!"

"I'm tellin' you, Chicken Shit is gone!" the Pro repeated. "It's like last year's bird's nest – it's gone!"

"Well, what happened to it?" the one-eyed hunter asked.

"It's a long story," the Pro said. "I don't even know where to start."

"Well, if it's that long, start at the beginning," said the Italian. "We're all here now, and it ain't like we ain't been waitin' all day to hear what you have to say!"

"I had no idea the stand was *that* close to Mr. Hogg's house," the Pro stammered. "When daylight came this morning, I couldn't believe that Chicken Shit was in such a terrible place. There was no sign of deer anywhere. There was nothin' to look at but pulpwood.

"I couldn't hear nothin' because of the blarin' from Mr. Hogg's television set. I got bored, lit a smoke and was about to blow the suds off my breakfast when all hell broke loose! A hot doe came hauling ass through the pines and stopped right in front of me! She was really ready!"

"How do you know she was ready?" the Italian asked.

"Because I was looking her dead in the eyes!" the Pro fired back.

"You mean to tell me you can look a doe in the eyes and tell when she's in heat?" the big, one-eyed hunter asked.

"I can tell you ain't spent much time up at the Legion Hall!" The Pro said with a big grin. "Anyway, about the time she spotted me, two big bucks come runnin' up and started the damnedest fight you ever saw! You know me – I got all excited – and before I knew it, I'd emptied my gun at them!"

"Go on," the Italian said. "Did you cut any hair?"

"Well," said the Pro, "when I got down and checked for blood, I couldn't believe it. Those two bucks had knocked so much hair off each other that I couldn't tell if I'd hit one or not. The ground was covered in hair and I was excited. I was shaking like a leaf. I got down on all fours and crawled around for at least an hour, but never found a speck of blood – or nothin' else."

"Ees that de end of eet?" the Islander asked. "And why deed Mr. Hogg bring you home and where your 4-wheeler at?"

"The ol' man already asked me that," said the Pro. "And why don't you just go put on your perfume or something! I should have let you sit Chicken Shit and you could be tellin' this story! He, he, he… Go call home or something! He, he, he!"

"Yeah," said the big, one-eyed hunter. "And what's the story about my stand being missing? I wanna know!"

"Aw," the Pro said, "I knew you were gonna ask me that! Chicken Shit and my 4-wheeler…Well, to answer your question, they're both gone. They kinda left together, if you know what I mean. We won't be usin' either one of them tomorrow!"

"Let's hear it," said one of the young hunters. "You done screwed up again, ain't you? Tell it all. We're all ears but we don't want it to take all night. It ain't like this is the first time you've screwed up!"

The Pro took a deep breath. "You see, I was really disappointed. I was on my hand and knees crawlin' around lookin' for blood or bone or anything when I started smellin' smoke. I looked back over my shoulder and I about had a heart attack. The woods were on fire all around Chicken Shit. I jumped up and ran toward the stand.

"I want to tell you this…"Boys that was the hottest blaze I ever saw… I took my coat off and started fighting those flames. The smoke and heat were awful but I kept fightin'.

"Finally, I realized I had to have some help. I made a dash through the smoke to get my 4-wheeler but it was too late. About the time I got her in sight, the fire ignited the gas tank and she blew. One fender went flying over my head and the seat barely missed me. Boys, there ain't nothin' left but four flat tires, two axles and some melted aluminum!"

"What about Chicken Shit?" someone asked.

"Well, about that time, Mr. Hogg showed," the Pro said. "We gave it all we had, fellers! We fought a good fight, but we couldn't save Ole Chicken Shit. It just wasn't her day…She went down in a flame of glory. When she hit the ground, sparks and ashes flew 50 feet in the air! You'd of been proud of her, though. She's laying over yonder now with her steel supports all warped and bent and one long leg sticking up in the air like she's trying to shoot a big bird to the sky. She's a sad sight, boys!"

"How'd that fire get started?" one of the younger hunters asked.

"Beats me," the Pro said. "It beats the hell out of me!"

"Deedn't you say you were smoking a ceegarette?" the Islander asked.

"Yeah, but ain't no way one little ole cigarette could have started a fire that big," the Pro responded. "And why don't you just go check your meat cooler... he, he, he... I can't figure out what happened! Stuff like this happens to me all the time. It's always me! I swear, I think I'm the most unlucky fellow in this whole club! What do y'all think?"

"Well, I think a deal is a deal and it's time for you to fess up on how you sort out your corn-fed deer from somebody else's," the big, one-eyed hunter said.

"It's easy!" the Pro said. "What you do is... You feed 'em all! And since it ain't against the law to shoot another hunter's fed deer, what I do is...I shoot at all of 'em!

"Those that I miss, I figure must've been mine... And all of 'em I kill, well, I suppose they must've been yours! Ain't nothin' to it! I've been doing it for years and it works every time!"

"Why you little sawed off, anemic looking, camel smoking, beer guzzling, yarn spinning ole fart!" said the big, one-eyed hunter. "You oughta' be ashamed of yourself! You done suckered me again! You tricked me into lettin' you sit in Chicken Shit and now my stand is burned up and all my huntin' over there is ruined for the season!"

"Don't worry about it," the Pro said. "I was thinkin' about going over there tomorrow and sittin' on the ground. You know how funny deer can be. Hell, with all that smoke to stir 'em up, ain't no tellin' what I might see!"

With that, the little ol' man poured the ice from his cup into the kitchen sink and said, "Boys, that's all the high-browed conversation I can listen to in one night." He looked at the Pro and said, "Damned if I don't believe this takes the cake! I'm just happy you didn't burn up Mr. Hogg and his house, too! What a day! What a day!"

As the little ol' man closed the cabin's front door, he could hear the laughter from inside. He knew things were back to normal and the Pro was going to be just fine!

CHAPTER 21

When the little ol' man walked into his house that night, his wife asked, "What's that grin on your face all about?"

"It's that crazy bunch of guys up there at the huntin' club," he answered! "They're insane! One of them set the woods on fire today and Mr. Hogg had to help him fight fire all morning. They said Mr. Hogg was about worn out from it too. They said he didn't look too good."

"Well," the little ole lady said, "Do you think he's alright? Maybe you need to check on him? He could be down over there and no one would know it for a week. You better go check on him. I'll put your supper in the oven."

"Okay," the little ol' man said. "I'll be back in a couple of hours."

"Why that long?" his wife asked. "It shouldn't take 2 hours."

"Aw, you know how Mr. Hogg is," he answered. "He'll start that story about the fire and it'll lead into three more tales and we'll wind up talking at least two hours!"

"I know," she said. "So go on and start your talking. I'll be asleep when you get in, so don't forget your supper."

The little ol' man heard her mumbling about his poor eating habits as she closed the door behind him.

The porch light was on as he turned into Mr. Hogg's yard. The old gentleman was sitting in his favorite rocking chair and enjoying the night air. A Maxwell House coffee can was sitting on the porch beside the rocker, and every now and then, Mr. Hogg would pick it up and deposit some of the sweetness from his Red Man chewing tobacco!

What a peaceful sight, the little ol' man thought.

"Hello!" Mr. Hogg hollered. "Get out and set with me a spell. Sho' is a pretty night, ain't it?"

"Except for all the smoke in the air," the little ol' man answered.

Mr. Hogg slapped the leg of his overalls and laughed out loud. "Damn sho' is smoky, ain't it?" he said. " The air smells like we wuz cooking up lard and stoking the fire with pine cones! Sho' is smoky!" he laughed.

"Yes it is," answered the little ol' man. "My wife sent me over here to see if you're all right. I mean, after fightin' the fire all morning."

"Your wife is a sweet lady!" Mr. Hogg said. "And you can tell her I said so! Yeah, I'm all right... I'm a little sore. Don't know whether it's from fighting fire or laughin' so much. It was the damnedest thing you ever saw, me and that boy trying to put out that fire by ourselves. We about wore ourselves out, but we beat it!"

"Hell, when that 4-wheeled motorcycle of his blowed up, I thought we both were goners. I got there just before she exploded! Parts and fenders were flying everywhere and about all the boy could say was, 'We gotta save Chicken Shit!'

"I didn't know what Chicken Shit was until we had the fire put out. I kept telling him, 'We got plenty of chicken shit out in the hen house! Let's just put the fire out!' That boy is something else. I laughed at him 'til my sides ached and tears ran down my face. He was fightin' the flames and yellin', 'They're gonna kill me if we don't save Chicken Shit!'

"Hell, I didn't figure it out until that three-legged deer stand crashed and burned. Man she fell to the ground like a wooden water tower and I thought that ole boy was gonna die! You'd a' thought it was his house burnin' instead of an ole deer stand!"

"Yeah," said the little ol' man, "that old stand had lots of memories for a bunch of them boys...Well, I'll run on now. I just wanted to check on you!"

"I do appreciate it," Mr. Hogg said. "But before you go, let me tell you about me and Slim fox huntin' last Saturday night... You know how Slim likes to fox hunt and he'd been after me to go for a week so I told him I would." You know ol' Slim is my brother and I just damn near rather not hunt than to go without him. We done been through a lot together, me and ol' Slim have! He's my brother but probably my best friend also, him and ol' Perry Williams up yonder."

"I thought you told me your fox dog had puppies," the little ol' man said.

"Well, she does," Mr. Hogg answered. "And that's what I'm about to tell you. Ole Pearl had puppies about eight months ago and they're a strange lookin' bunch! You see, Mr. Prather's Basset Hound dug in and got to her and she had five of the shortest-legged fox dogs you ever put your eyes on. Pearl ain't of the highest breedin' no way, you know, but she is the damnedest fox dog I ever saw. I ain't never seen a dog that likes to hunt more'n Pearl. Why, I've seen her run 'round and 'round the pen, half the night, barking all the while just because there was a fox on my television! I swear she could smell him on my television. I 'bout had to stop watching the Disney channel!"

"Anyway, Slim wanted to put that bunch of puppies out Saturday night and see if they would hunt. I told him, 'Slim, ole Pearl will just strike and run off and leave them short-legged chaps and we won't never find 'em!'

"'Hell,' Slim said. 'We'll leave her here.'

"Leave her here?" I said. "Why she'll dig out and be to us the first time them pups strike!"

"'We'll tie her up, then,' Slim said. 'Tie her to the outhouse with a chain and I guarantee you she'll stay here.'

"Well, that's what we done," Mr. Hogg continued. "We chained her up to the outhouse door, give her some water, a biscuit, and loaded them puppies up. Ole Pearl was pitchin' a holy fit as we pulled out of the yard. She was rockin' that ole outhouse left and right and the door was flapping to beat the band! 'She ain't going nowhere,' Slim said. 'She can't break that trace chain.'

"Well, we took them puppies way 'cross the swayback bridge on Sand Creek and no sooner did they hit the ground, than one of 'em struck! The whole bunch joined the race and them puppies was havin' a time.

"After a while Slim said, 'Brother, that's the damned slowest fox chase I ever did hear. Them short-legged pups can't keep up with nothing.'

157

"We listened for darn-near an hour and they never did run out of hearing. Sometime after midnight, Slim said, 'Brother, I'll just be kissin' 'yo ass if I don't hear ole Pearl behind them pups now.'

"I said, 'Slim, ain't no way, we chained her to the outhouse.'

"Slim said, 'I know it, but you listen and see if you don't hear her. Her voice is a little deeper than them chaps and she's way behind them!'

"I listened real close and sure 'nough, way behind them pups, I could hear ole Pearl singing out. She was lettin' it roll and you could tell she was gainin' on them half-blood Basset chaps. She was tearin' them woods and fields up and hitting some notes I ain't never heard her hit. In about half an hour, she'd done caught them puppies and man, the race picked up then.

"Them five puppies and their momma was givin' that fox a run! It was the most beautiful sounds I ever heard. Them Basset Hound voices blended in great with Pearl and I just closed my eyes and thanked the Lord Jesus that I got to live long enough to enjoy such a sweet sound...."

"Now wait a minute," said the little ol' man. "You say them pups was a keepin' up with Pearl?"

"Well," said Mr. Hogg, "about that time the race turned to the west and Slim said, 'Get in the truck, Brother, and we'll cut 'em off on the road before they cross at the Hutchinson Monument.'

"Well," Mr. Hogg continued, "we stirred up the dust in our ole truck and cut 'em off. We stopped in the road and you could hear them dogs acomin' and gettin' louder and louder and closer and closer. It was a sound and excitement that made chill bumps come up on my arms...."

"You mean, them puppies was keepin' up with their momma?" the little ol' man asked again.

"About that time, a big bore red fox crossed the road in the headlights," Mr. Hog said. "Ole Pearl was right on his ass. She was draggin' that shithouse door with them five short-legged chaps ridin' and all of 'em just a-yelpin' and a-yelpin' and singing sweet music like I ain't never heard before. Damnedest thing I ever saw. It's the truth if I ever told it!"

"Ah, you ole' goat!" the little ol' man said. "You had me believin' every word! Tell me it ain't so!"

"It's the truth if I ever told it!" Mr. Hogg said. "Well, all except for one little detail... It could have been a *sow* fox. He crossed the road in such a hurry I couldn't make out whether he was a boar or a sow but the rest of it's the truth. It's the damn truth if I ever told it and you 'oughta go with us some night. See, if you'd a' been with us, you'd a' seen it with your own eyes. They's some strange tales in them woods over yonder 'round Sand Creek. Me and Slim have seen some strange things! We've lived to tell about 'em and we ain't never been caught in a lie."

Mr. Hogg's eyes began to twinkle. "Did I ever tell you about the 'coon we run three nights in a row?" he asked.

"No," the little ol' man answered. "And I hope it don't take too long, 'cause my supper is warmin' in the oven."

"It won't," Mr. Hogg promised. "It won't take long a'tall!" He took a deep breath. "Well, you know ole Pearl will run anything that Slim puts her on, don't ya'? I mean if we take her down in the swamp and Slim starts talkin' to her and splashin' around in the creek, why the first thing ya' know Pearl will strike and we'll be huntin' 'coons the rest of the night! We can take her up on the high ground and Slim says whatever he says to her and next thing ya' know, she done struck a big red fox and we listen 'til daylight. Damn good dog, ole Pearl. Ya' know, I never saw her beat 'cept them three nights I'm telling you about.

"Yeah," said the little ol' man. "Three night in a row she let you down."

"Damn sho' did!" Mr. Hogg said. "Me, Slim and Perry Williams was 'coon huntin' way down Sand Creek almost to Whitesville. Ole Pearl had struck just below the old swayback bridge, and when she did, she went straight down Sand Creek a ways to the big beaver pond and she treed. It must have been two miles. Me and Slim started off in that direction. Perry didn't even get up off the stump he was a-sittin' on.

"You know how ol' Perry is," Mr. Hogg said. "He's been in the woods many a night and he ain't about to take off unless he knows something… Well, Slim turned around and held the lantern up high so he could see Perry's face. He was sittin' there in the dark smokin' a cigarette and whittlin' on a piece of hickory. 'Well,' said Slim, 'ain't you a-comin'?'

"'Ain't no need,' Perry answered. 'Ain't no need!'

"'No need, hell!' Slim said. 'Pearl is treed and I'd bet you a week's salary at the Saw Mill she has a big bore 'coon up a tree. She's down at the head of that beaver pond!'

"You could hear ole Pearl way down in the swamp. There was no doubt that she was treed and no confusion in her voice. She had him treed!" Mr. Hogg said.

"'What you mean, *no need?*' Slim continued. 'That dog is treed and she won't run no 'possum!'

"'I know it,' said Perry, 'but when you get down there, all you gonna find is a treed dog. You ain't a-gonna find no 'coon. She done struck ole Haint. I know… me and Billy Joe Kevette done tracked him down to that pond too many nights. Old Haint ain't a-gonna be there… Just you and Pearl!'

"'It might not be him,' Slim said. 'How you know it's that Haint 'coon?'

"'By the way he run,' Perry said. 'If he'd veered off down yonder and run any high ground at all, it might not be him, but he didn't. He went straight down Sand Creek and didn't go up none of them little branches or sloughs. I know… I done run him many a Saturday night! It's ole Haint all right, no doubt about it. Gotta be, and when you get to Pearl, she's a-gonna be on a big sweet gum 'bout five foot across.'

"Well, me and Slim left Perry sittin' on that stump and headed for the deep swamp," Mr. Hogg continued. "Just before we left, Perry screwed the lid off a pint Mason jar, took a deep draw of the liquid contents and said, 'Boys, you better get you a slug of this before you go because when you get back, it may be all gone!' Then he added, 'I'm a-gonna sit here on this stump in the *moonlight* and drink this-here *moonshine* 'til y'all get back with Pearl. If you bring a 'coon back with you, I'll kiss both your asses right here on this stump in the moonlight, and if there's any left, I'll give you the rest of my moonshine!'

"Slim took a big swallow, gave Perry a high five and we headed out. We must've crossed Sand Creek five or six times before we got to Pearl. It was so thick that you couldn't plow your way through. My overalls wuz torn to threads before we got there, and sure enough, there was Pearl on the biggest sweet gum I ever saw. It was sittin' just out of the water and so big around that me and Slim couldn't reach around it.

"'Well,' I said to Slim, 'shine him down and I'll put a .22 bullet in him. When he hits the ground, ole Pearl will have herself a time.'

"We threwed the light up in that big tree and no eyes shined back. We circled her a dozen times and couldn't see nuthin'. Pearl wuz singin' steady and Slim said, 'Brother, that 'coon has gotta be up there somewhere! Pearl ain't never told a lie like this!'

"We musta' shined that tree for an hour and never saw as much as an eye," Mr. Hogg continued. "Then we threwed the light out across that beaver pond and she was as still as could be. Nothing had stirred a ripple. All you could see was the fog driftin' and ain't no 'coon crossed it that night.

"'Damn!' said Slim. 'I hate to leave here like this. Perry is gonna laugh his ass off when we get back up yonder with no 'coon!'

"'I know it,' I said to Slim. But that's about all there was to it so we started back to where we left Perry. We 'bout had to shoot Pearl to get her off that tree. Slim 'bout choked her to death and even after we'd dragged her half a mile, she was still singin' and tryin' to get loose.

"When we got close, Perry flashed his light a couple of times and whistled. Slim answered him with the same low tone and when we got real close, Slim throwed the light on Perry. There he sat, right where we left him. He had a big grin on his face and the first thing he said was, 'I told you so! You rascals didn't believe me, now did you? She was treed on that big sweet gum, wasn't she? The one you can't get around for the water, and you ain't seen no 'coon. It's that Haint 'coon, boys! I knowed it was ole Haint alright!'

"'Something ain't right,' Slim said. 'Something just ain't right. Pearl said a 'coon went up that sweet gum and I don't believe in no haints. Now how he got down without leavin' Pearl a trail, I don't know....'

"Perry said, 'Boys, I been sittin' here a-thinkin' ever since y'all left. I been a-thinkin' 'bout how we can figure that scoundrel out and I think I know. What we need to do is come back tomorrow night. Brother Hogg, me and you will cross over from the other side of the beaver pond and hide so we can see that big sweet gum. We'll let Slim put Pearl out about 9:30 or 10 o'clock. We know she'll run him straight to that tree and we'll just see what he does!'"

The little ol' man said, "Mr. Hogg, how long is this story gonna last? I really need to get home."

"Hold on," Mr. Hogg said. "It gets better and you ain't got nothin' to do but go to bed."

"Well go on, then," the little ol' man sighed.

Mr. Hogg continued his story. "Well we did just that. Me and Perry dropped Slim and Pearl off on the road above Sand Creek. We parked way down yonder and made a big circle on foot. With the sweet gum in sight, we found us a log kinda out of the way and sat down to wait on Slim and Pearl. It was another pretty night and still as could be. There just weren't nothin' movin'. We sat there until about 10 o'clock, and then ole Pearl struck. She cut loose loud and strong. I said, 'Perry, that's him! She's still got his scent left over from last night and she's headed straight down Sand Creek to us!'

"Perry switched his flashlight on just to check it and said, 'I put new batteries and a bulb in this thing today. We don't want to miss nothin' tonight.'

"Well, ole Pearl kinda quieted down. We didn't hear nothin' from her for about 30 minutes and when she opened up again, she weren't 200 yards up the creek! I said to Perry, 'She's been runnin' that rascal closed mouthed tryin' to catch him. I've seen her do it before. You can't beat ole Pearl!'

"About that time, we heard something comin'. It was just a-scramblin' around in the creek and all of a sudden, we seen him! Perry switched the light on and I'm here to tell you he put that beam on the biggest bore 'coon me or him has ever laid eyes on! The ole boy went straight to that big sweet gum, and before we could say Jim Beam, he was 20 foot up it. He went clean to the top and disappeared out of the light. That ole gum tree must be 80-foot high, you know!

"Everything got quiet then, except for Pearl singing. We'd shined every limb in that tree by the time Pearl got there. Up on that tree she went and put out the sweetest music I ever done heard. Me and Perry looked and looked. There weren't no 'coon up there!

"'Well I just be danged!' Perry said. 'You seen him and I did too, but where in the devil did he go? There must be a hole in that tree!'

"'Yeah,' I said, 'but you seen him go clean to the top! He couldn't found a hole up there!'

"About that time, Perry turned and threw the light out across the beaver pond. What we seen sent chills up my spine and I said to Perry, 'Did you bring some bad liquor tonight or do you see what I see?'

"Ole Perry weren't sayin' nothin'. He was just steady holding the light on that big ole 'coon as he went across the water without making even a splash.

"'I told you he was a haint!' Perry exclaimed. 'The son of a bitch can walk on water! I ain't believin' it!'

"He was just moving steady and headed to a big dead pine in the middle of the pond. When Pearl seen him, she started whimpering and shyin' down like she done that night a pack of coyotes killed all the chickens at the house. We stood there and watched that big feller climb the dead pine and disappear in a hole about 40-foot up.

"Me and Perry was lost for words. Neither one of us could talk. Perry sat back down on the log and cut the light off. I could hear him fumbling with the lid of that Mason jar again and then I heard him blow hard and say, 'Hot damn, that's good! Here, have a drank, 'cause I ain't never seen nothin' like that sober!'

"Well, about that time, Slim showed up and said, 'Where is he, boys?'

"I started to tell him but I just couldn't bring myself to it. Finally I started and when I got to the part about that 'coon walking on water, Slim said, 'You two fools done got into that 'shine and you ain't seen nothin'!'"

"Is that all of it?" asked the little ol' man.

"No, there's more," Mr. Hogg said. "I told you in the beginnin' there was three nights of it. Just you be patient."

"Go on, then," the little ol' man said with another deep sigh.

Mr. Hogg picked up where he'd left off. "Well, we sat down on that log and Perry started talking. 'Ain't no way that Haint 'coon walked across that pond… Ain't no way! There's got to be more to it than that!'

"Finally, Perry got up and shined his light on the sweet gum. He said, 'I can believe he could've come down that tree on the backside and we could've missed him while we were shinin' them limbs, but how? Hell, I don't know how he done it!'

"We walked over to the tree and shined all around it. Nothin'... Just plain nothin'... Then Perry sat down at the water's edge and lit a filtered Winston. He was gazing at the muddy water. He musta' sat there for 10 minutes without saying a word. Then he got up, shined his light deep in the water and said, 'Come here, boys.'

"Perry was shinin' the water where it come up to the big tree. Low and behold, just below the surface, we seen a strand of barbed wire. Perry said, 'Well kiss my ass; I'll just be damned!' He shined down in the water again and you could see the wire fastened to a root about 6 inches below the water level. The wire stretched out across the pond toward that big dead pine, and it come up out of the water just a little bit.

"'He ain't no haint!' Perry said. 'That big rascal has done been walkin' that wire for years! And you know what? Ole man Gaylon Yates pulled that wire 15 years ago. You know he used to let his cows out in the swamp, and he pulled that wire when the neighbors got to raisin' Cain about them cows gettin' in their crops. That was way before the beavers backed up this swamp. Well, I'll just be damned! All them nights me and Billy Joe chased him... I'll just be damned!'

"Is that it?" the little ol' man asked.

"No, there's more," Mr. Hogg said. "I told you there was three nights of it...."

"Well please hurry," the little ol' man said. "Did y'all go back?"

"The very next night!" Mr. Hogg answered. "You know Perry. He don't give up on much. He wanted to go again the next night. I told him there weren't no use because to catch that ole bastard, we had to shoot him ahead of Pearl, or shoot him off that wire, and there weren't no sport in that. But Perry said, 'I'll be back tomorrow night and we'll see what happens.'

"We got back to our log about the same time the next night. We sat down and waited on Pearl to strike. Nothin' much was goin' on and Perry started tappin' the lid on his Mason jar. We took a slug and I said, 'Perry, that's the best liquor I've had in years. It reminds me of that wet year we had way back yonder. Hell, it rained all summer, and we couldn't get the grass out of our crop, and the worms had 'bout got to all the cotton. Me and Slim sat around the house for a week and it just kept on a rainin'.

"Finally, one morning, Slim said, 'Let's go to Drummon and get us a drank!' You know in those days, me and Slim didn't know what one drink was. I said, 'Slim, we ain't got no money.' He said, 'But we got them hogs out yonder in the pen.' So we loaded up a shoat hog that was about ready to kill, went over yonder in Drummon, and swapped him for three gallons of 'shine. Damn good 'shine too!

"Well, it kept rainin' and me and Slim kept drinkin' and after 'bout a week, Mr. Hopp Morgan pulled up in the yard. Me and Slim was laid out on the porch. Mr. Hopp said, 'Come on boys, I want y'all to take me down to the spring. I want some of that water to make sun tea with.' We had the best spring water in the county. Slim grabbed that last jug of 'shine and we started down to the spring. We both wuz about past goin' and had been for several days!

"Well, when we got to the spring, Mr. Hopp said, 'Boys, fill these two jars up with that spring water, hand them to me and then both of you get in that water and lay down. It's about time you sobered up!

"'Damn,' said Slim, 'I ain't gettin' in that cold water!' and he reached for our 'shine jug. Mr. Hopp pulled an ole pistol out of his back pocket, pulled the hammer back and when it went off, hell, I thought he'd done shot Slim. It scared hell out of me. Instead of shootin' Slim, though, he hit that 'shine jug dead center and mud, liquor, and glass went flyin' everywhere!

"I said to Slim, 'Brother, I think we need to take us a bath before we agitate Hopp! You know I've been a wanting to bathe for dang near two weeks now anyway!'

"Mr. Hopp said, 'Boys, I'm gonna sit right here 'til y'all get all sobered up!'

"Me and Slim stayed in that spring damn near all day and that night it stopped rainin'. We got our crop in. Weren't much to it though, and we didn't get nothin' for it. But we paid our seed and fertilizer bill so we could get another crop in the next year. Ole Hopp probably saved our hides. I know he saved that cotton crop. If he hadn't come over here, we would've stayed drunk 'til them hogs was all gone!"

The little ol' man said, "Mr. Hogg, get on with the 'coon hunt. It's near midnight now, and my ole lady will be out huntin' me if you don't hurry up and finish."

Mr. Hogg once again picked up where he'd left off. "We'd been sittin' on that log for the longest when Perry stood up and said, 'Give me a hand if you would.' He reached in his back pocket and pulled out a big red handkerchief and said, 'Cut me one of them bamboo poles over there. Cut the longest one you can find.'

"I did, and Perry wrapped his handkerchief all around one end of it and tied it in a knot. Then he reached in his other pocket and pulled out a jar of axle grease. He said, 'Hold this pole while I put this grease on my rag.' He put that whole jar of axle grease on that rag and said, 'Cut me another pole.' I did, and we walked over to the big sweet gum. Perry said, 'You hold the end of your pole.' And then he started wadin' out in that beaver pond while holdin' the other end of my pole.

"When he got to the end, he took the pole with the rag and grease on it and reached out as far as he could. All of a sudden, it hit me what he was doin'. Perry was greasin' that wire up good fashioned. He was standin' in water up to his neck and I just knew a big ole water moccasin was gonna be the death of him. When he finished, he said, 'Let's have another snort!' and before we got back to our log, ole Pearl struck. She struck loud and convincin', and although she was a good ways off, you could tell she was a-comin' our way in a hurry.

"'It won't be long now,' Perry said. 'And I can't wait!'

"Louder she got, louder and louder. No doubt about it, she was right on that Haint 'coon's tail with every intention of catching him before he got to the sweet gum. Pearl sounded like she was just right out there in the dark, but no 'coon had showed. All of a sudden, out of the banks of Sand Creek, ole Haint come up with Pearl grabbin' after him on every leap. When he got to the sweet gum, hell, he didn't have time to climb it. He just gave it a good brush and jumped for the barbed wire.

"Ole Pearl was dead on his ass! Out that barbed wire he went with ole Pearl still doggin' him! She was half swimmin' and half leapin' and singin' a pretty tune.

"Ole Haint was obviously gettin' away and Pearl was losin' ground — that is, until he hit that stretch of greased-up wire! That big rascal about turned inside out. He was slippin' and a-slidin' upside-down and every which-a-way, holdin' on for dear life and ole Pearl was now steadily a-gainin'. When he realized somethin' was bad wrong, it was too late to turn back.

Pearl was between him and the sweet gum tree when it become obvious he was gonna get hisself caught!

"He baled out right on top of Pearl's head and such a fight you ain't never seen. Why, they'd stay under water for a full minute and come up with hair and fur flyin' ever'where. Perry kept a steady light on them and the sounds of that dog hollerin' and that 'coon hissin' and a-screamin' was something to behold. I thought he was gonna drown ole Pearl for sure! Probably would have if Slim hadn't called her off. She come draggin' up the bank of that beaver pond and collapsed on the ground by Slim.

"Her head looked like it had been in a meat grinder and she was completely give out. Perry threw the light back on ole Haint just as he caught holt of and crawled back on the strand of wire. As he scampered, he was kinda wobbly and off balance, but he was steadily making it toward the dead pine. 'Shoot him!' yelled Slim. 'Shoot that big son of a bitch! That's the biggest 'coon in the state of Georgia!'

"'No!' Perry yelled. 'Don't shoot him. He's a legend now. Ain't no need to kill him. That coon has brought too much pleasure to too many men and dogs to be shot!'

"Ole Pearl could see Haint in the light and all she done was whine. She didn't want no more of him. We watched as he shimmied up the dead pine and disappeared into a hole. The night became very quiet and still again. It was so quiet that you could almost hear the mosquiter wings a-flappin'!

"There was absolutely no sound at all and the beaver pond settled back down. As fog formed over it, and by light of the moon, we could see hair and fur floatin' in the water. The moonlight made that hair shine like new money, and that was the only evidence of the great battle that had been fought there.

"'Nobody spoke for a full 10 minutes! We were in a trance. It was like we had witnessed something very special and we wanted to see it again on instant re-play! Then Perry slapped his leg and said, 'Boys, I've seen it all now! That's the best damned 'coon fight ever and we seen it with our own eyes!'

"Slim said, 'Yeah Perry and I'm glad you are here 'cause that bunch up there at Harold's Store would say we're lyin' if it was just me and my brother tellin' it!'

"Perry said, 'I sure wish ole Billy Joe had been here for this. He would've enjoyed it as much as we did. Y'all know he died last week, don't ya'?'"

The little ol' man spoke up. "Mr. Hogg, that's the best tale I've ever heard you tell. How do you make all that stuff up?"

"It's the damned truth, ever' bit of it!" replied Mr. Hogg. "It's the truth if I ever told it. You ask Perry about it some of these days. He'll tell you. Or better yet, go out yonder and look at the scars on Pearl's head. It's the truth if I ever told it!"

The little ol' man looked at his watch and realized that it was now well past midnight. He reached his hand out to Mr. Hogg and said, "I've enjoyed it and I'm glad you're alright after that fire fight today."

With that, the little ol' man cranked Old Blue, turned her around in the yard and slowly made his way up Marshall Williams Road. Mr. Hogg was still standing in the shadows as the taillights disappeared. Under his breath, Mr. Hogg mumbled, "I wish he hadn't had to go. I meant to tell him the story about the night Pearl fell in that groundhog liquor still over yonder on the Drummon Road! Hell, Perry was with me that night too!"

CHAPTER 22

The four deer made their way through the night. They stopped to browse several times and watered in the branches of the Dink Elkew property. Little Sam was always in the lead and he was obviously anxious to get back to the Park. He had experienced all the excitement he could handle for a while, and he was ready for the tranquility of his own home territory. He wondered how they'd all be received by Big Sam. He wondered if Big Sam would be happy to see him or, if he'd still try to exercise his complete dominance. *Even if he does, it's still better than having hunters and poachers shooting at me day and night,* Little Sam thought.

Just before daylight, the foursome reached the junkyard on the McKeen property. Scrap said, "Wonder where that dog is and which junk car ole Tennis Shoes is sleeping in tonight?"

"Who knows?" Little Sam said. "We'll just slip through and don't you dare wake them up. We're too close to home for any train wrecks now!"

Scrap's playful mind began working. He raised his head and surveyed the junkyard. Another old Cadillac was resting next to a rusted-out Jeep and Scrap thought, *If Tennis Shoes is here, he's in the Cadillac. Everybody knows how he loves Cadillacs! I think I'll have some fun with Sally!*

Little Sam and Star were out front and Sally was standing close to Scrap. Scrap said, "Sally, there's a muscadine vine over yonder by that old car and it always has the biggest, blackest, sweetest fruit you ever tasted. I ain't all that hungry tonight, but you oughta' go try some."

Scrap moved on but Sally's curiosity got the best of her. She glanced over her shoulder and sure enough, she saw an enticing muscadine vine hanging in a tree by the old cars. She couldn't stand it; she had to go back. She was munching on late-season muscadines the size of a quarter when something got her attention. She heard a strange nasal sound nearby and her nostrils picked up the scent of a dog. She stood motionless while she tried to determine what the strange sound was. Some living and breathing creature was exhaling air very loudly, almost like a bear or a hog snorting or grunting. What could it be?

Sally stretched her long neck up into the vine and tugged on it with her teeth to reach more of the remaining late-season grapes. To her surprise, the whole vine tumbled down and landed on the top of the nearby junk Cadillac with a distinct thud. Seconds later, all hell broke loose and the old Cadillac seemed to come to life! Tennis Shoes sat up in the back seat and started hollering, "Don't shoot, Mr. Paul, don't shoot! Don't shoot! It's just me, ole Tennis Shoes again, and I ain't stole nothin'!"

Moments later, the junkyard dog came charging out from under the Jeep and Sally went into a panic. She literally leaped over an old New Holland hay bailer and a John Deer turning plow! Every hair on her body stood straight up. Then, in her haste to get away, she simply ran over the charging dog. The once snarling, angry mongrel ran off whimpering and moaning! He had never been run over by a panicked deer before and he was terrified. In the past, Mr. Paul Mckeen had run over him twice with a wrecker and it had never scared him that badly.

Floodlights came on everywhere and Mr. Paul's old shotgun began to bark. Sally was now in high gear. Just as she caught up with Scrap, a ragged old black man passed them both with the junkyard dog hot on his heels. The watchdog had no fear of Tennis Shoes. Two more shots were fired and then the floodlights went out.

As the four deer watched Tennis Shoes running along Highway 219, the churchyard dog came out and joined in the chase. The two dogs chased poor Tennis Shoes all the way past the Rock Store at the crossroads! A steady stream of profanity filled the night air. The dogs were barking, Tennis Shoes was running for his life and cursing, and even three wild deer thought this situation was very humorous. But the *fourth* deer was not so amused. When the sounds of the barking and cursing finally faded into the night, Sally turned to Scrap, stood up on her hind legs and gave him a severe pounding with her front hooves. She didn't think it was funny at all!

Scrap said, "All I did was tell you about the muscadines."

Sally replied, "You set me up and scared me to death. I may never get over this. My heart jumped out of my chest. That's the ugliest black man and the meanest dog I've ever seen!"

"Sorry," Scrap said. "I didn't mean to. I just wanted to introduce you to a couple of my friends!"

The four deer then focused on getting back to the Park. With Little Sam in the lead, they were all anxious to reach their intended destination.

CHAPTER 23

Perry Williams was sitting on his front porch when the little ol' man passed his house. Perry threw up his hand and the ol' man hit the brakes on his truck. He turned old Blue around and pulled up in front of Perry's house.

"Get out and set a spell," Perry said. "You ain't got nothin' to do nohow. Come up here and drag you up a rocker and talk to me."

The little ol' man pulled up a rocking chair next to Perry and said, "How you been?"

"Ah, fair to middlin'," Perry replied. "I can't complain. At least I'm still here. Lots a' folks ain't, you know!"

The little ol' man laughed. He loved Perry and always enjoyed casual conversations with him. Perry always made him feel good and was one of the funniest men he'd ever known! Perry could tell a tale with the best of them and the little ol' man would laugh 'til he cried at Perry's jokes and humor.

The ol' man said, "Perry, have you ever known Brother Charles Hogg to lie?"

Perry laughed out loud, slapped his leg and said, "Bro' Hogg tell a lie? Hell no! He might lead you on and tell some wild tales, but he ain't never just outright lied. Most of what he tells on him and Slim is the gospel truth. Some of it's hard to believe, but who's gonna deny it? They back each other up on all them huntin' yarns!"

"Well," the little ol' man said, "he told me that story of y'all treein' that 'coon he called Haint. Is there anything to that tale or did he make it up?"

"Ever bit of it's the truth!" Perry said. "I didn't hear him tell it to you but I was there that night. Man, that was years ago. Didn't much bother me back in them days… I could hunt all night and work all day milkin' them cows up yonder at Avery Dairy. When did Bro' Hogg tell you about that Haint 'coon?"

"About two weeks ago, I reckon," the little ol' man said. "Tell you when it was… It was the night after them hunters burned the woods up over yonder."

"I heard all about that," Perry said. "In fact, Bro' Hogg told that up at Hopp's Store just the other day. He got a big kick out of that ole boy he called 'the Pro.' Bro' can tell some stuff now, but the thing about it is, ain't nary a tale he's ever told been disputed. He's just seen a lot in his day, I guess! Say, did he ever tell you about the night ole Pearl got into that liquor still over in Drummon?"

"No," the ol' man answered. "That's one I ain't heard."

"Well," said Perry, "it's been a while back. Me and Bro' decided to take Pearl and put her out on that branch that crosses the Drummon Road over yonder past the Ridgeway place. It was cold as hell and a big full moon. We put her out and she didn't strike until about 10:30 or 11 o'clock. We were just about to call it quits when she cut loose and headed over toward Drummon. Bro' said, 'It's about time! I ain't never known her to go this long without barking up somethin'.'

"I know Bro' Hogg told you ole Pearl wouldn't run nothing but a fox or a 'coon but she would sometimes! At least she did that night. When Pearl first opened, she sounded like she always did, but the longer she run, I could tell a difference! She just didn't act like she was as into it as she usually did. Anyway, we sat there in the dark and listened for the longest and then she treed! 'That's him,' said Bro'. 'She's got him!'

"I said, 'Bro', she ain't treed! She's bayed!'

"Bro' said, 'Now how in hell can you tell the difference in a treed dog and a bayed dog a mile away?'

"'Just listen,' I said, 'Sounds like she's in a hole. She ain't up on no tree.'

"'It don't make no difference,' Brother said. 'We still gotta go to her. If we don't, she won't never trust us again.'

"So we struck out down the branch. We walked about 30 minutes, I reckon, and I could hear her on down the branch just a-singin' and every now and then, a-growlin'! I said, 'Bro', that ain't no damned 'coon.'

"'If it ain't a 'coon, what in the devil can it be?' he asked.

"I said, 'I don't know, but I ain't got but two cartridges for this ole .22. Hope there ain't three of 'em!' About that time I got a whiff of something that smelled plum awful."

"Bro' said, 'Perry, I smell a liquor still.'

"I said, 'I smell it too, but there's something else out there as well!'

"Ole Pearl was just steady singing! I threw the light along the branch bank and there was Pearl, both front feet up on the rim of an open vat of sour mash. The head of the vat had been removed for repair. She was singing her head off! 'Well I'll be damned,' said Bro'. 'Pearl has done treed a gol'dern groundhog!'

"I said, 'Bro', there's got to be more to this than that. There's something else here!'

"'Hell, there could be a dead black man in that still,' Bro' said. 'I've heard of folks throwin' corpses in a still before!'

"'Naw,' I said, 'Ain't no dead man in there. It's something else.'

"'Well,' said Bro' Hogg, 'But you know how Pearl hates a nigger!'

"About that time, something moved on the backside of that big vat of mash and we saw it crawl up from behind the firebox. I threw the light beam on it, and low and behold an old momma skunk and five little'ns was sittin' on the rim. All five of 'em turned their tails toward Pearl. The ole dog was havin' a fit, and every time Pearl would lunge like she was gonna cross over that vat, all five of them bastards would spray her at the same time. About half of it would hit Pearl in the face and the rest went in the liquor still!'

"Bro' Hogg went hysterical. 'A god-dammed polecat!' he said. 'That bitch has done bayed a polecat! She ain't worth killing. I ain't feedin' a polecat-runnin' wench!'

"I thought Bro' was gonna kill her right there. Well, this went on for a full 10 minutes. Every time Pearl lunged, them skunks let her have it and the whole place smelled terrible. I said, 'Bro', if this keeps up, that vat is gonna be full of skunk spray.'

"'What're we gonna do?' asked Brother. 'You know a man will cuss you for messin' with his wife, but he'll flat-out kill you for messin' with his liquor!'

"'I know it,' I said. 'And we gotta do something fast and get out of here.'

"We both knew Pearl weren't gonna leave them skunks 'til we did. I said, 'Bro', we could cut us a pole and stick 'em....'

"When I said that, ole Pearl thought I said 'sick 'em,' and she baled off into that vat of mash and started dog-paddlin' toward them skunks. They were steadily lettin' her have it all the while. She swam across and grabbed that momma skunk by the ass and pulled her down in the vat! Mash was flyin' ever'where, and such a fight I hadn't seen since she'd caught ole Haint that night.

"They fought 'til both of them gave slap out. I guess that's what it was... Either that or they'd swallered enough mash so that they 'wuz both drunk. Anyway, ole Pearl swam up to the edge of that vat and when she did, Brother grabbed her by the collar, dragged her out, and slung her out across the woods. She was spinning like the blades on a helicopter and hit the ground with all four feet pointin' in different directions.

"The momma skunk crawled out of the vat and gathered her bunch together. When they passed by Pearl, all of them in a row behind their momma, they raised their tails and gave her one last dose of spray! Pearl had all of them that she wanted! As they passed by her, all she could do was growl and show them her teeth. I could read her mind, though, and I figured she was thinking, 'You stinkin' little bastards done got me in a world of shit with Mr. Hogg!'

"Is that the end of it?" the little ol' man asked.

"Not exactly," Perry answered. "In fact, some of it had just begun. That was the stinkin'est dog that God ever let live. I don't know which smelled the worser – ole Pearl, or all of that stale sour mash laced with polecat spray. Either way, Ole Pearl was soaked to the bone. Even with the windows rolled up and her in the back of the truck, we about got sick and both of us gagged all the way home. Bro' Hogg said the only way he could stand her after that was to tie her up down near the branch! But even then he could smell her clean to the house every time it rained!

"Ain't nothin' smells worse, you know, than a wet dog, and if she's been soaked in skunk spray, why it's even worse than that! Ole Pearl stunk damn near 'til Christmas that year and I don't know if the smell ever left her or if Bro' just got used to it! But at any rate, he eventually stopped talkin' about it!"

***

"Christmas Eve that year I was sittin' at the table drinkin' a cup of coffee and readin' the Sunday-morning paper. About 8:30, somebody started blowin' a car horn in the yard and I said to my wife, 'Who's that? Why don't they knock instead of sittin' out there blowin' the dadburn horn?'

"She peaked out the blinds and said, 'It's ole Cissero!'

"'Wonder what he wants?' I queried. 'I don't owe him nothin'!'

"You know Cissero used to do a lot of credit liquor business and he always collected his money on Sunday mornings. But I had him paid up. I went out to his car. You know Cissero always drove them long, fancy cars: big Chryslers, Cadillacs or Oldsmobiles! They might be beat to hell and have 200,000 miles on 'em, but they were big and long with shiny hubcaps and long radio aerials. Anyway, Cissero got out and he had on his usual red flannel shirt, khaki pants and bright suspenders. He was a striking old cuss and had made lots of money! You know how he made it don't you?"

"No, not really," the little ol' man answered. "I guess, foolin' with 'shine?"

"Well," said Perry, "some of it but most of it he made off corn. Everything he's got come from corn he made down yonder in them bottoms. Cissero ain't nobody's fool. Everything he's got come from corn. He knows how to grow corn and turn it into money. You see, he takes that corn, mixes it with barley, hog shorts, yeast and sugar and turns out some of the best 'shine I ever had. He sells it for good money.

"Then he takes them leftover skimmin's, beer and mash home in a 55-gallon barrel and feeds it to that lot of hogs he's got. Then he bar-b-ques them hogs and sells high dollar bar-b-que all over Troup County. His ole lady has about 25 laying hens that she let's run behind them hogs. Them chickens make a good living eatin' droppin's. That's the layin'est bunch of Rhode Island Reds I ever seen.

"She sells eggs in every store between Whitesville and LaGrange and they say the yellow of them eggs is as bright as a gold dollar. When them ole hens stop a-layin', Cissero rings their necks, dresses them, boils them down with some of that pork and sells Brunswick stew. Now, you tell me that ain't makin' money! Every bit of it comes from that bottomland corn. He don't buy nothin'!"

The little ol' man was puzzled. "Perry," he said, "Don't that mash make them hogs drunk?"

"Drunker'n hell!" Perry answered. "I've been up there when the whole lot was drunk! One Saturday evening I dropped by there to get me a pint and Cissero said, 'Boy, come on out here. You ever seen a billy goat fuck a sow?'

"I said, 'No, but I paid a dollar one time down at the Columbus fair to see a monkey nail a bird dog!'

"Cissero laughed out loud and led me out back to the hog pen. Low and behold, his ole stud goat, Billy, had jumped in the lot with them hogs and loaded up on that beer and skimmin's. The whole lot of them was about drunk and that billy goat was about right!

"Cissero said, 'I bar-b-qued all my nannies last week and that ole boy has been after everything on this place ever since.'

"About that time, ole Billy jumped a sow and I ain't never seen nothin' like it. She squealed to high heaven, and when she did, the whole rest of them hogs came staggering to her defense. They was all huffin' and snortin'! Ole Billy crawled off her and eased back to the trough of mash. Soon as things settled down, he ambled back over where she was and nailed her again. The second time, there weren't no more squealing! I guess he must've flung a cravin' on her.

"'Don't that just beat all?' Cissero said.

"'Yeah, it does,' I said. 'But ain't you gonna do anything about it? Hell, I'll help you get him out and we'll whip his ass!'

"'Naw,' Cissero said. 'Jest let him be. He'll sober up after a while, see how ugly she is, and feel bad enough about his own self without us having to whoop him. Just look at her. He picked the ugliest one in the lot! The ole fool could've at least picked one of them gilts!'

"That's a lie!" the little ol' man insisted. "You made that stuff up!"

"It's the truth," Perry said. "Every last bit of it is the truth! If Cissero was alive, he'd tell it the same way! Anyway, back to that Christmas Eve Sunday. Me and Cissero was standing out there by his car and he said to me, 'Boy, we done over-made over yonder!'

"I said, 'What do you mean *over-made?*'

"'Well, I mean we done made more than I can sell,' said Cissero. 'We done over-made. I come by here to see if you wanted some good liquor for half price.'

"'Half price?' I asked. "You ain't never sold no liquor for half price. Not since I've known you.'

"'Yeah,' he said, 'but we done over-made! Christmas is tomorrow and won't nobody in this community want any whiskey after Christmas, except maybe them Hogg boys over yonder.'

"I said, 'Now Cissero, what's wrong with the liquor? Tell me the truth.'

"'Ain't nothing wrong with it,' he insisted. 'It'll make you drunker'n hell and it beads up real good!'

"'Well let me see then,' I said.

"Cissero popped the trunk of his big, long Chrysler and that trunk was slap full of pint and half pint bottles of clear white 'shine! He had them packed neat as could be in saltboxes and I'll bet they didn't even rattle when he went down them dirt roads. I got to thinking: *Now he wants to get shed of that liquor so bad, must be something wrong with it.*

"I reached in and picked up a pint, turned it upside down, shook it up hard as I could, turned it back up and them pretty beads rolled and disappeared the best I ever saw. I asked him what he wanted for a pint and he told me. It was half what he normally asked. I said, 'Okay, I want a pint but I'm gonna' take it in two half-pint bottles.'

"He said, 'Hell no! I told you this whiskey was half price, but I never said nothin' about two for one!' He said, "I don't fess to know nothin' about money but I know a heap about liquor and I ain't about to give you two for one!'

"I said, 'All right, Cissero, just let me have this pint bottle and we'll be fine. By the way, you don't mind if I borrow two of them empty half-pint bottles you got there do you? I'll swap them out with you next time I'm up your way.'

"'Sho, sho boy, take as many as you need and drop them off anytime.'

"I paid him and was about to pour my full pint into them half-pint bottles when Cissero got excited. He said, 'Well boy, let me be gettin' on. I got a lot of bottles to get shed of today. Let me be gettin' on.'

"I knew he got in a hurry to leave for some reason and just before I opened my bottle, I said, 'Cissero, you sure ain't nothing wrong with this stuff?'

"Just before the seal broke, Cissero said, 'Well, I tell you Mr. Perry, it does have a little *whang* to it now and then!"

"A *whang?*" I asked. "What in the hell is a *whang?*"

"'Well,' he explained, 'when you first take a whiff of it, it don't smell jest right, but you see how clear it is and how it beads up and I know it'll make you drunk. It's got a little ole familiar smell but I can't quite put a make on it. It's alright though. I promise you that!'

"Well," Perry said, "I took the top off that bottle and what hit me right square in the face was something I'd tried for six months to forget – stale skimmin's, skunk spray and ole Pearl!

"'Damn, Cissero!' I yelled. 'What in hell have you sold me? This stuff smells like a wet dog soaked in skunk piss!'

"'I know,' Cissero said. 'I know it, but I swear, Mr. Perry, we made this jest like every other batch we ever made. For the life of me I can't figure out where that *whang* is a-comin' from! Sho' do smell funny, though, don't it? Sho' do smell funny! I don't know how liquor could be so bright and bead up so fine and smell so bad. That and the fact that we over-made is the reason I got this half-price special going. You sure you don't want two, three or more of them pints poured up in them little bottles?'

"No," I said, "I don't think I do."

"'Well then,' he said, 'I'll be going on. Y'all have a nice Christmas! And by the way, I'm gonna jest give you another pint to take Bro' Hogg tomorrow, y'all bein' kin folks and all that. I know you be seein' him tomorrow being it be Christmas and tell him ole Cissero said he hoped ole Santa brought him some new overalls! In fact, here's *two* more pints, one more for you and one for Slim. Hope y'all enjoy it, and don't ever tell nobody ole Cissero ain't never give you nothin'!'

"Well," Perry said, "He turned that long-assed Chrysler around, went down my driveway a-wavin', and turned out on the main road without even lookin'. I can't prove it, and I won't never know for sure, but I'll always believe ole Cissero knew me and Bro' Hogg had something to do with that bad batch of 'shine. All I learned from that experience is – you can boil the fool out of skunk spray, and it still stinks to high heaven!"

"Perry," the little ol' man said, "you take the cake! I knew if I stopped by here you'd tell me a good'n and you did! Reckon I'll head on down the road. I was goin' to Pine Mountain but it's too late now. Think I'll just go on back home."

And he did!

CHAPTER 24

The sun cast long bright rays of light in the oak trees as the four deer made their way across the Steve Morgan farm.

"Stop!" Scrap yelled. "Right out yonder in that patch of briars is where I was born and right down yonder by that branch is where Mrs. Morgan ran me down and caught me. It seems like yesterday, yet it was years ago. Don't think she could catch me now!"

"So this is the Morgan fescue field," Sally mused.

"Yep," Scrap said. "This is where it all began for me. The day the little ol' man carried me out from over here, I never thought I'd see this place again. Strange how life is, you know! Never can tell what's in store for you. Who would've believed that I'd ever get hooked up with Star and live in the Park again! I could've just as easily been one of the exhibits in an amusement park or the little ol' man could've given me to a zoo!"

"Yeah," said Little Sam, "and you could've eaten all the dog food you wanted then!"

Scrap bowed up and Star said, "You two stop it! We don't need y'all needling each other now. Last time I checked, Dad could still whip both of you, and I just hope he's in a better frame of mind now."

They made their way to the logging road that went up through the giant oak and hickory trees of the Park. As they started up a long hill, Star stopped abruptly, threw her head up, winded the morning air and gave a shrilling nasal blow! She was staring at something ahead. At the top of the hill, and standing in the middle of the road, was a big, big doe. The four deer stood motionless, gazing at the imposing figure before them. Finally, Star twitched her tail and said, "I believe that's Mom!"

"Me too," Little Sam agreed.

The doe didn't move. She simply stood and gazed. After a couple of minutes, she dropped her nose to the ground and quickly raised her head again.

"That's her!" said Scrap. "And Sam has to be around here somewhere. Man, I hope he's settled down by now. Star took a few steps forward and then moved on toward the big doe. The others in the group followed her as they made their way up the logging road. The big doe turned away and took several strides as if to run, then stopped and waited for the four approaching deer to come near. When she picked up their scents, she lowered her tail and greeted them with dominate body language typical of her status in the herd. Her initial red-alert behavior soon turned passive and she welcomed her family warmly.

"It's so good to see you, Star," Grace said. "How have you been? You've been gone so long, I thought you'd never come back!"

"We're doing just fine, Mom," said Star. "I'll tell you all about it later. Where's Dad?"

Grace dropped her head, and her eyes showed considerable sadness and stress. "Sam's not well," she said. "Your dad is in bad shape and I'm glad you're here!"

"What do you mean in bad shape?" Little Sam asked. "Where is he?"

"He's bedded down over yonder in those woods you call the finger. He's been there for two weeks."

As the deer started walking in that direction, Grace explained Sam's predicament. "Well, your daddy had a rough rut," she said. "He did some foolish things. My estrous period started the day after y'all left, and we had a wonderful courtship. It was just like always, but after it was over, he got restless and started roaming all over Harris and Troup counties. Any ole barren doe showed up and your daddy went frigging crazy over her."

"What's a barren doe?" Little Sam asked.

"Son," Grace said, "it's one of those old does that never seems to be satisfied. They never bear young and come in season two or three times during the rut and just drive old bucks like Sam crazy! They're always fat and slick and never seem to get enough. They ramble from one territory to another and most bucks can't resist them. They're the cause of so many disharmonies and the break-up of deer family units.

"Anyway, an attractive barren doe showed up over here one day and your dad followed her clear across the Avery farm to the Jim Woods property. Two strapping 3-year-olds jumped him over there and really worked him over. He's not as young as he once was, you know! They battered and bruised him up something terrible! He was gone three days, and when he finally showed up back home, he'd lost 40 pounds and the old gunshot wound in his shoulder had opened up again and it was a mess."

"Is that all?" asked Scrap. "Or is there more?"

"There's more," Grace said. "He got over that in time, and I thought he was going to be fine. He picked up some weight and behaved for a while, but then about two weeks ago that same doe showed up again. The old fool took to chasing after her and this time she led him across highway 18, all the way to the Hewitt property. He was gone four days and then I went looking for him! We met way back yonder behind Jim Wood's house and I convinced him to come home. That old barren doe was still in a teasing mood and there must have been a dozen yearlings after her. Your daddy looked like a complete fool and I told him so! You know there ain't no fool like an old fool, don't you?

"We were making our way back home in the middle of the night when it happened. I crossed highway 18 with no trouble. No cars were in sight and when I got on the other side I looked back for your dad. He was standing there looking over his shoulder for that sorry wench of a doe! I stomped my foot several times and when he turned to cross, he bolted out in front of a car. The lady did all she could to miss him, in fact, she almost wrecked her car. Your dad has forgotten that he has aged and can't do some of the things he once did – like dodge fast moving vehicles!

"The woman who was driving the car is one of the finest people in our territory. A sweeter lady I've never seen. She was heartbroken about the accident. They say she cares about people like the ol' man cares about us. She's a pillar of the community and everyone loves her. She has helped so many folks around here and she's tender hearted. Tears were running down her cheeks when she stopped the car and saw your Dad suffering!

"When it happened, Sam was one step from safety and Miss Linda was one mile from home. There was simply no way she could have avoided hitting him. I hated it for Sam but I also had feelings for the sweet lady! It hurt her in a different way. They both suffered from Sam's wayward behavior.

"It was your Dads' fault and that abnormal whore was his down fall! He simply cut it too close. When he made his last lunge to clear the highway, his hooves slipped on the asphalt and the car caught his right back leg and hindquarters. He plowed a furrow in the ditch and landed up on the bank. He managed to get up and hobbled along behind me for the remainder of the trip. He's been bedded down over yonder in the finger ever since. He won't eat and he seldom goes to water.

"His old teeth are worn down to the gums, you know, and he can't eat just anything. He's lost so much weight now that he doesn't even resemble his old self. What's worse, his spirit is broken! He says he just wants to be left alone to rest. I'm worried that he might be giving up! I do hope seeing y'all will lift his spirits."

"But he was so strong and healthy when we left," Star said. "He was the picture of strength!"

"I know," Grace said. "But at his age, and with his injuries, he went down quickly. You don't bounce back like you used to when you get older."

"I want to see him," Little Sam said.

"Don't expect him to be his old self," Grace said. "He's in great pain and his will to survive has gradually gotten weaker. I'm really scared for him. You know, when you rule the woods as long as he has, and you start failing, it's hard to take. Your dad has not adapted well at all!"

When the four deer reached Sam's bedding area, Scrap said, "Where is he? I don't see him. I scent him but where is he?"

"Look closer," Grace said. "He's right over there behind that log and in that brush pile."

Scrap strained his eyes and finally made out the tip of Sam's nose. Then everything else came into view. Sam was resting with his great horns laid back against his shoulders and all you could see was the tip of his nose and the underside of his neck. He was virtually invisible from a few feet away and he had used this position many times to avoid danger.

As the four deer approached, Sam twitched an ear but made no attempt to get up. It was obvious to all that he was in considerable pain. Star eased in toward her dad and gently groomed his face and neck. She licked his nose and muzzle, showing her love and affection for him. Sam's spirits seemed to rise and he tried to get to his feet. After a third effort failed, he settled back down in the bed and rested.

The five deer looked on in amazement. Here was the king of the woods, so weak that he couldn't get to his feet. There was a hopeless and helpless feeling in the air. Scrap thought, *I'd rather have him chasing me and kicking my ass than to see him laying here in this condition.*

Sam said, "Y'all go on now. Don't stand around here. You might give away my hiding place. You never know who or what is watching. Come back early tomorrow morning. Maybe I'll feel better and be stronger. Y'all go on now. Don't worry about me. Take care of yourselves and be careful. I'll be fine in time. I just need rest. I just need rest...."

They left Sam in his bed as directed and he continued to rest quietly. He'd been injured before. He'd been shot once and who knows how many brutal battles he'd been involved in. Often, in those battles, his opponents had not walked away! His scars told the story of his life. He was scarred from head to tail but never had he been hit by a car. Never had he been so seriously injured.

Sam had always been the eternal optimist. However, he was also a realist and he knew that these were serious times and that his days were numbered. His mind drifted off to the past and he thought about his sweet mother and Big Sam, his legendary dad. He recalled the day Big Sam was killed. He tried to justify that untimely death by reasoning how noble it was. His dad died at the height of his power. He died at the height of his reign! He died when he was King of the Flat Shoals watershed area!

Then Sam became angry and thought: *This is no way to leave the Park! This is not the way a king should go. This is a coward's death, hiding and waiting for the final hour to come. This is no way to be remembered by my family. No way at all! I'd rather that car had killed me while chasing a whore than to die here alone and have the buzzards eat my carcass.*

This great set of horns will be eaten by the squirrels and rodents, and my bones will bleach in the sun. My existence will pass and soon be forgotten. Death can't be allowed to treat me this way! My life has been too noble to die here and quickly be forgotten. I don't need to die here! Not under these unbecoming conditions!

However, Sam was also enough of a realist to understand that when death came calling, it was a hard thing to cheat! Death was a worthy adversary, when it came knocking and like birth, one in which he had little or no control. He knew that the only way to gain an advantage over death was to get the drop on the old grim reaper before he beckoned! But had he waited too long? He couldn't bare the thought of Little Sam, Star, and the others watching him as he grew weaker and weaker. But seemingly, he had no choice.

Yes, he *had* waited too long, and death's doorbell was ringing in his ear! He could feel death coming with the pain in his legs and the weakness in his back. He could sense it pulling at his breath and gnawing away at his strength. He wasn't afraid, but he was very much aware that life, as he had known it, was quickly slipping through his grasp. He had been strong, dominating and a fearless leader: however, above all else, he was a "realist!" He recognized the situation at hand and there was no denying it!

CHAPTER 25

His alarm clock went off way before daylight that morning and the little ol' man lay there in bed thinking about the day ahead. His wife rolled over, took his hand and said, "Why don't you just stay home this morning and not go? You put so much pressure on yourself. You push yourself way too hard. You're getting older and you need to slow down some. There'll be plenty of other times to hunt. You need some rest."

"No," he said, "it's Saturday morning. I haven't been to the Park in a week and I'm going. I told you I saw Scrap, Star and Little Sam headed that way and I want to see if they've gotten home."

"Well," she said, "do be careful. I hate to see you go way over there by yourself. Something could happen to you and nobody would even know it. Do be careful. Please, you ole Goat, please be careful! I worry about you!"

"I will," he promised, and his feet hit the floor with excitement. It was going to be a bluebird morning and he couldn't wait!

He parked Old Blue – the trusted '87 Toyota, 4-wheel drive truck – in its usual spot. Old Blue had been in the woods with him so many times. The worn out half-ton truck was as much a part of his hunts as the .270 caliber rifle that he carried. Blue had gotten him out of many a tough spot through the years. The truck was old but it was tried and true! The ol' man equated it to his own life! Her youth was spent: but, her dependability had not faded! Her youthful shine had long dissipated: however, the scars on her fenders and body were evidence that she had spent her time in the real world. The ol' man put a lot of emphasis on scars! Often, when his friends attempted to give him advice, he responded by saying... "Show me your scars!" He believed that tough times in life left scars! And that a man without scars had experienced very little and was not worthy of passing out advice to others! His trust of ol' Blue was right up there with the confidence he had in his rifle. *What would I do without either of them!* he thought.

The ol' man checked his flashlight and slowly made his way down the logging road toward what he called his corner stand. He loved hunting from that stand because he could see across the Avery Farm pastures and cover the lush hardwood thickets of the Park as well. The beams from his flashlight bumped along the rough road, and every now and then focused on a big deer track.

"It's going to be a great morning!" he told himself. "There are fresh tracks everywhere."

About half-way up his ladder stand, the little ol' man was startled by a loud howl. Out in front of his stand, in the pitch-black darkness, a coyote was telling the world that he had the ol' man in his sights. The coyote would emit five or six deep barks with the last one ending in an elongated howling. The ol' man figured the coyote was out in the Avery pasture and as daylight slowly crept in, he saw the dog's dark figure skirt across the frost covered meadow and disappear into the darkness.

Things settled down with the coyote's departure and the ol' man had some time to think. He sat motionless and strained his eyes across the fields and into the darkness of the big timber. His thoughts drifted to his family and the wonderful life he had enjoyed. His wife and children were special to him. He thought about his two sons and all the joys they had shared; all of the wonderful hunts and all of the wonderful stories they now had to tell.

He thought about all of their successful attempts to harvest a good buck and all the many times they had been skunked. He was so proud of the men they'd become! In addition, his two daughters had always been his pride and joy. His mind slipped off into the distant past. It focused on the tragic night his oldest daughter skidded off a slippery highway and ended a most perfect life. All the pain of that night, and the days, months, and even years that followed brought him almost to tears! It was something he would never get over. *How fortunate to be blessed with such beautiful children and a wonderful wife,* he thought!

The beautiful girl he married had developed into a most perfect mother and lifelong companion. So special she was to him! So special she was to all who knew her. He thought to himself: *She always has the right things to say during tough times and always has the patience to deal with even the most trying of circumstances.*

Without question, she had been the wind beneath his wings and he loved and respected her with all his heart. *So many wonderful blessings,* he thought. *I'm so blessed in so many ways, and there's no better time to reflect about these things than when I'm sitting in a deer stand!*

CHAPTER 26

Sam saw the yellow glow of daylight coming. Behind him, to the east, the sky was becoming lighter and day was approaching. He squirmed around in his bed. He tried to muster up enough strength to get to his feet. His pain was great and the cold night air had added to his misery! After several attempts, he gained his balance, and soon found himself standing on all four legs.

He knew his family members would be there shortly and he didn't want them to find him down. Sam hobbled along and made his way through the thicket. He was in great pain and discomfort as he crawled under the bottom strand of barbed wire, and found himself standing in one of the Avery pastures. A day in the past and he would have simply bounded over the fence with ease!

But that was another day and another time. He was dealing in the present and this day was a painful one! He slowly began moving ahead. He passed one fence post at a time. He measured his progress by the post he passed and made his way toward the gap that separated the Avery pastures.

Just as Sam reached the fence line gap, Little Sam and the others bounded over the fence and raced toward him. They gathered around as if to make certain he was protected. Grace began licking and grooming his face. This felt so good and it brought back memories of younger days when he and Grace had met for the first time. It was in this very same Avery pasture that Sam had acknowledged the fact that she was the most beautiful thing in the world and that she was the one he intended to spend his life with!

The four deer continued to groom each other. Then, they slowly moved through the gap and browsed toward the western edge of the pasture. Sam found himself getting farther and farther behind. His hips and legs were cramping and it was obvious his condition had taken a turn for the worst. The group had moved far ahead and it was all he could do to keep them in sight.

The worried deer family looked back and waited for Sam to catch up. It was obvious to Sam that he was slowing them down, and his experience had taught him that a slow moving deer was a prime target. In fact, he well knew that a slow moving deer often turned into a dead deer. His spirits were as low as they had ever been!

The group waited for Sam to close the distance. When he reached them, Grace threw her head up high in the air and gave a shrill, nasal blast. She stomped her foot and blew again. The others stood motionless and winded the air. She turned on her heels like a good quarter horse and blew again. Then she spotted him! Her nose led her eyes straight to his. He was sitting quiet and motionless high in his ladder stand in the edge of the woods. It was the little ol' man!

Even though she had long trusted the ol' man, they were too close this time and she knew it! The rule had always been to trust him, but stay out of his way, and they were far too close. She blew again. She did everything in her power and used every trick she knew to try and get the ol' man to move and give his location away to the others. He didn't and he wouldn't!

Sam took a painful step forward, lifted his nose and winded the little ol' man. He raised his big head proudly and his eyes met those of the old hunter. Sam thought: *Here we stand in the wide open field and he could have shot us a dozen times. He could have shot me or Little Sam a dozen times before now and didn't. Why?*

Sam's mind began to race. The thoughts of the previous evening found their way into the present and the memories of his dad, Big Sam, raced through his head! He thought about how he had admired his dad and found him so noble, even in death! Sam feared that he would become a burden to his group. He feared that he would become a feast for some cowardly coyote or buzzard. And once that happened, he knew his unique and beautiful antlers would succumb to the squirrels, chipmunks and mice and that his life would soon be forgotten.

Before he allowed himself to have another thought, a deep calm came over him. His body suddenly became energized and with his last bit of strength, he started hobbling toward the little ol' man. Grace continued to blow and stomp her foot. She ran around in circles. The other four deer broke and ran.

Sam hobbled on toward the little ol' man in the deer stand! He knew this was the way it had to end. This was the way it had to be! This was the way it was supposed to be! Sam stopped at the pasture's edge and looked up at the ol' man! For a brief moment they stared at each other. It was as if the eye contact allowed each to see deeply into the very soul of the other. Then Sam turned his head and thought: *Do it! Do it! Go ahead, Do it! Why will you not do it?*

The ol' man couldn't believe his eyes! Here was the huge old dominant buck he had known for years standing right before him! He probably carried the biggest set of horns in Harris County, and he was standing in front of him just a few yards away. It was then that he realized the extent of Sam's injuries. The little ol' man almost cried when Sam dropped to his knees and painfully crawled under the pasture fence. He could almost feel that pain as Sam struggled to his feet and hobbled toward the logging road!

He studied Sam's bulging ribs and noted that his sagging backbone was bare of any fat cover. Then he thought: As *magnificent as this buck is and has always been, he's not going to make it through the winter. The coyotes will drag him down and he'll die a horrible death. He deserves so much more than that....*

Tears began to roll down his face. He didn't know if he had the courage to take an old friend's life, but he knew it was the right thing to do!

Sam instinctively started to circle around the ladder stand. By now he was almost behind the ol' man and he wondered: *Why won't he do it? Why?*

As the little ol' man turned in his stand, his heart began to race. Like so many times before, the automatic pilot began to take control. His hands became sweaty, his back tightened up and he could feel a burst of energy from the adrenaline in his body.

Grace stood alone in the pasture, continuing to stomp and snort. Her perked ears were in high-alert position as she watched Sam. She was confused. What was he doing? Why did he walk so close to the little ol' man? Didn't Sam recognize the potential danger?

She tensed up as she watched the ol' man turn in the stand and place the gun to his shoulder. Then it suddenly became clear to her. Sam knew exactly what he was doing! He was choosing the best way out of a terrible situation. He was taking the high road. He was choosing to die a hero's death rather than suffer a long, miserable end. She stopped her commotion and stood quietly. She waited as her whole life passed through her mind! She waited as all the wonderful memories of Sam and their life together absorbed her. As she waited, her love for Sam consumed her. She watched with full awareness that life as she had known it for so long was about to end!

She remembered the first time she and Sam met and their courtship. She thought about the birth of Little Sam and Star and about the great father Sam had been to them! She remembered all the fights she and Sam had through the years and would have given anything to erase some of the things she had said to Sam in anger! Above all, she remembered their love for each other and the good times they had shared. However, she too was a realist and the reality was that Sam's time was near! Grace was aware that all good things in life have a beginning and end. And that even life has an inevitable closure!

The ol' man had turned completely around in the stand and found himself in a very awkward position. He had twisted to the extent that one foot was off the steps and he was leaning over the back of his ladder stand. When the cross hairs of his scope crossed the exact perfect spot on Sam's shoulder, his gentle pressure on the trigger sent the old reliable .270 slug roaring on its way. The big buck fell to the ground, dead before he knew what hit him. The little ol' man heard a crash!

CHAPTER 27

He felt a warm hand around his and recognized the kiss on his forehead. He heard familiar voices whispering. To no avail, he strained to open his eyes. He drifted off again. Again, he felt a warm hand. Using all his strength, he opened his eyes. The surroundings were strange. However, he recognized the faces and voices. The familiar voice of his wife said, "I think he's coming around."

The doctor said, "This might be the day!"

"Where am I?" the little ol' man whispered.

"Don't worry about where you are, just rest!" a strange voice said.

"Where am I?" he asked again.

"You're in the hospital. You've been here for two weeks." the strange voice answered.

"What happened to me?" he asked.

His wife said, "You fell out of a deer stand Saturday was two weeks ago and you've been unconscious ever since. They've had you on medication to keep you sedated."

"Where am I injured?" he asked.

"Broken leg and a severe concussion," she answered. "We won't talk about the cuts and bruises."

"How did I get here?" he whispered.

"When you didn't come home for lunch that day, I sent the hunters

197

from the camp up yonder to go look for you," she said. "You were on the ground under your stand. They found you unconscious."

"I've never fallen out of a deer stand," he said.

"Well, you have now," she answered. "And you're fortunate to be alive!"

He opened his eyes wider and saw one of his sons standing at the foot of his bed.

"Dad, did you shoot that buck?" his son asked.

"What buck?" the little ol' man answered.

"The big one they found in the logging road not 40 yards from your stand!"

The little ol' man didn't answer. He just grinned and drifted off again.

"He still ain't right," his son said. "If his mind was clear, he would remember that deer!"

"Don't worry him," the wife said. "Give him more time! Just let him sleep."

Later that morning, his eyes opened again and he asked, "What deer?"

"They found a huge buck near where you were hunting," his son said again. "But you don't need to be concerned about that now. You need rest, lots of rest and quiet time."

He drifted into another deep sleep!

***

The following morning, things seemed a little clearer and the little ol' man was full of questions.

"What deer?" he asked again.

"Dad," his son said, "apparently you shot a huge-racked buck that must have been really old and going downhill. They say he was nothing but skin and bones but he had a huge rack of horns!"

"How did I get here and how did they get me out of the woods?" the little ol' man asked?

"In the back of Old Blue," he answered, "They put you and the deer in there side-by-side and hauled y'all out together! Your buddies, Roger and Robert, went over there and got you! When they got back to camp, they didn't know which one to hang up and skin first, you or the buck!" His son said that and then he laughed out loud! The ol' man grinned because he knew his son's humor was a chip off the old block!

"Did they have to drag him far?" The ol' man asked.

"Not too far," his son answered. "Said the deer was an easy pull, and you'd have been too, except you didn't have any horns!"

The little ol' man chuckled!

His son continued, "Said they had a little problem. The game warden stopped them up at the crossroads and gave them a ticket. Said they should have tagged you both. Said an old codger with really thick glasses peeped over in the truck and said, "This'n on this side must be a doe... *He* ain't got no balls!"

The little ol' man chuckled again.

His wife came into the room about that time and said, "Well, you must be feeling better, you're laughing."

"Laughing?" he answered. "Yes I am. I'm happy to be here –alive that is!"

"I'm surprised some of these nurses haven't already killed you," his wife said.

"Why?" he asked?

"Because you've been a mess!" she answered. "You've had one nightmare after another and you've talked in your sleep constantly! You've been dreaming and talking for two weeks solid. You've been hunting and telling hunting tales. We about had to tie you down one morning. You were gonna fight two hunters you kept calling *"Carpet bagging Yankee sons of bitches,"* over a deer you shot. Your language was terrible! It was so unlike you using such foul words! I have never seen that side of you before!"

"No way!" he said. "I didn't do that! I couldn't have used any bad words!" He said that and then winked at his son who was grinning from ear to ear!

"Yes you did," his wife said. "And that isn't the half of it. It's been a circus around here! I guess it's the morphine they had you on. You've been out of your head, speaking to deer, and acting like a big buck was talking back to you! Who in the world do you know with the names like Sam, Sally, Scrap, Grace and Star? You've talked nonstop about Sam! We don't even know anyone named Sam. Not just Sam, but Big Sam and Little Sam too!

"One night, you talked about Mr. Charles Hogg. You kept calling him

Bro' Hogg! Several times you laughed out loud and who is Pearl for heaven's sake? Mr. Hogg has never had a dog that I know of. I thought you'd really turned for the worse when you talked about a big ole 'coon you called Haint!"

"You talked to Perry Williams for three days. I called him to see if any of the stuff you were saying was true. Perry denied all of it. One morning I almost pulled the plug on you myself. It was the morning after your worst night. You had talked to Cissero Moss and Perry Williams forever. I was so worried about you! Your vital signs were declining and you seemed to be getting weaker. I leaned over you and said, 'Honey, can you hear me?'

"Did I answer you?" the little ol' man asked.

"Yes you did," His wife said.

"What did I say?" He responded.

"You said, 'Woman, have you ever seen a Billy goat fuck a sow?' I almost killed you myself. You were hallucinating something terrible! Where in the world could all of that crazy stuff have come from? Then you kept saying, 'Get that wet dog out of here. She smells like skunk piss!'

"You embarrassed me to no end! The nurses finally got to where they didn't want to come in. You called one of them Sally and the other Star. You kept saying, 'When I get up from here, I'm going to find y'all a buck. I think the both of you are coming in heat!'

"Do you remember any of that?" she asked.

"Naw," he said. "I don't remember any of that! It sounds like y'all have all been drinking 'shine liquor! All I remember was leaving home that morning, gettin' into my stand and seein' those deer. There were six of them that morning."

His son spoke up and asked, "Dad, as much as you've hunted over there on our lease, have you ever seen that big buck before?"

The little ol' man's eyes gleamed. He looked as if he were concentrating on something very far away. He didn't answer!

His wife spoke again and said, "And then the morning the Preacher came to see you, you said, 'Fix him a drink. It may taste like skunk pee, but it'll make him drunker'n hell!' You embarrassed all of us! You kept calling your doctor 'the Pro!' You asked him one morning if he could blow smoke out of his nose and if he had missed any *big'ns* lately? That's when he suggested we call in a psychiatrist. We did, and when he came in, you accused him of burning Chicken Shit. What in the world were you thinking, and, just exactly what is Chicken Shit?"

The little ol' man grinned and said, "Honey, you gotta know what Chicken Shit is! I'm the one who fell out of the deer stand!"

For some reason, she didn't think that was as funny as he did! His son spoke again. "Dad, you didn't answer my question. Have you ever seen that deer before?"

Again, the ol' man's eyes focused on something far away and he said, "When I saw that buck, I wondered where he came from, who he was, where he'd been and why he was so emaciated! I wondered how a buck that thin could have grown those magnificent horns! I was thinking those thoughts when I pulled the trigger."

"Dad!" his son asked again. "Have you ever seen that deer before?"

The little ol' man's face became radiant. His eyes sparkled and he focused on something that only he could see! A warm and peaceful smile adorned him. Then he answered, "Yes, yes, yes, I have. I've seen him many, many times. He's been in my heart and mind all my life. His name is 'Sam' and he's a Harris County legend!"

THE END

FINAL THOUGHTS

The characters in this story and the circumstances surrounding their adventures are as real as we want them to be. If this story isn't true, it could have been. If it isn't true, maybe it should have been! The fact is – reality is often in the mind. If we can dream of great bucks and wonderful hunts, the mental satisfaction is just as rewarding as the real thing.

After many years of hunting, studying, and enjoying the great outdoors, I've graduated to a higher mindset. Observing deer is more rewarding to me than killing them! A truly mature trophy hunter finally realizes that the joy and thrill comes in the chase and that once the kill is made, the chase is over forever and ever!

Some of the happiest days of my life have been spent in the pursuit of giant-antlered whitetails. On occasion, I've been successful, but most often, the big buck I was hunting figured out my plans and won our game of tactics. I've made some mistakes along the way. I've taken three of four deer that should have been left to mature! I've never been on a paid hunt and have only hunted on my own land or leased properties. I've never fed deer other than natural cover crops for conservation practices in my farming operation! I believe in the fair chase rule and anything other than that is wrong!

On the few occasions when I have taken an immature buck, I made the age-old mistake of letting my eyes fool me or letting my ego get in the way. I can remember each of those hunts vividly, and the disappointment of those days shadow the thrills felt when the "right one" was mine!

The legacy of Big Sam, Sam, Little Sam, Scrap and the does could go on and fill volumes. These characters live in my heart and I can have a great hunt by simply closing my eyes and letting my mind wander!

The human characters in this story are somewhat, fictitious in nature: however, they are very real to me! I've hunted with them for years and they are my family and friends. They are as much a part of my hunting experience as Sam and Nasty Pete are of my imagination.

The Park in this story is a special place of leased property. I have hunted it for many years. The descriptions of it, in the story, are pretty much as it really is. It's a special place where does and young bucks are allowed to mature without the fear of being hunted prematurely.

The territory that Big Sam roamed is a real area that surrounds the community of Jones Crossroads in Harris County, Georgia. The Flat Shoals Creek community is very real and all of the landmarks, mentioned in the story, exist. Big Sam could have easily roamed those roads, woods and fields. And who knows? Maybe he did! Or maybe he's still out there! I can close my eyes in a quiet deer stand on a cold, crisp fall morning and make him appear anytime I want!

Big Sam, Sam, Little Sam, Scrap, Star, Grace and Sally are real in my mind and who knows, the next time I'm in the Park, they may just pay me a visit!

Ed Oliver,
June, 2010

Made in the USA
San Bernardino, CA
13 December 2012